The Berlin

David O'Donnell was born in Scotland. He is a qualified lawyer, and has both practised and taught law. He lives in rural Scotland with his wife Fiona and black Labrador Niamh. When Niamh is not taking him for a walk, his passion is cooking French and Italian dishes. *The Berlin Gambit* is his first novel.

The Berlin Gambit

David O'Donnell

Polygon

First published in Great Britain in 2023 by Polygon,
an imprint of Birlinn Ltd

Birlinn Ltd
West Newington House
10 Newington Road
Edinburgh
EH9 1QS

1

www.polygonbooks.co.uk

ISBN 978 1 84697 628 5

British Library Cataloguing-in-Publication Data
A catalogue record for this book is available on
request from the British Library.

Typeset in Dante MT by Initial Typesetting Services, Edinburgh

Those who begin by burning books will end by burning people.

—Heinrich Heine

For my beautiful wife Fiona, who has always loved and believed, and my dear friend Bill Macreath, whose help has been invaluable in so many ways.

Poland, December 1942

What can you offer a man with less than two hours to live? What levers can you pull to bend him to your will? Rolf Schneider had been pondering this riddle as he waited for such a man to be brought to him. He didn't have an answer.

Schneider had travelled a long and dangerous road to meet this man. He had given no warning of his arrival as that would only have shortened the man's lifespan even further. At the gate, he had shown the magic piece of paper bearing the scrawled, almost indecipherable signature. He was admitted. Schneider took the path towards the commandant's office. Every eye followed his passage with the usual interest of those condemned to the drudgery of routine, and who welcome any break from that monotony. But he sensed something more in the stares. It was something he couldn't quite define, an absolute fear, an unremitting terror, but of what, he didn't know. Then he realised it was of him, or rather of the uniform he was forced to wear. To these pitiful watchers, all such uniforms, and those who wore them, meant death itself walked among them.

When he reached the office, he had tried to clear his head of the smell. He doubted it would ever leave him. Burnt flesh, human waste and disease had combined into an indelible olfactory memory. But at least the piece of paper had again worked its magic, and now, finally, the small, emaciated figure of the man he had come to see stood before him. And still Schneider didn't know what he could offer him. Life? He doubted if he would be believed. Even the paper had a limit to its powers. Money? It was meaningless to this man. There had to be something. Then the man's eyes gave him the answer. They were fixed not on Schneider nor his uniform but on an apple lying on the desk. Schneider picked it up. The man's eyes followed as if attached by an invisible string.

'Would you like this?'

A nervous nod.

Schneider passed the piece of fruit over and it was devoured, core, pips and all, in less than ten seconds.

'Would you like another?'

The same nervous nod.

'First of all, I want to ask you something. Is that all right?'

Schneider had found his lever. He bluntly ignored all other considerations. He was the best policeman in Germany. He had been given a task to do. He would do it. It wasn't his job to get mixed up in politics.

But even as he passed the fruit over, he knew he was only fooling himself. He already wore the black uniform with the Death's Head emblem. And to come to Auschwitz extermination camp, bearing a paper signed by Adolf Hitler himself, meant he was more than mixed up in politics. He was at its very heart.

Berlin, the same day

Heinrich Himmler finished burning the letter. A man of infinite caution, he ground the ashes into dust before flushing them down the toilet. The thin lips twitched into a smile. Everything was going according to plan. Soon now, very soon, it would be time. But then he didn't know that at that very moment, an old man was hungrily devouring his third apple.

*

Another man had also just finished reading the same letter. But he didn't destroy it. He kept it in a file. He also believed things were going well. He walked to his window and stared out into the night as if trying to see across the distances that separated them. The time was getting close.

Berlin, October 1941

'I think our man is a soldier. He is someone who enjoys killing. He is cunning and extremely dangerous. He is probably also completely insane.'

Chief Investigator Rolf Schneider of the Berlin Criminal Police Department took a final look at what had once been a young woman. What remained of her now lay at his feet. He didn't need to be the best detective in Berlin to have arrived at the final part of his conclusion. The head that had been almost severed from the body, and the terror in the dead eyes, gave silent testimony to the frenzied nature of the killing. But maybe it was a jilted lover rather than a madman? No, only a madman would have carved the religious symbol on the chest of his victim. Only a madman would have butchered the stomach to leave the bloody internal organs exposed.

His assistant, Hans Albert, had done his best to ignore the horror but had finally lost that battle, and his breakfast. Now, wiping his mouth with a handkerchief, he tried to redeem himself by emulating his boss's deductive reasoning.

'Maybe if we check which army units were in the city at the time of the other five killings, we could narrow down who we are looking for. Then if we interview those soldiers to see where they were on the nights in question, we might get lucky?'

It was almost as though Schneider hadn't heard him. He was looking at the dead girl's identity card as if it could tell him something more than the printed information it held. Evidently it could, for suddenly Schneider snapped his fingers, a habit of his when he had made a breakthrough.

'Of course, of course. It's been staring me in the face all along. I think I know where to look for our man now.'

He started back to the car, ignoring Albert.

'Should I ask the army for details of the units that were here?'

Schneider stopped, as if he had heard him for the first time. Perhaps he had. He gave Albert a look that somehow managed to be both dismissive and encouraging at the same time.

'How many soldiers do you think pass through Berlin on their way to the Russian front? Do you think the army high command would have such details as we require? And even if they did, how long do you think it would take for us to get them? Our man could well have committed another six murders by then. In any event, how do you know he is a soldier?'

'But you said he was.'

'And do you always believe me?'

Hans Albert nodded. Of course he did, just like every other policeman in Berlin.

Schneider sat in silence on the journey back to police headquarters. He was obviously deep in thought and clearly didn't require any help from his assistant. So, Hans Albert allowed his own mind to run over the investigation to date. And to thank God that he had been assigned to work with the man now regarded by many as Germany's greatest detective.

The first murder had been carried out more than two months earlier. The woman's throat had been cut and she had borne the same mutilations as today's victim. In wartime, lots of people die and there is little time for detailed forensic investigations, so the marks had been put down to other wounds inflicted during the attack. It was only when another two victims were discovered within the space of a week that Schneider had been called in. No other murders took place in August and there was a hope that the killer had either stopped or was no longer in the city. Maybe he had even been killed in an air raid. Schneider had said this man would never stop until he was caught or killed and that, sooner or later, he would strike again and that it would only be in Berlin. He had been right. Since the last week of September there had been three more killings, all bearing the same gruesome hallmarks.

The victims were all respectable women in their mid-twenties. All were married and had apparently led completely normal lives. None of them had children and none had criminal records. While some had belonged to the Party, none were known to be die-hard Nazis. In short, they were all unremarkable and ostensibly sharing only one thing in common: either by chance or design, they had all fallen victim to the same killer.

Yet Schneider seemed to have seen something in the last victim's identity card. But that was so typical of Schneider. Hans Albert looked across at the unremarkable face of his boss. He was forty-six years old, and it showed. He was single, had no known vices nor interests and lived only for his job. He spent every day and some nights in his office. His home, if it could be called such, was a small one-bedroom flat. No one had ever been invited there and Schneider had never been known to accept an invitation to a colleague's home. He had no female friends, and some said he had no friends, full stop. His life was his work and his work his life. It was almost as if the man didn't exist some of the time, leaving only that brain and its deductions. Whether Schneider was aware of how others viewed him was debatable. What was certain, however, was that he didn't care about the views of others, be they colleagues or criminals. The man who had written that no man was an island had clearly never met Rolf Schneider. He had joined the police as soon as he had been old enough and the myth of Schneider had slowly been born.

Hans Albert mused that, if truth be told, his boss was a bore, perhaps even an eccentric, and would have been treated as such except for his unique ability to solve crimes. In that, he was a genius.

*

Back at headquarters, Schneider quickly obtained the information he wanted from all six files. He didn't explain to Hans Albert what he was doing or looking for, but that was his normal way. Albert knew that eventually Schneider would explain, and then maybe he could for a fleeting moment see into and share the mind of genius.

Schneider was poring over the files he had extracted from the well-ordered filing cabinets. The light was dim, in keeping with war-time economics, but German efficiency still prevailed in the filing system. Every crime was recorded, and every citizen had a personal file. And these records were Schneider's territory. He could sift through them for hours, apparently seeing connections that escaped lesser mortals. Albert moved a little closer and noticed that Schneider seemed to be concentrating on the husbands of the victims. This seemed strange to him as he knew that only one of them had been in Berlin at the time of his wife's murder. And it was obvious that the man had been destroyed by her death. In any event, he had an alibi. He was visiting his sick mother in hospital at the time of the murder, and this had been verified. So, what was so special about these absent husbands? Albert knew all he had to do was wait.

Schneider made what seemed to be a final check and then snapped his fingers.

'I think we are getting close. So, Hans, tell me what you deduce from the following pieces of information. One. The victims are all married to soldiers in the same regiment. Two. Only one of those soldiers was in Berlin at the time, and we know he is innocent. Three. All the victims are mutilated in the same way.'

Schneider might just as well have asked him to explain the theory of relativity. His blank expression was answer enough for Schneider.

'Nothing obvious? Then let me help you a little more. Did you notice that this regiment has been stationed in Russia, attached to "police duties" behind the front line? Do you know what "police duties" are, Hans? Of course you do. It means working with our friends in the SS, dealing with "enemies of the state", whoever they are. Does that help you any further?'

Some men might have been embarrassed by this sort of questioning, but Hans Albert knew that was not Schneider's intention. It was more akin to a kindly teacher encouraging a slow but keen pupil. Since he still hadn't made any sense of the clues, he said nothing.

'A little more then. Did you also note that it was the first murder victim whose husband was here? And did you note what the pathologist told us had been removed from every single victim? Her womb. So, putting all this together, what does it tell you?'

Hans Albert shrugged. It was still beyond him. But he knew he wouldn't be alone in that regard. Perhaps the only man who could get something out of this information was Schneider himself. Whether it was by reasoning or some intuition beyond the ken of mere mortals, Hans Albert didn't know.

'Well, my dear Hans, it tells me that the unfortunate husband of the first victim knows who the killer is. We only need to ask him. So, get onto army headquarters and find out the current location of Sergeant Helmer. I suspect the poor man will still be in hospital. And if he is, find out from that hospital which of his comrades-in-arms has visited him the most.'

*

As usual, Schneider was proved right. Helmer had never really recovered from his wife's death and was now in a clinic just outside Berlin. The doctors doubted if he would ever make a full recovery. Albert noted with interest that Schneider asked if the killer being caught would help the recovery. Schneider had never been known for his small talk or idle speculation; to ask this, he must be close.

As they waited for the patient to be brought to them, Hans Albert saw the first signs of the effect of a lengthy war. Doctors were noticeable only by their absence. Order had been replaced by disorder: beds were left unmade, patients were propped in chairs anywhere a space could be found. Nurses rushed and voices were raised, a sure sign of growing chaos. Worst of all was the constantly braying martial music that only served to remind these shattered men of what they once had been and never would be again. Albert hoped he didn't take ill soon.

Sergeant Helmer was less than happy to see Schneider again. The thick-set neck sank even lower into the broad shoulders, and the narrow brow furrowed its displeasure. The eyes still held a trace of the insanity that had brought him here. Deep down among all the other nightmares that must be filling his every waking moment, he knew that at one time he himself must have been a suspect. To be suspected of doing that to your own wife was not something you forgot.

Schneider ignored the sullen anger of the broken man opposite him and tried to make him see that it was normal police behaviour to investigate those closest to the victim. He explained that most victims know their killers, but it was difficult to tell if anything of this got through to Helmer. Finally, Schneider asked the questions that he needed to, knowing the last one could, and probably would, send Helmer completely over the precarious edge of sanity that he was clinging to.

'I think you had a friend with you from the regiment on the day your wife died, didn't you? Who was it?'

Helmer seemed surprised at the question. 'How did you know that?'

'I don't know that. I'm asking you now.'

'Peter Berger. He was new to the regiment, and it was his first leave. He seemed a little lost, so I took him to our house. We had something to eat and then he left for the station to get his connection.'

The eyes became misty. He was starting to remember the last day he saw his wife alive. Schneider had to be quick.

'And I take it that this Peter Berger was less than enthusiastic about your duties in Russia?'

It snapped Helmer back. 'What do you know about our duties in Russia? We only did what we had to, what we were told to do.'

'I'm not criticising you. You were a soldier. You will be one again. I just want to know what Berger thought of what you were doing, that's all.'

Helmer's face mirrored the memory of Russia as his mind took him back to a time when he had been a man, a proud member of the Aryan master race. It hardened as he remembered who had been in charge then, amongst the Jews, amongst the eastern *Untermenschen*, the subhumans.

'We did what was necessary. It was a hard job, but it had to be done for the Reich. But Berger? He was young, from the country. He never liked it, not from the start. He said it was wrong to kill people like that. That God would punish us. So, in the end, we gave up on him. We'd do the shooting and let him organise the burials and so on. Now I come to think of it, I don't think he ever shot any of the Yids himself. I didn't like it that much myself, but orders are orders. But I sort of felt sorry for him and knew he could end up at the front line if he wasn't careful. So, I sort of took him under my wing, I suppose. Why are you asking this? What's he got to do with . . . with . . . what happened to her?'

Hans Albert was unable to hide his shock at what he was hearing, but Schneider's face was a mask as he pressed on, ignoring the question. He was almost there.

'On the day you took him to your home, did you tell him that you and your wife were planning to start a family?'

Helmer slumped back in his chair as if struck by some invisible force. His lips puffed as he breathed out once, then twice. The eyes bulged until it seemed the sockets would be unable to contain them. And as they grew, the madness in them grew too. The scream that finally broke through the furiously working mouth only confirmed what Schneider already knew.

After they were out of the ward, Schneider asked Albert if he had discovered where Berger's regiment was stationed in Berlin.

'How did you know they're back here?'

Schneider gave him a knowing look and then Albert got his reward. As if a light had suddenly clicked on in a darkened room, he put it together himself.

'Are we going there to get him now?'

Schneider nodded. You didn't leave a murderer on the loose for any longer than was necessary.

*

Army barracks have that same look the world over. Grey, cold and masculine. Outsiders were not welcomed, and Schneider and Albert were clearly marked as outsiders. They could be nothing else but police, and to the soldier on rest and recuperation that spelled only trouble.

With a very obvious show of bad grace from the guard on duty, they were shown to the commandant's office. He was a man used to giving orders, not taking them, but when he heard Schneider's name his attitude softened. It must be serious if he was here. It took less than a minute to confirm that Peter Berger was indeed in the barracks, and a guard was dispatched to summon him to the commandant's office. The three men waited in silence until the knock at the door announced Berger's arrival.

'Private Berger, these men are from the police and would like to ask you some questions.'

Peter Berger was everything the idealised German soldier shouldn't be. For a start he had black hair and brown eyes. He was short and thin with the face of an innocent. His eyes held the kindly, almost submissive look of a country boy rather than those of the Aryan conqueror. At the mention of the word 'police', those

15

same eyes had taken on the concerned look of someone who might have unwittingly broken some minor law. They were not the eyes of a serial killer.

Schneider sensed that his assistant was starting to doubt his own conclusions and a small smile played across his lips. He himself had no such doubts.

'My name is Schneider. I am here to arrest you for the murder of six women. Do you have anything to say?'

It was an old ploy of Schneider's. No gentle introduction, no circuitous questioning, but rather a brutal, all-out assault. Over the years he had seen many reactions to this tactic. Some had hysterically denied any knowledge of the charge, other had started to cry, and some had even confessed on the spot. But whatever they did, they always did something. Peter Berger did nothing. It was as if Schneider had spoken a foreign language.

'You have nothing to say, then?'

Slowly the head shook, indicating no. There had been absolutely no change on the young soldier's face. No change at all. He meekly accepted the handcuffs and walked out to the car between Schneider and Albert. He could have been going for a stroll. And then they heard it. Softly, almost inaudibly, Berger was singing. It was a hymn.

*

Schneider and Albert went to an interrogation room and waited while Berger was being booked in. Like all new prisoners, he had to be searched and examined by a doctor to ensure he was up to interrogation. While they waited, Albert risked a question.

'Why do you think he was singing?'

'Because he was fulfilling his destiny. He thinks of himself as a martyr now. He has only been serving his God, and the unbelievers – that's us, by the way – will now make him a martyr. So, he was singing to his God.'

'Then you think he is insane?'

'Who knows what insane means these days? I don't really know what you would call him. But whatever he is, he is our man.'

They spent the best part of an hour trying to get him to talk, but Peter Berger was now beyond such earthly matters. He sat staring blankly, his mind elsewhere. Albert thought that they should simply hand him over to the shrinks. Not that it would matter in Nazi Germany. Insanity would not excuse him from the firing squad. But Schneider was determined to get a response. He decided to try a different tack. Maybe the cold interrogation cell was wrong. He told Albert to give him ten minutes and then to bring Berger up to his room. It was to be one of the few mistakes that Schneider made in his long career.

Schneider told Albert to leave him alone with Berger. Now in the cramped but more human atmosphere of his room, Schneider tried to get inside the mind of the other man. He hitched his chair closer, and his hands began a strange rhythmic wringing motion. The eyes had taken on a strange intensity that Hans Albert would not have recognised. Nor would he have recognised the voice. Low, almost a whisper, yet strangely staccato, as if the words were coming too fast.

'I thought it would be better if we spoke here alone. The others wouldn't understand, you see. I can't pretend to understand why you did what you did, but I know it must have been the right thing for you to do. I know that the Lord works through you. I have prayed for years that I might also become an instrument of His will. Could you tell me how I can do this? How did the Lord choose you?'

Berger still showed no reaction, so Schneider pressed on, both the hands and words moving faster now.

'Maybe I'm unworthy in some way. But I want to do the Lord's will. Maybe it is to help you to carry on with His sacred work. Do you want me to let you go?'

That brought a reaction. Berger was now staring at him. Schneider's voice dropped to an even more urgent whisper.

'I can, you know. I'm in charge. I can simply say that I was wrong, that you are innocent. Is that what the Lord wants? Tell me, we don't have much time.'

When the voice came, it surprised Schneider. It was soft, almost without any intonation, but overlaid with the guttural sounds of a strong Bavarian accent. It sounded like the voice of a lost soul.

'I want to go home. I want to see Mittenwald again before I die. I don't deserve to live. What we did in Russia is wrong. It is a sin crying out for vengeance. They made me kill those people. Just because they were Jews. I watched them taking off their clothes and standing there while we shot them. They never tried to stop us. Somebody said it was almost as if they wanted us to kill them, that we must be doing God's work. But that was when God spoke to me. He told me that this evil that is Germany must end. So, I stopped the killers from fathering more killers. I took their wives in atonement for what we had done in Russia. And now I just want to go home.'

Before Schneider could stop him, Berger rushed towards the window. He went through it headfirst. By the time Schneider reached the window, Berger was a broken heap in the courtyard forty feet below, the dark blood stain already starting to spread beneath him.

When he got down to the courtyard, Schneider looked at the smashed face and twisted body. Already he was asking himself why someone could do the things this boy had done. And then to kill himself. Maybe Berger was insane, but he hadn't always been. What had changed him? Schneider felt his mind going back to what the young man had told him about the happenings in the east. He knew it was something he had ignored before and insisted others did the same. But could he do it now? What sort of police officer would do that? What sort of man could do it? Before he could muse further, a car roared into the courtyard and screeched to a halt beside him. An SS officer leapt out. He ignored the human wreckage lying only feet away, as if it was an everyday occurrence for him.

'You are Chief Investigator Schneider? You have a Peter Berger in custody. Obergruppenführer Heydrich has deemed the matter one of state security and I am here to take him with me. Where is he?'

Schneider nodded to his feet. 'There he is. I don't think you're going to get too much out of him.'

Schneider wondered why someone like Heydrich would be interested. He put it to the back of his mind, but he didn't forget it.

*

'The body has been taken to the morgue. What do you want done with it after they are finished with it there?'

Schneider seemed to have been affected by the suicide. He had been happy to let Albert tie up the loose ends.

'Why don't we send him home to Mittenwald? That's what he wanted. Find out about his family and try to keep the worst from them if you can.'

Albert hesitated before asking the next question. You could never be too careful. Instinctively, his eyes checked that they were alone.

'Have you . . . eh . . . thought what you're going to put into the report to the SD?'

Although the matter was purely a criminal one, every major crime had to be reported to the Sicherheitsdienst, the Reich security service under the command of Reinhard Heydrich.

The question seemed to bring Schneider to himself. 'You mean, am I going to say anything about what Berger told me was happening in Russia?

'It doesn't really have to go in, does it? It doesn't really have that much to do with the killing. He was just insane, wasn't he?'

'Hans, Hans ... Yes, he was insane, and yes, it would be so easy to leave it at that. But he told me why he did it. I am a policeman. It's not for me to get involved in politics. That's for others. Now leave me to finish this, and then I'm going home for a long sleep.'

As he was writing the report, Schneider mused whether he should accurately report what Berger had said about Russia. The thought had occurred to him, even without his assistant's prompting. He had always stayed clear of politics. Politicians just talked endlessly, they never actually did anything. He talked only when necessary. He was a doer. Talking served no purpose unless it was followed by action.

The coming to power of the Nazis had meant little to him. Wars start and wars finish, but crime is constant. Like everyone else, he had heard the whispers and the rumours about what was happening in the east and in the concentration camps and, like most other Germans, he ignored them. It was the safest course of action. In any event, what could he do? Speaking out against what was happening would achieve nothing apart from his dismissal from the police, and he was arrogant enough to think that was not in Germany's interest.

He had seen the yellow stars of David appear, and the disappearance of Jewish police officers and lawyers. He didn't want to think about it. It was the law, after all, and he was a police officer, nothing else. But should a law like that even exist? Such matters were for the politicians or the philosophers, not for the likes of him. But now he couldn't put Berger's words out of his head. He felt it would almost be betraying him not to report what he had said. He put Berger's final words into his report. Let them do what they want with it and with him. He threw the report into the typing basket and headed home.

If you had told Schneider that in less than a year, he would be investigating the SS itself on the direct order of Adolf Hitler, he would have thought you as insane as Berger.

– 2 –

Berlin, 20 January 1942

The fifteen men made their separate ways to the attractive but anonymous villa in the prosperous suburb of Wannsee. They greeted each other warmly, secure in their positions of authority in an authoritarian state. They made small talk and boasted about their latest purchases from the conquered territories. They complained about their long and demanding working days, as middle managers do everywhere. The meeting was set to start at noon and chairman Reinhard Heydrich, head of the SD, was the last to arrive. He glanced at no one as he took his place at the front of the room. A hush had fallen with his arrival, and the fifteen took their seats and waited for him to begin.

They were an unremarkable group, comprised mainly of middle-aged bureaucrats. It could have been a gathering of executives from any large industrial company, except for the black-uniformed senior SS officers scattered among them. Only Heydrich noticed the small, insignificant-looking man who remained on the periphery of the others. He wore the collar studs of an SS colonel, which put him well down the pecking order. Most of the other delegates, even if they were aware of his presence, simply ignored him. Out of politeness, a few nodded a greeting and received the grateful, fawning response of the classic sycophant. Adolf Eichmann had turned obsequiousness into an art form and was quickly dismissed by the movers and shakers around him. He simply blended into the background. Only Heydrich knew his true worth, and Eichmann was content with that. At least for now.

Heydrich rose to his feet and the murmur of conversation died. His athletic physique was enhanced by his sharp features and blond hair. Here was the perfect specimen of Aryan manhood. His eyes passed coldly over the gathering before him, probing their inner thoughts, and few chose to meet his gaze. Not for nothing had he been called the handsome young god of death. His eyes finished their survey of the faces and minds before him and he began. As was his habit, he wasted no time on preliminaries.

'I have been appointed the plenipotentiary for the final solution of the Jewish question. It is our purpose here today, gentlemen, to decide how best we can implement this plan.'

If Heydrich's words shocked any of those present, it didn't show on their faces. Such men were well schooled in the practical politics of the Third Reich. Showing nothing was usually the best course of action until it became clear which way the wind was blowing. If they even suspected what 'final solution' meant, they hid that suspicion very deeply.

Heydrich went on to briefly summarise the history of the Jewish problem to date. He reminded them that the original plan had been to forcibly remove all Jews to the island of Madagascar. Unfortunately, the war had now made that impossible, and so the Führer had charged him with finding another solution. That solution was to be the forced evacuation of all Jews to the east to work as slave labour.

'Undoubtedly, the majority will fall through natural diminution, but a hard core of Jewry will remain. That hard core will be the product of natural selection and so will be the most dangerous to us. They will, therefore, have to be treated accordingly.'

Heydrich didn't spell out what 'treated accordingly' meant but then he didn't need to elaborate any further to such an audience. They were senior Nazis, after all, but even Heydrich was surprised at how readily his audience appeared to be accepting his plan. Quickly he turned to numbers. He had calculated that there were eleven million Jews in Europe, and all of them would be moved east. It was clearly going to be a mammoth undertaking, but it must be done.

All the while, Eichmann had sat and listened. He knew what 'final solution' and 'treated accordingly' really meant because Heydrich had told him. These euphemisms were only for the minutes of the meeting. As far as he was concerned, it didn't really matter what words were used. He had been given an order and he would obey it. As Heydrich continued, he was already thinking of the logistical problems of moving so many people. Clearly the railways were the only practical solution. He must ensure that he had absolute priority in this area, as that would be vital.

Heydrich was almost at the end of his speech, and Eichmann was looking forward to lunch. It would be a rare chance to meet important people and ensure that they remembered his name. Such opportunities should never be missed. If he did it well then surely further promotion could not be far off.

He was brought back to the present by Heydrich's raised voice. One of the bureaucrats seemed to be daring to argue with him.

'I do not agree with Obergruppenführer Heydrich's analysis. It seems to me that to take such a view would be very dangerous. I would propose a much simpler solution, I would—'

But Heydrich cut him off. It was clear to Eichmann that a problem had arisen.

'I have made my position clear. It represents the will of the Führer. I do not see that any further discussion is required on this topic.'

Heydrich brought the full power of his lynx-like blue eyes to bear on his opponent. His gaze was pitiless and had terrified countless numbers of friends and foes alike. He was known to be completely without pity, without any humanity. He was a man you did not cross. But the other bureaucrat was confident enough of his own position to argue further. And, incredibly, it was he who was arguing for the more radical solution.

'But we all know of the Führer's great humanity. And he has so much on his mind just now with the Russian front. So, I think that we, his faithful followers, should remove this burden from him once and for all. It seems to me that all Jews, irrespective of how much Jewish blood they have, should go east. That would be the real final solution.'

Eichmann realised that the argument was over the definition of a Jew. Even in Nazi Germany, there was still the pretence of laws and courts. Perhaps such a pretence was absolutely necessary to allow the good burghers of the country to sleep easily at night. The Jews had to be dealt with legally. It was necessary, therefore, for a law to be drafted, and laws require definitions. A Jew was a Jew, but were the children of mixed marriages Jews? So, there were laws about how much non-Jewish blood was needed to make one a non-Jew. What the bureaucrat was saying was what a lot of people really felt. But clearly not Heydrich. Eichmann knew of the rumours about Heydrich's own bloodline, of how he himself was tainted with Jewish blood. Was this why he was protecting those of mixed race? But that was inconceivable. How could you personally take responsibility for the extermination of an entire race of eleven million people and yet think that you may share some of that bloodline yourself?

It was clear that others at the meeting felt the same way. They would all know of the rumours about Heydrich. Maybe they were just testing him. It was a dangerous game and, ultimately, an unsuccessful one.

'Do you really dare to think the Führer has not thought this out? Have I not also personally devoted much of my own time to this plan? So, tell me exactly where you think I have made a mistake. I presume you do not intend to suggest the Führer has erred in some way – or do you?'

The question could not be answered, as everyone there knew. It was enough to quell any further discussion. Certain categories would not be going east.

After that, the meeting ended quickly and the participants enjoyed a leisurely buffet lunch and brandy. Eichmann mingled and flattered. No one there, apart from Heydrich, knew his true function. No one cared. Eventually, the party broke up and these fifteen men went their separate ways. Their consciences were clear. They were simply obeying the law of Nazi Germany.

As he travelled back to his office, Heydrich was troubled. Not by what had been decided. He had no scruples in that direction. Nor by the difficulty of the mixed race question. He was too powerful to let the rumours about his own bloodline affect him, and they had no idea of why he thought this important anyway. He was troubled by the whereabouts of his boss, Heinrich Himmler. Where had he been instead of at the conference? What could be more important to him than the final solution of the Jewish question?

At that moment, Himmler was also leaving a meeting. It had taken place in the Hungarian embassy and was indeed infinitely more important to him than the Wannsee conference. And it had to be kept more secret, much more secret.

*

Serendipity. Making discoveries by accident. It does not matter the lengths that men go to keep secrets, for on occasions serendipity will override every plan. It is likely that Himmler's meeting would have remained a secret from Heydrich but for a chance remark. Upon his return to headquarters, Heydrich requested a meeting with Himmler to report on the conference. This was immediately granted, and Heydrich found Himmler looking as relaxed as he ever did. The inscrutable eyes, shielded by the pince-nez, showed nothing of what was going on in the mind behind them. Physically, the two men were at opposite ends of the spectrum. Himmler was short, podgy, with receding brown hair and pitifully weak eyes. But mentally, they were on a par, each fully aware of the danger the other carried and also, in a strange way, each feeling a camaraderie with the other, as only men in their positions could.

Heydrich gave a brief report of the meeting. He used this as an opportunity to ask Himmler why he did not attend himself. He didn't expect to find out anything of value, but you never knew if you didn't try.

'I have every confidence in you and so my attendance wasn't necessary. And I had one of my migraines this morning.'

'I hope the Reichsführer is feeling better. Is there anything I can do?'

Heydrich's voice carried sympathy, but the eyes were cold, watching like a hawk. But Himmler was at least his match and betrayed nothing.

'Thank you, Obergruppenführer. But I am quite well now. I am afraid that I had to rest here all morning, but I am fully recovered now. So, I have much to attend to. Is there anything else?'

There wasn't and Heydrich left. Who knows what Himmler had been up to? Maybe he was even telling the truth. He did suffer from migraines. Heydrich would have dismissed it from his mind except that he met Himmler's chauffeur-cum-bodyguard in the corridor. Heydrich was a good boss to work for if you produced results. The chauffeur had once worked for him until stolen by Himmler. He had been a good driver, and Heydrich always had a word for him.

'So, you've had a quiet morning then, Erich, eh? Sitting with your feet up reading the papers, I suppose?'

It was an innocuous question just made in passing. The chauffeur was only too aware of the rivalry between Himmler and Heydrich to ever reveal what his master had been doing. But Heydrich had just left his master's office. Clearly, he was aware of what Himmler had been doing.

'I'm afraid that the Hungarian embassy doesn't have any papers that I would want to read. And as for the temperature there . . .'

Heydrich passed on without a flicker on his face. Well, well. So, Himmler had been to the Hungarian embassy rather than in bed with a migraine. Something was happening. All politicians, or those seeking power, need information. Like an insect's antennae, they gain such information by constantly sensing what is happening around them. If they lose this sense, they lose power. In Nazi Germany if you lost it, you would probably also lose your life. Heydrich had never allowed anyone to surprise him. His senses were acute as were his myriad sources of information. He had his own source in the Hungarian embassy. It was time to give him a call.

*

His contact in the embassy had been less than happy to hear from Heydrich again. His diplomatic passport offered him no protection against the likes of Heydrich. The photographs of him in bed with a young boy safely locked away in Heydrich's secret files ensured his co-operation. Such behaviour was not tolerated in Hungary and carried a lengthy prison service.

31

Heydrich's request had been simple and to the point. Find out how often the Reichsführer had visited the embassy and, more importantly, whom he had seen there.

He had his answer that same day. His contact had access to the embassy day book, which recorded all visits. It disclosed that Himmler had visited the embassy three times in the last four months and had always met the same man, a Victor Meznik. He was a middle-ranking embassy official who seemed to be of no great significance. But the Reichsführer SS does not meet a man of little significance three times. Clearly, there was more to this man than met the eye. Heydrich thanked his contact and assured him that his secret was safe, at least until the next time he needed him. He now needed to find out more about Victor Meznik.

Heydrich called for the SD files on the embassy staff. He let it be known he suspected a British spy was there and wanted to check any ties the staff might have to Britain. Heydrich was infamous for checking almost everything himself, so his request raised no suspicions. To have asked for Meznik's file alone could have got back to Himmler, and that would have been as dangerous to Heydrich as it would have been to Meznik.

Alone in his office, Heydrich extracted the thin file headed Victor Meznik and started to read. Like everyone in Germany, whether citizen or visitor, the

SD maintained a biographical file on them. Most were bland and restricted to routine information. But a diplomat's file held details of all his postings and any indiscretions that the SD were aware of.

Victor Meznik had been born in Budapest in 1907. He had attended university and joined the Hungarian diplomatic service in 1931. He had served in three different embassies and had an unremarkable record. There were no other details recorded. But on a different sheet of paper in the file, Heydrich found what he had been looking for. He made one phone call to someone loyal to him and him alone in a different department of the Reich security service. He had only to wait now for the trap to be sprung.

*

Four weeks passed before Heydrich got the call he was waiting for. In that time, he had watched Himmler for any sign, any clue of what he was planning. But he simply didn't have enough information. In every way, the Reichsführer was his old self. But that meant nothing. The man was a sphinx.

Heydrich had made his plans in the four weeks. He knew what had to be done. He had his two most trusted men on standby for this day. They didn't know why they were to do the job, only that it had to be done. Heydrich had thought of many different ways it could be done, but all of them carried risks of it eventually being traced back to him. So, he decided to do it the old-fashioned way. People might have their suspicions, but there would no proof.

The two men waited at the airport. The drive from Tempelhof to the Hungarian embassy was not a long one, so it had to be done as soon as the car left the safety of the airport. Victor Meznik had not enjoyed his short trip back to Budapest. For a start, the weather was poor and he was airsick. He had literally only been in Hungary for three hours and didn't even have time to see his family. But he had collected the package as normal and was now returning with it in his briefcase. As he had diplomatic immunity, his bag was never searched and so he was the perfect courier. He didn't know what the package contained, nor did he wish to. Unbeknown, save to a few, Victor Meznik was Jewish. That alone would have been enough to cost him his post in Germany. But he also had many relatives in Germany, in his extended Jewish family. Unfortunately for him, one of the few who knew his secret was Heinrich Himmler. How he had found out, Meznik had never discovered. But instead of exposing him, Himmler had offered to protect not only him but his German relatives in return for occasionally acting as a courier for him between Berlin and Budapest. He had never known what he was carrying and knew better than to try to find out. Himmler himself collected the packages from him. He received anonymous phone calls advising him when it was time to visit Budapest again. As a diplomat he only needed a day to get his exit visa, and the package was always waiting for him at the Hungarian foreign office. He had no idea where it came from. Himmler would call the day after he returned to Berlin. He simply collected the package, assured Meznik his relatives were being cared for and left. It usually took only a minute, but Meznik had come to dread that odious little creep even being near him for that length of time.

The embassy car was waiting and Meznik climbed into its warm interior. He had just had time to pick up a bottle of plum brandy in Budapest and was looking forward to using it to ease his shattered nerves and churning stomach. The car appeared out of nowhere and careered straight into the side of the embassy car. The force was enough to throw Meznik against the door opposite. He lay stunned as the door was ripped open. His last memory was of a large hand with a black jack in it. When he regained consciousness the next morning, everything in his pockets had been taken. So had the briefcase.

— 3 —

Berlin, 20 April 1942

Schneider had tried to avoid the party. Every year since 1933 he had successfully pleaded pressure of work as a reason not to attend. But this year his pleas were ignored. The Reichsführer himself was attending. All the senior SS, SD and police officers in Berlin would be there to celebrate the fifty-third birthday of Adolf Hitler. That alone would have been more than enough reason for Schneider to avoid it. Greedy, ambitious men bereft of intelligence had never been his type. He also knew that he would be regarded as a curiosity among them, someone who had never joined the Party. Schneider hated being the centre of attention, and the idea of having to make small talk with these morons made him feel almost physically unwell. But this year he had to do it. He had checked his tie was straight in the old mirror in his hallway and set off. The thought that he could maybe feign illness after the first hour or so sustained him as he drove the short distance to SS headquarters.

But now, over an hour later, he was actually finding

it an interesting experience. First of all, he had been generally ignored by the other guests. He realised that in time of war he was no longer a significant figure and all the talk around him was of what was happening in the east. Domestic crime paled into insignificance when set against a world war. Whether the ubiquitous, overwhelming confidence in the final victory was genuine or simply the mouthings expected of these people, he didn't know and really didn't care. He was happy to be allowed to stand in a corner, keep his mouth shut and observe.

He observed the sycophancy and the posturing. He observed the winning smiles to faces and the killing looks behind backs. He noticed the currents of power that eddied through the room and the way people were drawn from one to the other. But there were two circles of power that dominated all others. In these circles, sycophancy was raised to new and almost unimaginable levels. Men who wielded the power of life and death in the capital of the German Reich hopped nervously like errant schoolchildren. They hung on every word of the men at the centre of these circles as if they were holy script. Schneider smiled to himself as he suddenly realised that it was exactly that to these hangers-on. He was the only person in the room who had not tried to enter the circles around Heinrich Himmler and Reinhard Heydrich.

He noticed that gradually the two circles were drawing closer together. Suddenly, like some joining of two separate organisms, they merged, and Himmler and Heydrich stood together. Schneider had spent his life observing people and now studied the two men less than twenty feet away from him. Himmler was short with closely cropped dark hair. His little pot belly ruined the cut of his black tunic. He was an entirely unprepossessing figure, yet power seemed to radiate off him. But that sixth sense that Schneider had but could never explain told him the power came only from his position and not from the man himself. It was a common failing of such men that they always felt the need to demonstrate their power. To a keen observer like Schneider, it only demonstrated their weakness. In some ways, however, that weakness made Himmler even more dangerous. He would wield his power ruthlessly against anyone who even suspected he was not the German superman he craved to be. He was a bureaucrat and no matter what post he held, he would have used its power first and foremost for his own aggrandisement.

Heydrich was a different proposition altogether. Tall, blond, with piercing eyes, he radiated genuine power. Here was a man who would go to any lengths to achieve his goals. It was the first time that Schneider had seen his two bosses so close. Despite himself, he was impressed with Heydrich. He would have been even more impressed if he had understood the nature of the conversation that was going on between them. Heydrich was probing like a surgeon searching for a tumour.

'I understand that the wallet and briefcase of the Hungarian diplomat have now turned up. They were both empty, of course. Do you think they might have contained anything of importance to the Reich?'

Heydrich watched Himmler closely for any reaction. He had personally sifted through everything that had been taken from Victor Meznik. He had found the letter in the briefcase. It was short but completely incomprehensible. For the last six weeks he had mulled over its meaning, having retained it word for word in his almost legendary photographic memory.

H.

I agree with your proposals. The problem is one of co-ordination. Direct communication is impossible, and the M. route takes too long. I propose we set the time and act accordingly. We should wait until after this summer's battles have been fought. Regardless of the outcome, their positions will both be weaker. I propose 30 November. Do you concur?

B.

The 'H.' must be Himmler, but he had no idea who 'B.' was. 'M.' was Meznik, unquestionably. The letter was typed in German on ordinary paper. Whose position would be weaker, and after what battles? What was to happen on 30 November? Eventually, Heydrich realised that to break this code he needed a cipher. And that could only be Himmler himself, for that was the only lead he had. So, he had let the police recover the empty briefcase. Himmler had shown no interest in either the original theft or the finding of the briefcase. He really was a master. Meznik had returned to Budapest to recuperate from his injury, and Heydrich presumed that on his return to Berlin he would bear another message. Himmler obviously felt he was safe to wait until then, but Heydrich hadn't climbed to his rarefied position of power by waiting for others.

'I'm surprised at you, Obergruppenführer. Do you really think that I have time to interest myself in such minor matters? What interest do you think I could possibly have in the matter?'

Touché. Himmler had met his opening bid and raised. Should Heydrich now raise further?

'I had heard somewhere that this Hungarian was known to the Reichsführer. Perhaps I was wrong?'

Bull's eye. The face remained impassive, but the eyes blinked twice.

'I may have met him at some diplomatic function. I really cannot recall. But no doubt if there is anything of importance, you will advise me.'

'Rest assured, Reichsführer, you will be the first to know.'

The die had been cast. Himmler knew that Heydrich would never have asked such a question unless he knew something. But what did he know? Himmler was suddenly stricken with one of his migraines. Heydrich knew they often appeared in times of stress.

*

Where Heydrich was bold, Himmler was cautious. He seldom, if ever, took a rash step. He spent two weeks carefully considering the entire situation. Heydrich had the letter, of that he was sure. But equally he was sure that he couldn't possibly understand its significance. Only two men knew that. He could wait and see what developed, but deep down he knew the problem had to be dealt with. Once he had made his mind up, he could be just as ruthless as Heydrich.

He used an alternative means of communication, one that was less secure but safe enough for this purpose. That loose end could be tidied up in due course, along with the others, like Victor Meznik. The plan was simple and quickly accepted. Now he only had to wait.

Prague, 29 May 1942

Among his many positions of power in the Third Reich, Heydrich was the Reich Protector for Bohemia and Moravia. Surprisingly, he was doing a good job. He treated the Czechs who were prepared to work for the Reich fairly, allocating them the same ration levels as German workers, but extracting bloody revenge on those who showed the least sign of resistance. By and

41

large, German rule was now accepted, and the streets were almost as they had been before the German takeover.

During his visits to the protectorate, Heydrich lived twelve miles outside Prague in Panenské Břežany, a château that had been confiscated from a Jewish sugar magnate. Here he could relax with his family. So confident was he of his position that he drove in an open car on a daily basis from the château to SS headquarters in the city. Himmler was aware of this act of bravado.

Today seemed like any other to Heydrich until he noticed the two men. The car had slowed to negotiate a sharp bend on the road. One of the men produced a machine gun and started firing, and the other threw something. That something exploded below the car, but Heydrich managed to climb out and even return fire at the disappearing men. Then he collapsed, his spleen riddled with fragments of horsehair from the car seat that had been propelled into him by the force of the explosion.

Upon hearing the news, Himmler flew immediately to Prague. Heydrich was still alive, and a wounded animal is even more dangerous. The would-be assassins had disappeared, but Himmler would deal with them later. First of all, he had to determine if Heydrich was going to live. He had brought with him his own doctors, who gave a guarded prognosis. Matters were on a knife edge, in more ways than one. Himmler's concern was not that Heydrich would die. Few would genuinely grieve for such a man. But if he lived, what then? How would he react to this attempt on his life? Himmler's main worry was the files. Heydrich kept files on everyone. No one knew the contents of those files, but their very existence engendered terror among the leading Nazis. Everyone has a secret, and Heydrich knew more than most. He had used these secrets in the past to control others. Now, if he lived, he might use whatever he had in those files to strike back at his enemies. Something had to be done. Heydrich, although in agony, was lucid. Himmler risked a confrontation. After the usual pleasantries the well give to the seriously ill, he got down to business.

'The doctors are not certain if you will survive this terrible attack. I simply cannot imagine being without you. But if it should happen then we must work together now for the sake of the Reich. I know that in the past we have sometimes shared different views but of one thing I am certain. We are both loyal to Germany. If your secret files were to fall into the wrong hands, it could be disastrous, not only for me but also for Germany. Will you not trust me with them in the hope that I will be able to return them to you on your recovery?'

Despite the pain, Heydrich smiled. He knew now that the letter must be priceless. If he could only survive, he would be one step closer to his eventual goal: to succeed Adolf Hitler himself. 'I do not know what

43

the Reichsführer means by secret files. Perhaps there is one particular thing that you are interested in?'

Himmler could gladly have strangled the crippled man. But he had to know where the letter was first. It was time for both of them to put their cards on the table.

'Let us stop fencing with each other. You may not survive for much longer. If I do not get what I need from you and you die, what do you gain? Nothing. And you should consider your family. It would be unfortunate if anything were to happen to your wife and children when you weren't there to protect them. But if I have what I need, I give you my word that I will personally ensure their wellbeing. And if you survive, you will be at my side, as always. Most importantly, you know the information you have is worthless to you.'

'You seem to be very concerned about something that is worthless. As for threatening my family, I have made enough arrangements to look after them. In any event, you know that they know nothing and cannot harm you in any way. As to your word, well, I think you know how much either of our words is worth. But perhaps if you tell me more about what you are planning, I may be clearer as to what would be the best course of action.'

'What I am doing will ensure the Third Reich's future. I can tell you no more than that. Now, will you tell me where it is?'

Heydrich stared at the persistent little man sitting at the side of his bed for well over a minute. Then he simply said, 'No.'

*

Heydrich died a week after the attack. He was unconscious for the last three days of his life, but Himmler, ever cautious, had placed a stenographer by the dying man's bed lest he reveal anything in his delirium. He didn't. The secret of the whereabouts of the letter died with him. Of course, Himmler had Heydrich's offices and files thoroughly searched, but to no avail.

But Himmler reassured himself that only Heydrich would have had the necessary skill to use the letter against someone like him. Even if it turned up, it would be harmless to him in anyone else's hands. Or so he thought.

In the week after Heydrich's death, his assassins were discovered hiding in a church cellar in Prague. Despite Hitler's desire that they be captured alive for interrogation, this proved impossible. Himmler had removed a risk to himself, as he had promised B. he would. In the same week Victor Meznik was discovered dead in his Budapest home. The cause of death was a heart attack. No one realised it had been induced by injecting Meznik with benzene. Another risk had been removed. Now only the letter remained.

At Heydrich's memorial service, Hitler described him as 'the man with an iron heart'. It was a fitting epitaph, along with the destruction of the Czech village of Lidice and its inhabitants, ordered in retribution for his killing. Himmler said nothing but held the hands of Heydrich's two young children throughout the service. Afterwards he said it was a strange feeling, holding the hands of two half breeds. But he was content. His plan was now safe.

Except that Rolf Schneider was now about to make his reluctant entrance onto the field of history.

– 4 –

Berlin, July 1942

All the talk was of the new offensive in the east. The German armies had struck south towards the rich oil fields of the Caucasus. Stalin would have been fooled by the Führer's brilliance in not attacking Moscow again. The success of this attack would surely mean the end of the war. When Russia was beaten, the Führer could then make peace with America and set up a new world order. Then he could deal with the stubborn English as he wished. He would make them pay for their bombing of Berlin. And if America was stupid enough to keep fighting then the new wonder weapons that Goebbels threatened would still ensure complete victory. Indeed, hadn't the Führer so far resisted their use out of simple humanitarian concern for the devastation they would cause?

Schneider listened to the chattering around him. He knew that beneath the arrogant outward confidence, a great fear was stirring in the German people. Their armies had been turned back at the gates of Moscow last winter. It was whispered that hundreds of thousands had died in the snow. The Gestapo had been ruthless in stopping such false defeatist rumours spreading, but the whispers still persisted. America, that industrial giant, was now an enemy. Of course, Germany was an ally of Japan, but had the Führer really been right to declare war on the Americans? Hadn't the Japanese attacked America first? Worst of all, the bombing of Germany itself had started to become almost a nightly occurrence. Where was Göring's Luftwaffe?

It was normal for people to worry in times of war, but Schneider knew that the fear that eddied around him was not simply of losing a war. Every German suspected that things were happening in the east that would bring an awful retribution on their entire race if they lost this war. Jewish neighbours and friends had all but entirely disappeared. It had been years since a Jewish doctor, lawyer or schoolteacher had been seen in Germany. People simply didn't ask where all these people had gone because, deep down, they knew. And knowledge meant guilt. Schneider knew he was no different, but still he tried to force his mind to ignore the anxiety and the gossip, particularly today.

Schneider was having one of his rare days off. He had recently finished a major investigation. Perhaps 'finished' was the wrong word. Gold was being smuggled out of Germany, a capital offence in time of war. With his usual thoroughness, he had relentlessly traced the source of the trade in gold back up its chain through the army and Nazi bureaucrats. As he got higher, more inducements were offered to him to stop his investigation. He could have become a very rich man. But he was a police officer first and only. He continued. The inducements turned to threats. Schneider continued. Behind the threats and the bribes, he could sense the alarm in those he was investigating. He was beyond their power, which seemed to be a novel situation for such men. He discovered the gold was coming from somewhere in Poland and there appeared to be an almost endless supply. He sought permission to go there to continue his investigation. He was surely getting close to the top man. Without warning, he was told to stop. He was ordered to hand over all his files to the SD, who would now take over the investigation. Schneider was advised to simply forget all about it. Indeed, he was *ordered* to forget all about it. He knew what this meant. Somehow the SS were involved, and they never washed their dirty linen in front of outsiders. The matter would be dealt with internally.

But Schneider wouldn't or, more accurately, couldn't forget. That had been over a month ago. The men who Schneider had already identified as being involved were now all back behind their desks. It was as if nothing had ever happened. And then Schneider knew that the whole thing obviously came from the top. For the first time, Schneider wondered if he could continue being a police officer in Nazi Germany. Could a man really claim complete political innocence in such a country? He had looked the other way for so long, had pretended he only had to follow orders to be kept above the mire. But every German was responsible in some way, and he was no exception. He thought that defeat might not be so bad, after all.

Another man might have confided in a friend, but he had none. He never had. Ever since he was a child, he had been alone. An invisible wall existed between himself and other people. Even his parents seemed like strangers to him. He was happiest when he was alone with his own mind and thoughts. Sometimes, on odd occasions, he felt something was missing from his life, but he didn't know what. It wasn't that he felt lonely or lacking in anything. It was just a feeling that there should be more to life than what he had. Over the years the feeling had diminished and now it raised its head only rarely. It had become almost like an old friend now, reminding him that he was something more, or perhaps less, than what he appeared to be to others. He knew that people to him were just like pieces of evidence to be examined and then discarded. No one had ever touched him personally. He didn't cry when his mother died. He watched others instead and tried to imagine what *they* were feeling, but he didn't know where to start. He had no frame of reference. Love was only a meaningless word or, at best, something that only other people felt. After his father's death, he cut off all contact with his extended family. His mind thought only of the investigation he was on. Deep down he knew something was very wrong in a country where people seemed to disappear, but no laws were being broken. He forced himself not to think about it. After all, what would that gain? It would only distract him from the job in hand. He was like a mirror coldly reflecting back all outside unwanted influences. So, he was always alone, but on some days, those rare days when the feeling came, he liked to go somewhere different just to observe people, perhaps even be near them. Today was such a day.

He had gone out for lunch at one of the city's more expensive restaurants. He had drunk a half-bottle of pre-war Mosel and washed his coffee down with an excellent Weinbrand, Germany's cognac. He had almost managed to ignore the chattering around him and was planning to take himself to the Tiergarten, the zoo, for the afternoon. Even the Nazis had been unable to brainwash the animals there. He reached for his wallet to settle the surprisingly expensive bill.

He became aware that a hush had started to settle over the restaurant. He looked at the tables around him and found all eyes locked on the door. An SS officer stood there scanning the diners. Clearly, he was looking for someone. Even here, no one felt absolutely secure. As the eyes passed over each table in turn, the diners dropped their gaze, only raising their heads when they felt the eyes pass on to some other unfortunate. Eventually, they reached Schneider. He held their gaze and was somewhat startled when they did not move on. Instead, the tall, elegantly dressed officer headed towards his table. A wave of relief seemed to wash through the restaurant. They were safe again. And now all eyes turned on Schneider. Eyes that held no pity at all. Clearly, this man must be an enemy of the state and was now about to get his just desserts.

'Chief Investigator Schneider.'

It was a statement rather than a question, so Schneider simply waited.

'Would you please come with me at once? I have a car waiting outside.'

It was an unusual arrest procedure, if that's what it was. But equally, the invitation was not one that could be refused.

'Just let me pay and—'

'That will not be necessary.'

He snapped his fingers and, as if by magic, the manager appeared and plucked the bill from Schneider's table. Schneider noticed that his hands shook and that his eyes flitted everywhere except on his customer.

Schneider rose and headed towards the door, his SS escort just behind. Already he could hear the whispers starting as he passed. No doubt it would give them something new to gossip about for a while. A large Mercedes was waiting outside. Schneider noticed that it carried the personal flag of the Reichsführer SS,

Heinrich Himmler. Maybe it was the unaccustomed brandy, but Schneider was unafraid. He had no idea why Himmler would want him, so he felt he had nothing to be afraid of. The doors slammed shut and the car roared off.

*

Himmler was a man used to keeping others waiting. Schneider sat for over an hour in the small waiting room at SS headquarters. He was treated courteously and given coffee. Newspapers and magazines lay on the highly polished coffee table. Smartly dressed, confident young women hastened by with files in their hand. High-powered men occasionally passed, deep in conversation. It was a hive of industry and the very model of German efficiency. It could have been a waiting room in any highly productive and well-run organisation, except for one thing ... no one could tell him how long he would have to wait. Indeed, the look he had received when he asked the question spoke volumes. He would wait as long as was needed. It was not for him to enquire as to the Reichsführer's schedule. The effects of his unusual lunchtime drinking were starting to wear off, to be replaced by a dull headache. Schneider wanted to go home and sleep, but in SS headquarters the wishes of one man only were obeyed. His eyes started to droop and he struggled to make himself more comfortable in the heavy wooden chair. Then the phone on the secretary's desk bleeped. She listened for a moment before looking over at him.

'The Reichsführer will see you now.'

Two perfect specimens of the Aryan race escorted Schneider along the corridor. Immaculately dressed in black, they towered over him. Every detail about them screamed physical perfection. Yet Schneider did not feel inferior in any way. He had looked into their eyes and seen the moral and intellectual vacuum behind. They were machines, nothing more.

They entered a small anteroom and Schneider submitted to the body search. He knew there was no point in arguing. His pistol was removed. One of the automatons knocked on the door opposite. A strangely familiar voice said to enter. Schneider was ushered towards the door and through it. The other two stayed outside, the door now closing behind him. He was alone with Heinrich Himmler.

The Reichsführer sat behind a large desk. There were two neatly arranged piles of files on the left and right sides. He was in the process of signing something in the open file before him and ignored Schneider for the time being. If it was meant to impress Schneider, it was wasted on him. He had used all these techniques and more to intimidate and dominate suspects. He himself was immune to them. So, he studied the man and the room. Himmler appeared even smaller behind such a desk. The room was spartan and tidy. It could have been the room of a headmaster at some provincial school. Except for the portrait. Behind Himmler hung an enormous oil painting of Adolf Hitler staring out into the room as if alive, watching and listening to every word. Despite himself, Schneider found himself drawn to the mesmeric stare.

'It is a very good likeness, don't you think? Sometimes I feel his presence, as if he is actually standing behind me. But I suppose, in a way, he is standing behind every German, is he not?'

Schneider willed himself not to come to attention. Whether for Himmler or the painting behind, he didn't know. If Himmler noticed this apparent discourtesy, he gave no sign. He carried on talking, almost as if to an equal, a kindred spirit.

'But you are as aware as I am of the pressures of our work. No matter how many files I look at, there are always more. I think that even if I could do nothing else but sign my name, still there would not be enough hours in the day. And the contents of the files themselves? Some are a pleasure to read, like this one just now approving a promotion. But others here are less enjoyable. Traitors can be found everywhere. We Germans are having to suffer undreamed-of hardship in order to fulfil our historic mission. Harsh decisions and actions are required of us all at this time.'

Himmler leaned across and picked up another file. Schneider saw it bore his name on its cover.

'I have read your file with interest, Chief Investigator. It is probably fair to say that you are Germany's greatest detective. Over the past twenty years you have solved some of the most difficult cases imaginable. You have my admiration. It is, however, a disappointment that you have never found it necessary to join the Party, although I do not hold that against you. Perhaps you will see the error of your ways. But we can return to your politics later. That is not why you are here. Do you know why you are here?'

The wisest thing was to say nothing. But something made Schneider challenge the little, so arrogantly assured man before him. 'Presumably because of my investigation into the gold that is being stolen. Have the SD managed to make any progress?'

Himmler's stone mask of a face cracked. Clearly, Schneider had hit on a sensitive spot.

'You were ordered to forget that investigation, Chief Investigator. It is something beyond your area of responsibility, far beyond it. The matter is in hand, and you can be sure that the proper steps are now being taken.'

Schneider couldn't let it go. 'My area of responsibility was to solve a crime. People were stealing gold. I would have caught them. Is that not what the SD are now doing?'

For a moment he thought that Himmler was going to jump to his feet. Easy, Schneider, easy. Don't forget where you are and who you're speaking to. Push it too far and you could just disappear today, like so many others. But Himmler seemed to regain control.

'I repeat: leave this matter alone. You cannot know what you are dealing with. But perhaps you will in the future.' Himmler seemed to find his final comment amusing, for some reason, and his eyes shone at some hidden understanding. Then he stood up and came round the desk to stand directly in front of Schneider. He pulled his shoulders back and stared into Schneider's eyes.

'I have to tell you something of the gravest importance. You have been summoned here today on the express order of the Führer himself.'

*

It took Schneider some time to believe what he was hearing. He must have looked so shocked that even Himmler felt it wise to offer him a seat. Then he had listened in growing astonishment to Himmler outlining the reason for Hitler's summons. It was only now starting to penetrate. Himmler was summarising his instructions.

'So, you see, Schneider, the Führer feels that a totally independent investigation is necessary into Heydrich's death. He decided that it was best for it to be handled like any other murder inquiry, and so he asked me who was the best detective in Germany. I advised him you were. And here we are. You are ordered by the Führer to carry out a full investigation and to report your findings to him. I may tell you now, however, that I do not expect you to reach any different conclusions from that of the SS investigation. It may also be in your own interest to clear any report with me before passing it on to the Führer. Have I made myself clear?'

'Very clear, Reichsführer.'

Himmler then appeared to hesitate before he spoke again, trying to find the right words. His eyes tried to take on a look of unconcern, as if it was a minor matter hardly worth mentioning.

'There is one other matter. It is believed that Heydrich kept personal files. Such files should not have been kept outside this building. Unfortunately, these files have never been found. I do not expect you to have any more success than my own men, but if by some chance you do discover these files then I am to be notified immediately. The files can be of no value, but I think it would not be in your interest to read them anyway, should you find them. Nor should you report their finding to anyone else. I do not want the memory of a great man tainted by some minor bureaucratic failure.'

Schneider couldn't resist asking the obvious question. 'What do these files contain, Reichsführer?'

Himmler's face took on a pained look. 'I do not know. No one does, but there have been rumours that he kept some . . . However, such matters do not concern you or your investigation. I wish you success.'

Schneider had also heard the rumours about these secret files; they apparently contained information about the leading Nazis that none of them would want made public. But he had a more pressing concern. In less than fifteen minutes in that office, he had somehow ended up trapped between the two most powerful and ruthless men in Germany.

*

Schneider was ordered to begin his new assignment immediately. Himmler told him that an office had been assigned to him at SS headquarters and that the SS report into Heydrich's death was there for him to read. If he required anything further then he should ask. He was then curtly dismissed.

Himmler was satisfied. This policeman would be no threat to him or his plan. The best police officer in Germany? Perhaps. But more importantly, an apolitical one. With no axe to grind, he would have no real desire to dig too deep. And with no political allies, he could be easily controlled. Himmler was very satisfied indeed. But if he could have read Schneider's mind, he would have been a worried man.

Schneider knew exactly why he had been chosen and how Himmler expected him to react. But he intended to get to the truth of Heydrich's death. More than that, he remembered the fat, smug faces of the men who stole gold while others died at the front. He remembered the face of a young man driven to suicide by what he had seen. Perhaps it was time for him to start making amends for his years of deliberate blindness.

5

Berchtesgaden, August 1942

The summons had been unexpected, shocking and almost terrifying. Yet it was nevertheless welcome. It was welcome on three counts. First, it got Schneider out of SS headquarters, where he knew that his every move, his every request, was being reported to Himmler. Second, it was a chance to meet Hitler. To every German, maybe even to every human being on the planet, Hitler was a mystery. An uneducated man, a simple soldier, he had sprung from nowhere to lead the German people simply by the power of his will and his unique voice. But that hadn't been enough. Now he was trying to conquer the world. Like Attila the Hun and Genghis Khan before him, he was as much myth as substance. To meet the real man was an opportunity few got. And third, Schneider had never been to Berchtesgaden. Since Adolf Hitler had built his country house there, it had become a Mecca for German holidaymakers. On reflection, Schneider realised he had never been anywhere in his adult life unless it was connected with an investigation. Holidays were things that other people took. So, he was looking forward to seeing this charming old Alpine town close to the former Austrian border.

The SS driver assigned to Schneider had collected him at Munich railway station. He had travelled on the overnight train from Berlin to Munich, and it only suffered two delays due to the bombing. Sitting in a dark train inside an even darker tunnel was an experience he didn't wish to repeat. Although he knew it was nonsense, he couldn't stop his latent claustrophobia pushing images of collapsed tunnels and mangled carriages into his mind. The other passengers on the train seemed less concerned than he. Indeed, he was almost certain that he heard the sound of lovemaking coming from a nearby soldier and the girl with him. It had only added to his discomfort. Eventually, his torment came to an end. No bombs had landed near the tunnel and with the dawn the skies cleared of the planes and he emerged into the light.

The road from the city to Berchtesgaden passed through some of the most beautiful countryside in Germany. It had so far been completely spared the effects of the war, and Schneider marvelled like a child at the towering mountains with their perpetual snow-covered peaks. Greens of every hue leapt from the meadows and fields. Cattle wandered and grazed at their ease, their large Alpine cow bells adding to the overall tranquillity. A man could live at peace in such a place. He could see its attractions for Hitler.

A man could forget his worries here, at least for a little while.

The drive to Berchtesgaden was so enjoyable that Schneider even found himself trying to make small talk with the driver.

'Have you ever been here before?'

'No, sir. This is my first time.'

'What do you think of the scenery?'

'Very nice.'

Eventually, he gave up. The driver obviously felt uncomfortable talking to him. It was a feeling he had encountered most of his life. Few people feel comfortable speaking to a police officer. But the driver felt uncomfortable for a different reason. He was Himmler's creature, sent to spy on Schneider. You didn't fraternise with the enemy, no matter how much they tried. Himmler would probably take it as a sign that Schneider was already proving just how harmless he was. Good, thought Schneider.

They reached the first roadblock outside the town itself. When the Führer was in residence, security around Berchtesgaden increased exponentially. To Schneider's delight, Himmler's driver was relieved of his duties at that point. Schneider's pass to travel to the Berghof, the Führer's house, was in order, but that did not cover his driver. Another SS driver took over. He belonged to the Leibstandarte Adolf Hitler, the Führer's personal bodyguard. Their first and only loyalty was to Hitler himself. Here, even Heinrich

Himmler carried no threat. The last that Schneider saw of Himmler's minion was his hurrying towards a phone, no doubt to advise his master of what had transpired. Schneider settled back to enjoy the incredible ride up to the Berghof.

Hitler had first come to this beautiful region of Germany in the early twenties. He had apparently fallen in love with the place and managed to buy the small mountain chalet, Haus Wachenfeld, where he had stayed. As his fame and fortune grew, the modest chalet was gradually transformed into the Berghof, his rural home. The whole mountain that the house stood on had eventually been taken over. It now contained several barracks, a hospital and hotel, and it was surrounded by the most unimaginable security. Other leading Nazis had also had homes built there, to be near their leader.

As the car climbed the almost one-in-three road to the Berghof, Schneider recalled the old newsreels of Chamberlain, the British Prime Minister, coming here. What must he have felt, driving up such a road? It was as if you were going up to see a god. Did Hitler think of himself in such terms? Schneider looked forward to forming an opinion.

The car passed through three separate security checks. The entire mountain was surrounded by three concentric rings of security. Only those with the highest clearance were allowed inside the final ring that protected the Berghof itself. After the final check, the car climbed the last and steepest part of the road, slowing to almost walking pace as it toiled against gravity. Looking up at the very top of a mountain, Schneider caught the reflection of the afternoon sun against glass. He screwed his eyes up to get a better view and saw, to his amazement, that it was a building.

'Is that the Berghof there?' he asked, astonished that a building could be constructed so high.

The driver's voice echoed with pride. 'That is the Kehlstein, the Eagle's Nest. It is where the Führer sometimes takes tea. You can see forever on a clear day.'

'But how could something like that be built?'

'With German engineering. A lift shaft was blasted out of the mountain and lined with copper. If you get the chance to see it, it is something you shouldn't miss. That's the Berghof itself now just starting to appear.'

Schneider saw the Berghof rising above the road as they turned yet another hairpin bend. But the car carried straight on past the house itself and came to a halt behind the small guesthouse that now served as the Gestapo office. The Berghof itself was set just a little further down, but only visiting heads of state were allowed to drive there. Lesser mortals had one final security check in the Gestapo office before being escorted down to the rear entrance. Schneider noticed that his briefcase was not searched, although he had to hand over his pistol. He thought this was a glaring lapse in security until he got to the Berghof itself.

Here he was physically searched and every item in his briefcase minutely examined by a team of SS guards. Satisfied, he was informed that as the weather was so pleasant, the Führer would see him on the balcony. He was shown to the biggest balcony he had ever seen to await Hitler's summons. He was stunned. The clear weather gave him a view over all the surrounding peaks stretching well into Austria, now known as the Ostmark. The air was fresh, birds were singing. It was idyllic. Could there really be war raging all over the world? But then he noticed the guards everywhere. On the corners of the balcony, at every door and also in the forest below. The whole mountain was covered in them, like ants on a nest.

He sat and enjoyed the view, for there was nothing else to do. In the distance he could see Salzburg. He remembered a school visit to Mozart's house and the special marzipan sweets made in his honour. Even then he had wanted to be a police officer, to catch murderers. Now he was sitting on the balcony of the biggest murderer in the world. But what could he do? He must have been lost in these thoughts because he did not hear the footsteps behind him.

'I also find the view quite intoxicating. If I didn't have other duties, I would spend the rest of my life here.'

The voice was unmistakable. Schneider leapt to his feet and turned. He was face to face with Adolf Hitler.

So great was the shock that Schneider just stared open-mouthed for what seemed to him to be an eternity. As if by its own volition, he felt his right arm starting to move, to rise in the Hitler salute. And then Hitler held out his hand and grasped Schneider's. The handshake was brief and somewhat limp, but it was enough to allow Schneider to regain control of himself. Later he learned that it was Hitler's invariable practice to shake hands with everyone he met. It was just his Austrian upbringing but, coming from the Führer of the Greater German Reich, it took most people by surprise.

'I thought we could talk here, as it is such a lovely day. I do not have much time, but perhaps we can have coffee together while you explain what you are going to do.'

Hitler signalled and immediately coffee and cups were produced. Hitler sat at the wooden table with his back to the view. Despite himself, Schneider was impressed at this thoughtful act. Hitler could see the view anytime. Schneider sat opposite and waited for the SS guard-cum-waiter to pour. He noticed that Hitler did not take coffee but rather some herbal tea. There were also some squares of chocolate, which Hitler began to consume with great relish. Schneider was surprised when Hitler started to make polite small talk with him, asking about his journey and commenting on the weather. He quickly realised that the man opposite was really two different men. One was the Führer, the leader, the great warlord. But the other was the *petit bourgeois* who felt obliged to go through the ritual for every guest. Without warning, however, the Führer returned.

'So, Schneider, the Reichsführer has told you why you are here. I wanted to see you personally, to see Germany's greatest living detective. The Reich is in your debt. But there is now more important work for you to do for the Fatherland. I want you to find out the truth about the murder of Heydrich.'

Schneider had been studying the man opposite. He had seen the face hundreds of times, emblazoned on banners, newspapers and books. And yet to see it in the flesh was disappointing. It confirmed what Schneider already knew. The Führer was a man, nothing more. And not a very impressive man, at that. Already the face was showing the signs of the strain the man must have lived under for the past three years. The skin had a washed-out, almost translucent look as if from lack of sleep, and the hair, unlike in the photographs, was now decidedly grey. There was a tremble in the hand when it reached for the chocolate. This was a man in the first and irreversible stages of old age, not the Führer-God of Goebbels' propaganda. Yet even now, Schneider was aware of those things that had propelled Hitler to absolute power. The voice was indescribable. Harsh, guttural, with a distinct Austrian accent, it was the voice of an uneducated man. But it carried a force, a certainty within it that brooked no opposition. Even now, when at its natural timbre, Hitler's voice was compelling. When raised in spellbinding passion, surrounded by thousands of believers, it must have been irresistible. Schneider knew that the magic in such a voice worked on individuals as well as the masses. It would take a constant deliberate effort on his part to resist its blandishments.

But the voice was not Hitler's only weapon. For behind the voice were the eyes. Eyes of the sharpest blue that seemed to penetrate to your very soul. To return their gaze for any longer than a second was impossible, but even in that first second Schneider felt their power. He had never believed in hypnotism until this moment. But in that one brief locking of eyes, he had felt himself drawn to this man, *his Führer*. Schneider deliberately shifted his gaze to the stunning peaks behind. Before Hitler came to power, some of the newspapers had suggested that he was pure evil. One had even called him the anti-Christ. Schneider had never believed in God or magic, but he wasn't so certain now. There was something almost mystical about the power that Hitler could wield. Schneider knew now how this man had been able to entrap Germany. He only hoped he could save himself.

'Heydrich was invaluable, almost irreplaceable,' Hitler was saying. 'Now I am left to work without him. Destiny has indeed given me a hard road to follow.'

Schneider glanced back at the man in front of him. Instantly, the eyes found his and he fell himself starting to fall under their magic. The voice was now tugging at his emotions, making him want to help this man. Schneider shook his head, desperately trying to clear it. The eyes were compelling him to respond. He knew he had to get away.

He was rescued by an interloper arriving on the balcony.

'Adolf, when can we take our walk? I've been waiting all afternoon.'

Eva Braun was slim, attractive and liked the simple things of life. Like an afternoon walk with the man she loved. Only she would dare to interrupt and call Hitler 'Adolf'. Hitler rose to his feet, again revealing his Austrian manners. Schneider, still trying to clear his head, followed more slowly. Like most Germans, he had never heard of Eva Braun.

'Herr Schneider, may I present Fräulein Braun. She is a guest here. Herr Schneider is our greatest detective. I will only be a few more minutes and then we can walk.'

Eva shook hands with Schneider, pouted at Hitler, and left. Remarkably, Hitler felt the need to apologise to Schneider for the interruption. The voice was now soft with emotion. Schneider intuitively realised that he had just met Hitler's mistress.

'Please excuse her, Schneider. She gets to see me so little now with most of my time being spent in the east. She is young, and the young have no patience for matters of state.'

The voice changed. He was the Führer again.

'Now tell me, what do you think of the SS report into Heydrich's death?'

Schneider spent the next ten minutes avoiding Hitler's eyes and prevaricating about the report. He still had much to do. He needed to visit Prague and to interview witnesses, but it was difficult to arrange this in the middle of a war. Perhaps the Führer could help . . .

Hitler suddenly interrupted. He jumped to his feet, clearly more comfortable in that position. The Führer of Greater Germany was not normally seen sitting.

'You are perfectly correct, Schneider. You must have full access to everything you need. Wait here a few moments and I will arrange for you to have the necessary authority. Please conclude your investigation as soon as possible.'

With that, he was gone. Schneider slumped back in his chair. He had survived and got what he wanted. Power to override Himmler. Now he could really investigate Heydrich's killing. And the other things.

He didn't know how long he sat there. He felt drained as if from some titanic struggle. He heard voices on the road below. Hitler and Eva Braun were setting off for their walk. Schneider knew he was now privy to a secret that could kill him. He looked back towards Salzburg. His youth seemed a long time ago, a lifetime ago.

He didn't have long to reminisce. An SS guard approached and asked Schneider to follow him to the interior of the Berghof. The rooms were large but lacked charm. It was like walking through a museum. He followed the guard to the rear of the house where the staff offices were. The guard knocked on an unnamed door and a voice within told him to enter. He stepped aside and ushered Schneider forward into a small study containing only a desk. A man was seated behind it, and the face was strangely familiar to Schneider, although he could not immediately put a name to it. Unlike most of the others Schneider had seen, this man was wearing the brown uniform of the Party rather than the black of the SS. He remained seated, staring at a letter he held in his stubby fingers. Then he nodded, coming to a decision. He lifted his gaze to Schneider. It was a cold, almost reptilian look, but it held none of Hitler's power. It was the gaze of a bully. And like all bullies, he had to show how important he was.

'I am Reichsleiter Bormann. I act on the Führer's behalf *in all matters.*' He had deliberately stressed the last three words to ensure Schneider knew just how important he was. His gaze returned to the letter in his hands. 'The Führer has asked me to give you this authority to allow you to carry out your investigations. I suggest you read it now while I explain some things to you.'

He slid the letter across the desk and Schneider picked it up. Bormann still hadn't risen nor offered Schneider a seat. But that would have been difficult because the only seat in the room was already under

71

Bormann's ample backside. Schneider was unimpressed. A bully always likes to show his power, no matter how petty the performance. He turned to the letter, which was short and to the point. It was printed on the official note paper of the Führer.

> *Chief Investigator Schneider is acting on my direct orders. I instruct all persons, regardless of office or rank, to render him such assistance as he requires and to treat such requests as my direct orders.*
>
> *Adolf Hitler*

Schneider forced his face to remain impassive. He didn't want to give Bormann the satisfaction of seeming to be impressed by the letter. But inside he was shaking. With such authority, he could do anything. Nobody could stop him.

Then Bormann spoke again. It was as if he had read Schneider's thoughts, and his words were like a splash of cold water on Schneider's face.

'Do not let the letter go to your head, Schneider. I drafted it. I can just as easily draft another, rescinding it. The Führer relies on me in such matters. I arrange all appointments for the Führer. So let us be clear about your duties. By all means find out everything you can about Heydrich's death. But before you report anything to the Führer, show it to me first. We do not want him unnecessarily troubled. I would also suggest that you keep me informed of any developments on a regular basis. Do we understand each other?'

Schneider understood Bormann only too well. But he also knew Bormann would never understand someone like him. He was being squeezed between Bormann and Himmler in a competition for power. For a moment he toyed with the idea of calling Bormann's bluff. After all, he had the letter. But it was too soon. He would just let the game play out. He would carry out the investigation. He could worry about the rest later.

'Yes, Reichsleiter. I am completely clear as to what is required.'

He had deliberately come almost to attention. Let Bormann think he was cowed if he wanted. Why make another enemy just now? He looked again at the letter in his hand.

'I suppose this letter can at least arrange a car back to Munich for me? And a flight to Hamburg?'

Bormann was surprised at this. 'And why do you want to go to Hamburg?'

Schneider couldn't stop himself from showing a little resistance. 'When I have something to report, I will.' But he didn't say to whom.

Bormann accepted this small show of spirit. Schneider was of no consequence to someone like him. He could swat him as easily as another man might a fly.

6

Hamburg, the following day

Schneider had been driven down the mountain out of the security zone. Bormann must have arranged for him to be taken straight to Munich airport. By the time he got there it was too late to fly, as the air raids would be starting soon. So, Schneider had found a cheap guesthouse nearby to spend the night in. Maybe his letter could have got him somewhere better, but it never occurred to him to use it. The next morning, he was at the airport at first light and found a plane waiting for him. Whether this was thanks to the letter or Bormann, he didn't know and didn't really care. He was on an investigation and needed the plane to get to where his first witness was waiting. It also gave him the chance to re-read the SS report on the flight. He also thought carefully about the questions he intended to ask when he got to his destination. The SS report was to be his bait. As a police report, it was useless, filled with assumptions, dead-ends and faulty conclusions. But at least it gave Schneider the clues he needed to really carry out an investigation.

According to the SS report, Heydrich had been slain by three Czech resistance fighters parachuted into the country by the British, who also supplied the weapons and explosives. The three men had been found by the authorities, but it was impossible to capture them alive. Ballistics proved their weapons had fired on Heydrich's car. More explosives of the same type that had been thrown at the car were also found. It was an open-and-shut case. The British and the Czech resistance were responsible. It was all so glib and easy.

Schneider knew it was all a complete fabrication, but superficially it was credible and that was all that mattered in a totalitarian state. He knew it didn't add up because it lacked the one thing that any murder investigation needed: a motive. The war wasn't enough. This was directed against Heydrich personally. Why? Why not assassinate Himmler or Göring, or even Hitler himself? The answer was because wars were not conducted by assassins but by generals. And politicians didn't try to assassinate each other, even in times of war.

Schneider thought for a moment that it might be a better way of waging war. Let the leaders fight if they wished. He knew very few people who welcomed war, so how did they start? Leaders let them start, so maybe they should finish them also. It was a nice thought, but fantasy. Why was he thinking like this when his mind should be on the investigation? It was most un-Schneider like. He returned to Heydrich.

What was the real reason for his death? To begin to find the answer, he had to get to know the man. So, he was going to see the person who probably knew Heydrich best: his wife. Following Heydrich's death, she had returned to the family home on the Baltic island of Fehmarn, and it was there that Schneider was heading, unannounced and unexpected.

Schneider had used the aeroplane radio to contact an old colleague in the Hamburg police and arrange for the use of a car. He could have used the letter, but something held him back. The less people knew about him and his investigation, the better. They landed at Hamburg airport and the plane taxied to a small parking area well away from the constant military take-offs and landings. He told the pilot to wait for his return and was not surprised that his orders were accepted without question. Whether he would be back in an hour or a week didn't matter. It was clear this man would wait until a higher authority overrode the order, and there was no higher authority.

Schneider collected the unmarked police car that was waiting for him and set off for Fehmarn. He drove through the beautiful Baltic town of Lübeck, so far untouched by the war, onto the plain leading to the island. As ever, a wind was blowing. Schneider had never understood why so many of his country-men spent their holidays here. It was remote, cold and featureless. Even the people were different and spoke an almost unintelligible language to the outsider. He reached the bridge across to the island and drove through the small town. He had little difficulty in finding the Heydrich family home. It was an unremarkable house on a quiet street of equally unremarkable houses. Whether any of the houses were occupied was difficult to tell. The streets were deserted and there was not even a curtain twitch to hint he was being watched from any of the windows. He had expected to be challenged, but to his surprise he found the Heydrich house completely unguarded. It seemed strange and he wondered if perhaps the family had moved; but with Heydrich dead, why did they need protection now? He parked a little along the street and walked up to the front door. As far as he could tell, neither he nor the house was under any kind of surveillance, but he couldn't be sure. At this point it didn't matter anyway – it would still just look like a standard police investigation. He rang the bell.

Lina Heydrich answered the door herself. Schneider showed her his police identification and enquired if he could ask her a few questions. She seemed surprised but readily allowed him into the lounge. He could see that her eyes were red from crying. She must be one of the few crying for Heydrich.

Like any good middle-class German housewife, she offered him coffee and cake, which he accepted. It also allowed her time to recover herself. While she was in the kitchen, he studied the room. It was unpretentious.

There was nothing to indicate the nature of the owner. Lina Heydrich returned and served him some cake. He noticed it was not home-made, so the family must still enjoy some privileges. She had washed her face in the kitchen and her eyes were less red.

'So, Herr Schneider, what can I do for you?'

'First of all, may I thank you for seeing me without an appointment. I can say I did this for your own protection. Certain people may not have been too happy about this and tried to prevent it. Now it is too late, and there is no risk to you after I leave here.'

She had not been Heydrich's wife without learning about such matters. 'Herr Schneider, I think I am perfectly safe. I was Reinhard's wife, not a professional associate. I know nothing of his work because he made sure I didn't. Although my husband is gone, he has made certain that I and the children will not be harmed. So, I do not think you need concern yourself on that front. And I may decide to report your visit to me anyway. That will depend on what the question is.'

'That is your right, but first of all please let me show you two things. Afterwards you may ask me to leave or report my visit to whoever you choose. But please, look at these things first.'

'What are these things?'

'One is a letter. I have also brought with me the SS report into your husband's death. Do you wish to read it?'

That got her attention. As Schneider suspected, she

had been given almost no information about the killing. She stretched out her hand.

*

It took her fifteen minutes to read the report. It really was that short. Her face was a mask, and even Schneider with all his experience couldn't guess what she was thinking. At one point she blanched, and for a moment her anguish was clear to see, but only for a moment. When she had finished, she returned the report to him without comment.

'And what is this letter you want to show me?'

He showed her the Hitler letter. Again, her thoughts were her own.

'So, Frau Heydrich, you now know my authority. I could demand your co-operation, but I ask it instead. If you refuse, I will leave and you will never see me again.'

Tears were now in her eyes. The details of her husband's injuries and suffering had been detailed in the report.

'What is it you want to ask me?'

'One question to begin with. Do you believe the report you have just read?'

Schneider waited, hardly daring to breathe. For a long spell she stared at him, trying to judge whether he could truly help or not. Then she just said, 'No.'

Schneider spent the next two hours questioning Lina Heydrich. By the time he was finished, the sky was darkening. He knew it was crazy to fly at night during the RAF bombing raids, so he phoned his colleague in Hamburg and arranged to stay with him. He knew he wouldn't be questioned about what he was working on and could enjoy a decent meal and a bed that was clean. He also phoned the pilot and said he intended to fly to Prague at first light tomorrow. By now he was almost getting used to his orders being obeyed without question. Perhaps the adage was right, after all: power does tend to corrupt. But he knew his power was transitory and doubted he would have it long enough to need to worry on that score. On the drive back to Hamburg he went over what he had learned from Heydrich's widow, or rather what he hadn't learned.

He had asked her the most obvious question of any murder investigation: who did she think would want to kill her husband?

Both she and Schneider immediately saw the incongruity of such a question in relation to someone like Heydrich. It helped in some strange way to release the tension, and Schneider was sure that he saw the shadow of a smile play over her drawn face.

'Some people would say that everyone in the Reich, or even beyond, might have wanted my husband dead. But I presume you mean who in the leadership might have done this. My husband had several enemies, as you probably already know. They were his enemies for any number of reasons. Fear, envy, or just hate for something Reinhard had done. Sometimes I think it was for no reason at all, that some of these people just hate for hate's sake.'

Schneider instinctively looked around, expecting Gestapo men to suddenly appear on hearing what was a treasonous statement in the Third Reich. But presumably no one would dare to bug Heydrich's house. Schneider felt a chill run up his back. Who knows what is happening now that he is dead? He could only hope Heydrich was able to protect his family even from the grave.

'Herr Schneider, any of the leadership would have wanted my husband dead. You see, just before he left for Prague, he told me something that the Führer was planning to announce on his return: my husband was to become the Führer's chosen successor.'

Schneider immediately grasped what this meant. Göring was to be replaced as successor; clearly, he had a motive. Himmler was being overtaken by his own most dangerous subordinate; he had a motive. And where did people like Goebbels and Bormann stand in all this? Were their positions threatened? Did they have a motive? Now Schneider had two clear suspects and maybe two others. It was a start.

Lina Heydrich didn't know who knew about Hitler's plans, but Schneider was sure that Bormann at the very least must have known. Had he told anyone else? And who knew what spies Himmler had? It was now starting to take the shape of a real murder investigation. He had let Lina Heydrich talk on, most of what she was telling him being irrelevant. But he didn't stop her. Because he wanted her to answer one more vital question. When the time was right, he asked it.

'Do you know where your husband's secret files are?'

She froze, her cup of coffee suspended before her mouth. Her eyes showed her surprise and also something else. Fear? No, not that. It was amusement.

'Herr Schneider, you may be the best police officer in Germany, but you will never go far in politics, at least in this country. No one would ever ask such a direct question of me. I could easily tell you that I don't know what you are talking about, and then what would you do? But I have heard the rumours about these files as well. Believe me when I tell you that I have never seen them and have no idea where he kept them. Even if I did, do you think I would tell you?'

She looked at him as if sudden revelation had come.

'Although maybe I would, because I think you are the only man who will try and get to the truth about my husband's death. To you, the papers mean only that. But I don't know where they are. Do you believe me?'

Schneider did because Heydrich would never expose his wife to unnecessary danger. And such knowledge would be lethal. He had asked everything he needed. As he was leaving, however, she gave him something else.

'My husband was a very intelligent, very careful man. You can be sure that if these papers exist, they will be somewhere that the likes of Himmler will not find very easily. No one will. But perhaps I can give you a little help. Reinhard trusted very few people. Some say he trusted no one, but I know that isn't true. Anyway, there was one secretary that he trusted above all others. They seemed to have some kind of special bond. I know it wasn't sexual, for he told me about her himself. I even met her, and believe me, a wife knows such things. But he trusted her in some special way. Maybe she can help you further. I know that she has been questioned by Himmler. But maybe you could find out something he didn't. Her name is Anna Weiss.'

*

The next morning was cold and grey with a chill wind coming off the sea. Schneider was glad to be leaving. He arrived at the airport to find his plane and pilot ready and waiting. If the pilot was surprised at the change in destination, he didn't show it. He filed the new flight plan and ten minutes later they were airborne. Schneider suspected that he had also phoned his master with the news. Whether this was Bormann or Himmler, Schneider didn't know. For the moment it didn't matter. He could even afford to let his future movements be known.

'I am returning to SS headquarters in Berlin. I expect to be there for a few days and have cancelled my visit to Prague. You may return to your other duties after we reach Berlin.'

He drove directly to SS headquarters and spent the

rest of the day pretending to be studying files relating to Heydrich's death. Fortunately, Himmler was not in Berlin, so he was spared a summons. He went home to his flat and had an early night. Tomorrow might be a long day.

Berlin

The next morning, Schneider went to Heydrich's old offices. Ernst Kaltenbrunner had been installed as Heydrich's successor. A tall, scar-faced Austrian, he was everything that Heydrich hadn't been. He was a fanatical brute and totally lacked Heydrich's natural intelligence. Yet this man had a PhD and gloried in the title of 'Doctor' almost as much as his SS rank. He had progressed through the SS on the classic route of cunning and brutality. Within two minutes of arriving, Schneider was summoned to his office. He was even taller than Schneider realised, standing at well over six feet. The duelling scars on his cheek made him look like a gangster, and Schneider found it hard to believe he was a qualified lawyer.

Kaltenbrunner knew of Schneider's appointment to investigate Heydrich's death, but he wasn't going to have anyone interfering in his fiefdom. When you had power in Nazi Germany you hung onto it.

'What's the meaning of this, Schneider? How dare you question my staff without my permission. And stand to attention before me.'

Schneider reached into his pocket and threw Hitler's letter onto the desk between them. He didn't have time for Kaltenbrunner nor his ego. 'Read this, now.'

It was a command. Kaltenbrunner flushed, the scar standing out a vivid white on his cheek. No one ever spoke to him like this. But he picked up the letter and read. The change was remarkable. He proffered it back to Schneider as if it would bite him.

'Please excuse me. I had no idea. Is there anything I can do to help? My entire office is at your disposal.'

'I know it is.'

Schneider let the words hang between them for a moment or two, just long enough to show who had the real power here. Then he turned and left the giant standing with his mouth gaping. Kaltenbrunner knew nothing of interest to Schneider.

Schneider asked for and got the list of staff attached to Heydrich. He made a pretence of studying this for a while and then chose four people he wanted to interview. One of them was Anna Weiss. The three others were brought to him in short order and Schneider passed a wasteful hour asking them about Heydrich's previous trips to Prague. But he had to keep up the pretence that he still had no definite line to follow. Indeed, he 'let slip' to one of them that he thought Heydrich had become somewhat careless with his security. That ought to keep Himmler happy for the time being. After he had finished with the third one, he asked for Anna Weiss. The secretary who was helping him said that she was no longer here, that she had been transferred to a different department shortly after Heydrich's death. She didn't know where. It made it very difficult for Schneider. If he showed too much interest in her, others might wonder why. But he had to speak to her.

'Tell Obergruppenführer Kaltenbrunner that I want to see him again.'

Schneider enjoyed ordering someone such as Kaltenbrunner to come to him. The smile on the secretary's face told him she enjoyed it as well. Kaltenbrunner arrived in under a minute. Clearly, the letter worked. Schneider made it seem that he was giving him a report out of courtesy. He was Heydrich's successor, after all.

'I am finished here. Please don't quote me on this, but it seems your predecessor had become over-confident. God knows how many people knew about his travel arrangements. It was only a matter of time, I suppose, before the resistance found out.'

Kaltenbrunner watched him under hooded eyes. Schneider knew his every word, his every action, would be reported to Himmler within minutes. But he also had the Hitler letter. Kaltenbrunner saw no harm in currying favour. Just in case, just as Schneider had expected one such as him to behave.

'Of course. Everything you tell me will be treated in the highest confidence. The Obergruppenführer is a sad loss to us all. He had many great qualities, but perhaps he grew careless. It is something we all must guard against.'

He waited to see if Schneider was going to impart anything else of value, but Schneider seemed to be finished, putting the last of his papers into his briefcase. Then he stopped as if he had just remembered something.

'There is one other thing I would like to check just a little further about these travelling arrangements of Heydrich's. They were handled by someone called Weiss. But I am told she no longer works here. Where is she now?'

Schneider was watching Kaltenbrunner closely to see his reaction. But there was none worth the name.

'Ah yes, her. I got rid of her myself. She really wasn't what I was looking for. I don't know what Heydrich saw in her.'

'So, where is she then?'

The pleasure of the memory was clear for Schneider to see.

'I sent her somewhere she didn't want to go. I sent her to Dachau.'

Schneider struggled to remain calm. Everyone had heard of the concentration camp just outside Munich. He couldn't show any unusual behaviour, do anything that would be considered strange. So, he made a joke.

'On what grounds did you send her there? Surely it needs more than bad typing?'

Kaltenbrunner laughed. It was a horrible sound but suited the man perfectly.

'Oh no, you misunderstand me. She isn't a prisoner there. I sent her there to work. Is she important to you?'

'Not at all. It's just that I like to tie up all the loose ends. But it really doesn't matter. I'm sure she could tell me nothing that isn't already in the files.'

Schneider made his farewells. He had let it seem that it really wasn't that important he speak to this girl – maybe he would the next time he was in Munich, if he had some time. But he made it appear as if he had almost finished his investigations anyway. He thanked Kaltenbrunner and left. He could picture him racing to contact Himmler to give him the good news. Neither Kaltenbrunner nor Himmler would have been so happy if they knew what Schneider's real intentions were. He had decided to drive to Dachau that very night.

Dachau

The new autobahns allowed Schneider to reach Dachau by the next morning. His police authority gave him access to all the petrol he needed for such a journey. There had been only one checkpoint, just outside Würzburg, and again his police ID was sufficient to allow him to pass without any delay. He had been thinking as he drove about how he was going to get to Anna Weiss. He could use the letter to get into the camp, but then Himmler would know within minutes, and he couldn't risk that at this stage. She was the only lead he had at the moment. Something told him that Anna Weiss would probably meet with an unfortunate accident if he showed too much interest in her. And then it came to him. It was so easy when you stopped thinking like a police officer. When you lived and worked among gangsters, you had to think like them as well. And that was exactly how things worked in the higher levels of the Third Reich. Never mind laws and rules, never mind normal behaviour. All that mattered was getting what you wanted without being caught.

He found a phone and roused Hans Albert from his bed. His assistant only knew that he was working on something top secret, nothing else. It was better that way because what Hans didn't know, he couldn't tell. And that was his safeguard if Schneider's plan went wrong. He told Hans to go immediately to the police record office and find out the current address of one Anna Weiss, a secretary with the SS. He also asked for a description. He told Hans he would phone him later that day at the office to get the information. He didn't have to say to tell no one: Hans had been his assistant for long enough. Schneider mused that sometimes a totalitarian state had its advantages. The central police record office in Berlin kept the current details of every citizen of the Reich. Any changes, such as a new address or job, were routinely made. Anna Weiss couldn't commute from here to Dachau, so she must have changed her address.

Schneider parked at a little guesthouse on the edge

of the village. He showed his police ID and said he needed a room for the day. The proprietor was happy to oblige, particularly when Schneider offered to pay cash rather than force the owner to face weeks of bureaucracy to get paid. But behind the effusive thanks was suspicion. The police in Germany didn't usually behave like this. Schneider looked around, obviously checking they were alone. He moved closer to the proprietor, gesturing with his finger that he should listen very carefully. He spoke to him man to man, trying to ignore the smell of the other man's meaty breath.

'Perhaps you can help me further. This is – how shall I say? – an informal police matter. It would be better if no one knew I was here. Do you understand me?'

'I think so, Chief Investigator. But you know better than me that I must report every guest to the local police. What can I do?'

The man's eyes were fixed on Schneider's still open wallet or, rather, the notes that Schneider was extracting.

'I realise you are a good citizen, but this is a personal matter. I shall be bringing someone back with me this afternoon, a young woman, and it would be better if no one knew I had, eh, interviewed her here. I'm sure you understand it is a matter of state security.'

The notes lay between them, an unspoken invitation. The large hand of the owner accepted it.

'I know my duty when it is a matter of state security. I hope your interview goes well.'

He winked lasciviously at Schneider, who even

returned it. Now all he had to do was get some rest. He went to the room, pulled off his jacket and trousers and was asleep within seconds.

He woke up three hours later, as he had planned to. He woke up fully alert, conscious of where he was and of what he was doing. He quickly washed and shaved and had a simple lunch of *bratwurst*, the ubiquitous German sausage, and bread. He was the only guest. Dachau was not a place many people would willingly come. He prevailed upon the owner to use his phone by producing another note from his rapidly thinning wallet.

'Hans, did you get it?'

'Yes, sir.'

He could hear Hans reaching for his notebook and he stopped him before he could say anything else. 'Hans, leave the office and go to a nearby shop. Phone me back at this number.'

Hans did as he was instructed. He knew that almost every official phone in Nazi Germany was probably tapped by the Gestapo. It took him less than ten minutes to find a small bakery with a phone. His police ID and ten Reichmarks were enough. The operator connected him to the number he had been given and Schneider answered.

'No names, Hans. Just say the address and the description, nothing else.'

'Medium height, dark hair and eyes. Twenty-eight years old. Very slim. A small scar on the forehead. I'm sorry, but that's the best I can do without a picture.'

'Thank you, Hans, that will be enough. And the address.'

'There was none. There were two red stars on the file.'

Schneider knew what this meant. Anything concerning Anna Weiss was to be reported to Himmler himself. Now why would Himmler be so interested in a secretary? But Schneider already knew the answer to his own question.

*

He walked through the village. It was a typical Bavarian village; that is, it was pretty and clean. And yet there seemed to be a pall hanging over its inhabitants. You could almost feel it, a sense of unease, as if they were trying to hide something. Everyone knew that Germany's first concentration camp had been built here in 1934. And then Schneider had it, he had seen it so often before. It was a sense of guilt. Like other Germans, Schneider could only guess at what went on inside the camp. The police had no authority in such places, and he had never been near a camp, never mind seen inside one. Goebbels had told the German people that the camps were used to punish the guilty and to rehabilitate them, to make them good Germans again. But how many people had come back? Schneider knew he had avoided such obvious questions till now. He still tried to, but standing here face to face with reality made his deliberate blindness more difficult to maintain, let alone justify. But some people knew what went on inside. The inhabitants of Dachau village knew, and that was the source of their particular guilt. He still hoped he wouldn't have to find out personally why they felt so guilty – and felt guilty himself even as the thought entered his mind. He returned to the guesthouse and picked up his car. The drive to the concentration camp didn't take long. He parked as close as he dared and took his first look into a concentration camp.

The camp was situated near the centre of the village but was surrounded by an electrified barbed-wire fence. He could see the huts inside and even some of the prisoners shuffling in the yard. Apart from their uniforms, it could have been an army barracks. The villagers must pass the camp every day, must see what is happening. How could people just carry on as if this place didn't exist in their very midst? No wonder a sense of guilt was palpable. He knew it should pervade every man, woman and child in Germany, because all of them had turned the other way, pretending not to see what was happening in their country. Would that absolve them? Maybe here, in this life, but if there was a God, Schneider doubted if their guilt could be so easily assuaged before that court.

Now, his own guilt overwhelmed him. Who was he to condemn others when he had done exactly the same? He knew what was happening here was wrong beyond any normal measure, and with a sudden, keen insight, he knew his days of looking the other way were gone for ever.

He didn't want to go any closer, in case he was challenged. He checked his watch. He only had ten minutes to wait. Even in a concentration camp, the Germans were a regimented race. Office workers stopped at five p.m. Shortly thereafter, the first of them started to leave. All of them were stopped and their IDs checked before they were allowed through the double gate. Some wore the SS uniform, others civilian clothing. Most were in groups, talking like any crowd of workers on their way home. Schneider found it hard to believe that they could really be discussing what was for dinner, or some family problem, after leaving such a job. But maybe they saw it just as that, a job.

Then he noticed a woman on her own. She seemed not to have enjoyed her day's work. The slump of her shoulders and the lowered head spoke volumes to a trained observer like Schneider. At the pavement's edge, she raised her head to check for traffic. She matched Hans's description, although he was unable to see the scar from a distance. He followed her until the other workers had all gone their separate ways. He caught up with her.

'Anna Weiss?'

She looked startled. 'Yes.'

Schneider breathed a sigh of relief. She was alive. At least for now.

7

Dachau

It took only moments for Schneider to convince Anna Weiss to come with him. He was surprised at her willingness to accompany an unknown police officer to a guesthouse rather than the local police station. Maybe she had heard of him, but she hardly glanced at his police ID when he produced it. He could have been anybody.

During the short drive she just stared straight ahead. No questions, no worried looks. That was very unusual, for everyone, no matter how innocent they might think themselves to be, always asks something, or shows some reaction. While he studied her for any sign of what she was thinking, he noticed that Hans's description of her had only been partially accurate, for it did not say how attractive this young woman was. Schneider normally only noticed those things that suggested guilt or innocence. He saw the blinking of eyes, the sweating, the nervous impulsive movements of hands. Now he was noticing the colour of eyes and the fullness of lips. It had been a long time since he had

95

noticed these things on a woman. Maybe it was her vulnerability that he noticed rather than her looks, for her eyes held some deep sorrow which anyone, never mind Schneider, could readily have seen. He sensed that she was defenceless, that she had given herself up to him to do with as he wanted. For some reason he felt protective. It was strange because this young woman had been a confidante of Heydrich and now worked in a concentration camp. Schneider reminded himself of these facts as they climbed the stairs to his room. The fat proprietor saw them and gave Schneider an approving nod after running his eyes over Anna Weiss. This time Schneider didn't return his gesture.

He locked the room door and invited her to sit on the one chair.

'Do you know why I've brought you here?'

If she was afraid, she didn't show it. In fact, apart from her sorrow, she showed nothing at all.

'Yes. But I can't tell you anything I haven't already told you. So, if you are going to kill me, please have the decency to do it quickly.'

Schneider was confused. Clearly, so was she.

'But I've never asked you anything before, and I certainly have no intention of killing you. I got your name from Frau Heydrich. She thinks I might be able to get to the truth about her husband's death. She thinks you may be able to help me.'

'Then you haven't come here to kill me? You're not from Himmler?'

Hope flashed momentarily into her eyes but was almost instantly extinguished. Hope was not something to be relied on in Nazi Germany. But her reaction had been enough to explain her behaviour. She had thought she was being brought here to be killed. Or worse. Schneider tried to reassure her that her fear of him was groundless.

'On the contrary, I think I may be the only person who can save you.'

He fingered the letter in his pocket. It showed he had the power to do what he was telling this girl. But what would she make of such a letter? Would she trust him? He knew he had to show he could help her, and his words would never be enough. He reached into his pocket.

'I think you should look at this letter and then maybe we can have a long talk. A very long talk.'

*

After two hours of questioning, Schneider was sure of only one thing: Anna Weiss had been totally loyal to Reinhard Heydrich. He found such devotion to someone like Heydrich inexplicable. How could someone who appeared so gentle be devoted to such a monster? Schneider decided to leave that conundrum, but only for the moment. His instincts told him that if he could solve that, a lot of other things might also become more apparent. In the meantime, he would try to unsettle her a little, something he had singularly failed to do so far.

'How do you like working in Dachau concentration camp?'

The question was thrown in without any warning. It had nothing to do with Heydrich or his death. For the first time she looked uncertain.

'I don't know what you mean. What has that to do with anything?'

Schneider put on his interrogation face. His voice hardened. 'I ask the questions here. Do not forget on whose authority I act. Now answer me.'

Anna Weiss looked as if he had slapped her. For two hours he had nursed her gently through his questions, never pressing, never demanding. If she couldn't remember or was uncertain, that was all right. She had almost come to believe him. Now he had shown his true colours.

'I do my duty. I was sent here. I didn't ask to come.'

'What kind of answer is that? I asked if you liked your job. Do you like it?'

'I do my best. No one has ever been dissatisfied. I work hard. I . . .'

Schneider sensed something. It would be so easy for her to simply say yes. Why wouldn't she? He tightened the screw to see what would happen.

'I find your answers disappointing. And alarming. After all, aren't you doing the greatest service anyone can give to the Reich in dealing with its enemies? Perhaps you need more direct contact, more hands-on experience, to show you the full value of your work. I think I will have a word with the camp commandant to see if you can be transferred to such duties. I am sure some time spent with these enemies of the Reich is just what you need.'

'Please, you do not know what goes on in the camp. I beg you, please don't do that.'

Schneider didn't know what went on in the camp. As far as he knew, it was a severe prison regime for those people deemed to be the ubiquitous 'enemies of the Reich'. His doubts resurfaced about what was happening in Germany. He truly didn't know what went behind the barbed wire, but he suspected. A pain was beginning to throb in his temple, but he didn't want his mind to be cluttered with such doubts. He forced his mind back onto its usual single track of investigation.

His suggestion had obviously touched a nerve with Anna Weiss. Reluctantly now, he pressed home his advantage.

'So, tell me what goes on. You have seen my letter of authority. Tell me.'

'You think it is some kind of prison, don't you? That's what everyone is supposed to think. A place where prisoners are worked hard but fairly, so that they may someday be rehabilitated back into our glorious Reich. But it's all a fairy story, or perhaps I should say a horror story. Dachau is a place where people disappear. They are shot, hanged, or worked to death. And then their bodies just disappear. And the worst thing about it is that nobody cares.'

Schneider found it incredible. He was a police officer. There were laws and courts and judges. People just couldn't be killed and then disappear. The throbbing in his temple increased tenfold. He knew his veneer of denial was being ripped apart. Desperately he fought to retain some shred of honour.

'So, where do these bodies disappear to? There must be a big graveyard in Dachau if what you say is true.'

'Use your nose. Don't you smell them? They are turned to smoke. That's how they disappear.'

Schneider refused to believe it. His sanity could not permit it. He even argued with her, telling her to stop this nonsense. But even as he was saying it, he knew why he was telling her she was lying. For the first time he was being forced to come face to face with what his country had become. So, she told him how he could be sure. Didn't he have a letter in his pocket that gave him access to everything in Germany? Why didn't he just go in and see for himself? That answer told Schneider several things. First, that he was dealing with someone of intelligence, who was able to cut right to the heart of any problem. This was probably one of the things that Heydrich valued in her. It was something that Schneider liked as well. It also told him that she was telling the truth. Because Schneider could easily check, using the Hitler letter as she suggested. And lastly it told him that she had no regard for her own safety. If he did check, Himmler would know in minutes that he had spoken to her. That would probably be her death warrant.

But her answer still didn't tell him why she had been so devoted to Heydrich, who had effectively been in charge of all concentration camps. If she found the camps so appalling, how could she have been so attached to Heydrich? For two hours he had asked her about Heydrich's relations with Himmler, with the other leading Nazis, and about his files, but she had remained evasive. Maybe it was time to ask her about the man. Schneider tried to put what she had just told him about the camp out of his mind. He had always managed in the past to compartmentalise even the most gruesome facts of a murder case, so that he could concentrate dispassionately on doing his job. It needed all his will to achieve it this time. And he didn't know how long he could do it for.

'I'm sorry, but I had to try and find out what you really thought. Although I find it impossible to believe what you have told me, I also know it must be true. I do not need to check your word on it. And there is another reason I will come back to. But for now, would you please answer one more question?'

Schneider couldn't be sure if she believed him or not. But she nodded.

'I know you find what is happening in the camp totally and utterly wrong. But Heydrich ran the camps. How could you work for him?'

'You are right. He was in overall control. But he

wasn't a monster to me. I saw only a kindly, cultured man, who was a good boss. I know it's no excuse, but I hadn't seen inside a camp until I was sent here. Are you any less guilty than me? You work for the security services as well. If I tell you that he had more than enough reason to harm someone like me but that I also knew he never would, would that answer your question?'

Something about what she said was ringing a bell in his mind. Why would Heydrich ever have wanted to harm her? Was she a former lover? Was she blackmailing him in some way? He dismissed both ideas as soon as they entered his mind. She simply didn't fit the bill for either a mistress or a blackmailer. So, what was it? Then he had it.

'Some people say that Heydrich had Jewish blood in him. If he had been anyone else, he might have ended up in a camp himself. But he wouldn't harm himself, would he? Is that why you still revere him, even after seeing what you have seen? Because he made sure it didn't happen to you? Who else knows you are Jewish, Anna?'

She didn't seem surprised at his conclusion. Nor did she try to deny it.

'Only you. My mother was Jewish but became Christian when she married my father. But that doesn't matter. A half Jew is still a Jew as far as the law is concerned. What are you going to do with me?'

'I told you there was another reason why I wouldn't

visit the camp. If I did, Himmler would know about my meeting with you and that would put you in danger. What you have just told me means that your life is now completely forfeit. If Himmler or anyone else finds out, you're dead.'

'I've known for a long time that this day would come.'

Still she seemed uncaring, resigned to her fate. If she didn't value her own safety then Schneider would have to. Was it because of her value to his investigation? Perhaps. But it was more than that, much more. She was vulnerable and he wanted to protect her. He wanted to be the only one to protect her now.

'I'll tell you what I'm going to do. I'm going to see the commandant and show him my letter. I'm going to tell him that I need you to work for me in sorting through some of Heydrich's files. What could be more natural than a former secretary doing this? It's the best I can think of just now to keep you alive. Do you agree?'

She had no choice. Both of them knew that Himmler wouldn't be satisfied with such an explanation. But that would have to wait. One problem at a time.

'You can work in my office. I think that would be better than going back to your old office. Do you have somewhere you can stay in Berlin?'

'I gave my room up when I was sent to Dachau. Perhaps one of my friends might be able to help.'

Schneider made a decision. 'You'll stay in my flat. And before you start to think your virtue is under threat, I'll stay in my office. I have a bed and everything else I need there. Anyway, I think we'll be spending a lot of time travelling for the next few weeks.'

Schneider felt a little embarrassed, almost like a pubescent schoolboy. The sensation was as surprising as it was pleasant.

Anna watched him and then for the first time since Schneider had picked her up, she smiled. Clearly, her honour was not in danger from this man. Her own surprise was the disappointment she felt.

*

Schneider dropped the room key into reception and drove to Anna's flat. She packed her few belongings and, as it was late, they spent the rest of the night there. Schneider endured a fitful night on the small couch in the living room. He woke several times, his sleep disturbed by dreams of people in prison uniform disappearing up chimneys while he stood by and watched.

They had a simple, silent breakfast together of stale bread, margarine and what passed for coffee in the fourth year of a war. Schneider loaded the car and they set off for the camp. He had explained to her what he intended to do. For the first time he heard her laugh. It pleased him. This time Schneider drove right up to the camp gate. The overweight, rather slovenly guard clearly didn't like being summoned by Schneider's leaning on the car horn. His protests were cut off by Schneider sticking the Hitler letter in front of his face. Seconds later, Schneider was inside Dachau concentration camp. Anna directed him straight to the commandant's office. She seemed like a different person, almost like a young girl again. Mischief played in her eyes.

'Can't I come in with you? I'd really love to see that pig's face.'

'No, it's better if you stay here. I'll be quicker on my own, as we agreed.'

Schneider strode up the steps to the office. He entered without knocking and said he was here to see the commandant. The thin-lipped secretary blustered about being occupied and appointments, but Schneider ignored her and opened the commandant's door. He certainly was busy.

The commandant's face was buried in the groin of a boy, no more than fourteen years old. Schneider understood the scene instantly. The thin face was still pretty, even with a shaved head. The ravenous eyes had been fixed on a tray of freshly baked morning rolls lying on the desk, as if not really a part of what was happening to the rest of his body. Slowly, the eyes swivelled to Schneider. They held no shame for what was happening and, after a second, they returned to the rolls. The commandant was too engrossed in what he was doing to notice that someone had come in.

'What is going on here?'

Schneider had to start somewhere.

The commandant struggled to his feet, hindered by his open trousers and swag-like stomach. His victim continued to stare at the rolls, only the rolls. Schneider noticed the redness on the man's face, whether from his exertions or embarrassment he didn't know. But this was the commandant of Dachau concentration camp. He was not a man to trifle with and certainly not to embarrass.

'What the hell is the meaning of this? Who are you? How dare you enter my office!'

'Shut up and read this.'

The letter thrust into the sweating face worked its wonder again. Fear now replaced outrage in the piggy eyes. Against the power of that piece of paper, his position was as nothing. He started to stutter some explanation.

'I was just . . . It wasn't what . . . I don't . . .'

'I told you to shut up. Get rid of the boy and, for God's sake, make yourself decent.'

Schneider turned his back while the commandant hurried to obey his orders. The boy was even smaller than he had seemed earlier. He moved past Schneider without a glance at him, as if nothing untoward had happened. Schneider realised that in such a place it probably hadn't.

'Wait.'

The boy stopped and turned.

Schneider nodded towards the rolls on the desk. 'Take them with you.'

After the boy had gone, Schneider simply told the commandant that he was taking Anna Weiss with him to assist him in an investigation. Other than that, he didn't need to know anything else. The matter was top secret and was to be reported to no one.

'Oh, I'm sure that you might think about telling someone, just to cover yourself. Maybe the Reichsführer, for example, or Kaltenbrunner. Well, I suggest you don't. You see, they don't have much time for homosexuals, particularly if they're also child molesters. So, let's just keep that our secret for now.'

It had worked out even better than Schneider had thought. The letter would not have guaranteed his silence, but what had happened with the boy would. It gave him a little more time.

Berlin

The journey back to the city was uneventful. They arrived at Schneider's flat, and he let Anna unpack a little while he made a simple supper. Both of them were aware of the barrier of secrets that lay between them. Schneider's questioning of her in Dachau had not answered the questions he needed answered. He also sensed the distrust she still felt for him. After all, how many people in Germany worked directly for Hitler? Schneider knew that he had to find a way to remove that barrier. All day he had thought of how he could do this and hadn't been able to find an answer.

He decided to take a chance. When all else fails, truth may be the only solution.

He pushed the remains of his half-eaten dinner away. She had only picked at hers, and he didn't think that was entirely down to his culinary ability. It was time to get the answers or else give up.

'Anna, I know you don't trust me, and I don't blame you. You hardly know me. I could just be after Heydrich's papers and using you to get to them. Hitler has given me the letter I showed you. So, maybe I'm a fanatical Nazi. How could you tell the difference? I can think of only one way of convincing you. Let me tell you how I became involved in all this. Then if you still don't trust me, I'll just have to accept it, and you need never see me again. How does that sound?'

He could see the suspicion in her eyes. Was this to be another of his attempts to get the information he wanted using some other ploy? All he could do was hope.

He told her everything. He told her he had been picked because he was completely apolitical. He told her everything about his meetings with Himmler, Bormann and Hitler. He told her about a young man who had thrown himself to his death for reasons he didn't understand, and how this had been his real aim when he got Hitler's letter. Then he had met Lina Heydrich, who had put him onto her. Something about Heydrich's death wasn't right. He was still a police officer and if he could, he wanted to get to the truth of that as well. If she truly cared for her former boss, she would help him. Because only she could give him the information he needed.

She studied him for a long time after he had finished, trying to find a way to judge his story. There was no such measure, and at the end of the day she could only rely on her own instincts.

'I don't know why, but I believe you.'

Schneider sighed in relief. He didn't want her simply to disappear out of his life. Now she had chosen to believe him, she went to the heart of his investigation.

'What you want to know is where Heydrich kept his secret files, yes?'

'That's where I think we'll find the answer as to why he had to be killed.'

'But he kept files for years on all the leading Nazis. No one ever tried to kill him before, as far as I know. And to kill him risked the files being used against them, for he must have taken steps to protect himself. That was his safeguard. So, why would someone kill him now and run that risk? Maybe it was the British, after all?'

'It was the British. But they had help from someone here. As to why it was now, it can only mean that Heydrich discovered something recently. Something so important that it outweighed all other risks they might face in killing him. Something that only Heydrich had discovered but the full significance of which he obviously didn't understand, otherwise he would still be with us today. Something as yet incomplete but so important that Heydrich had to die for it. I'm only hoping that I'll find it in his files. And there's another thing. He's been dead for over three months now. What has happened to the safe-guards he must have put in place to prevent his being killed? No one has used the files. Maybe they've already been discovered by the person who arranged his death?'

Anna shook her head.

'The files haven't been discovered. I know where they were kept. I also know why they haven't been used.'

★

The evening slipped into the early hours of the morning as Anna recounted the whole history of her relationship with Reinhard Heydrich. She recalled coming to work for him in 1934 when he was just another middle-ranking member of the still small and unimportant SS. Then came the Röhm assas-sination, later called the 'Night of the Long Knives', which catapulted the SS and Heydrich to a new level of importance. In 1936, Heydrich became head of the SD and chose Anna to be his personal secretary.

'One day he called me into his office and asked if I'd heard the rumours about him being partly Jewish. Everyone had, but what could you say to a man like Heydrich? So, I just told him I had. He asked if I believed them. I don't know why, but I said I didn't know. I expected to be sacked, but something – perhaps my own Jewishness – made me say it, wouldn't let me deny it. In any event, there were still Jews in Germany at that time. I thought the worst that could happen would be losing my job.

'Heydrich seemed to find my answer amusing. He just sat there and laughed. Then he showed me the file he had been reading. It was my file. My mother was named as a Jew. I thought he was so cruel to tease me like that and told him to his face. He just sat there and listened, the most feared man in Germany. Eventually, I calmed down and told him to send for his guards. But he told me he had known for months that I was Jewish. He told me he had another plan for me that required great courage, a courage he believed I had, given that I had kept my Jewish blood hidden and yet worked for the likes of him. My outburst had only confirmed him in that view. He said he had the power to make the report about my mother disappear, if I wanted. I asked him what he wanted in return, and he told me, "Your silence." He explained there were lots of files like mine containing information that was best kept secret. Most of the files were about the little people that Heydrich used, but he also kept such files on all the leaders of the Reich. That was how he controlled them. And now he controlled me too. He asked me if I would be the courier who took the files to where they were secretly stored. In return, he told me he would remove my Jewishness from my record and always protect me. So, I agreed.'

Schneider was amazed at how simple it all was. But there was one question he was curious to know the answer to: 'Did you ever find out if Heydrich was Jewish?'

'We never had such a conversation again. I think he really didn't know himself, even after all his investigations into his own background. And that's what used to drive him mad, I think. He wanted to know everything about everybody but couldn't find out about himself.'

'So, where were these files hidden? You know that Himmler has looked everywhere.'

Anna smiled. 'He thinks he has looked everywhere, but even he didn't understand the kind of man he was up against. One of the things that Heydrich hated above most others was religion. He was always pushing for more action to be taken against the churches. He even said once that all ministers and priests should be sent to concentration camps and that Germany needed no other religion than the Führer. I don't know if this hatred was genuine or not. But no one could be in any doubt that Heydrich would never have anything to do with any church. So, I took the files to the last place anyone would ever think of, even Himmler. I took them to a priest. It was really so simple, and I'll explain how it worked in a minute. But you remember I said that I know why the files haven't been used?

It's because the priest has been arrested. Just before I was transferred, I found out he is in a camp in Poland called Auschwitz.'

Schneider had never heard of the place. But his mind was taken back to the young soldier who had flung himself from his office window. Hadn't he told him that terrible things were happening in the east? Schneider realised with a sudden clarity that he was somehow going to face the harshest of Nazi Germany's truths and that his time of looking the other way was gone forever.

'Remember, I have the letter from Hitler. I can use it to get to the priest if need be. Now tell me how Heydrich's system worked and where this priest comes in.'

'I was brought up a Christian, a Lutheran, to be exact. Heydrich told me it was time I became a Catholic. He told me to go to a small church on the outskirts of Munich but close enough to my flat so that it wouldn't seem suspicious. I was to see a certain priest there who would "instruct" me and oversee my conversion. This took place fairly quickly because I never intended to become a Catholic. I then started attending confession, as Catholics should, but always saw the same priest. If there was something to be delivered, Heydrich gave it to me just before I left the office. I took it to the church and handed it over in the confession box. I don't know where the priest kept it after that, but it must have been in the church. It would be far too risky for Heydrich to have the priest carry such files around with him. Anyway, if they were going somewhere else, what was the point of my going to the priest? I could just as easily have taken them somewhere else.'

Schneider could see that the simplicity of the plan also made it effective. He wondered who this priest was and what he was to Heydrich, but he would get to that eventually.

'Let's assume the files are still in the church for now. Do you know what these files were?'

'I never looked inside the sealed envelopes. I already knew what they were anyway. Heydrich had told me. They were his files on the other leading Nazis. Some people even said he kept a file on Hitler. Anything untoward about these people would be in these files. Anything in their past that he could use against them would be there.'

'And now the priest has been arrested. Why?'

'Oh, it was nothing to do with the files. He really is a priest, and he said too much in a sermon about what was happening to the Jews in this country. He had been warned about this several times but wouldn't listen. So, the Gestapo came for him.'

'When was this? Sometime after Heydrich's death? I suppose he was protected by Heydrich until then?'

'I don't think he was. The last thing Heydrich would have wanted was to draw attention to him. No, he was arrested just before Heydrich was killed. I went to the church with a delivery, but another priest told me what had happened. Heydrich was going to Prague that night, so I never got a chance to see him again.'

'And I suppose you destroyed the file?'

Anna smiled, a smile he was growing to like more and more.

'I suppose I should have, but I didn't. I've kept it at home since then among my underwear. I suppose that wouldn't have stopped Himmler for long if he had ever suspected, but it was the best I could think of. I didn't want to destroy it because I always hoped that someday somebody might find a good use for it. I think that somebody has come. I brought it with me here – shall I go and get it?'

*

Schneider had read and reread the file. It gave a concise account of what Heydrich knew about Himmler and his contacts with the Hungarian embassy. It also contained the original letter to H. from B. Schneider wondered what it meant. He knew now he had three things to do. To find out what this letter meant. The answer to that would give him the answer to who killed Heydrich. And then he could find out what he really wanted to know. The young man's smashed face lying in the courtyard was never far from his mind. And the route to the answers all started at the same place. Auschwitz.

Himmler was clearly the chief suspect. But there

was one other suspect he needed to eliminate first. The current successor to Adolf Hitler may have known he was about to be replaced. That would certainly be a strong motive, as strong as anything Himmler had. Hitler's deputy was vain and deadly protective of his position as 'second man of the Reich'. It was time to pay a call on Reichsmarschall Hermann Göring.

— 8 —

Carinhall, near Berlin

Schneider had seen the fabulous wealth of criminals that sometimes was their undoing. Their need to flaunt their ill-gotten gains usually led to a prison cell. He had thought he had seen all the excesses of Mammon, but he had been wrong. Here he was in a completely different league.

He was waiting to interview Hermann Göring, Reichsmarschall, head of the Luftwaffe and deputy Führer, only a few among the myriad of titles he had amassed. Like most Germans, Schneider had found Göring the most acceptable of the Nazis. Known affectionately before the war as 'Fat Hermann', he was the human face of the Nazi regime. He was a hero of the First World War, being the last commander of the famous Richthofen fighter squadron. Large, fat and apparently fun-loving, he was the antithesis of Himmler. Maybe it was because of this that Schneider had not felt the trepidation he had before his first meetings with Hitler or Himmler. Maybe it was his growing belief in the power of Hitler's letter of authority. Nevertheless, he reminded himself that you didn't rise to be the second man in the Reich without the ability to deal ruthlessly with anyone who opposed you. After all, it was Göring and not Himmler who had set up the Gestapo and been its first head. It was Göring who had engineered the Anschluss, the takeover of Austria, and who had been Hitler's closest political ally.

In recent years his prestige had declined, along with the declining fortunes of his Luftwaffe. Its failure in the battle of Britain, followed by its continuing failure on the Russian front, had seen Göring slip almost into obscurity. No longer at the Führer's right hand, he was an outcast at military conferences. Consequently, more and more of his time was spent at his country house. When Schneider contacted Luftwaffe headquarters to find out his whereabouts, he had learned that he was presently at a house just outside Berlin. He contacted Göring's adjutant, ready to quote his authority to him, but for some reason he was readily granted an interview without even needing to mention Hitler's letter. It was almost as if his call was expected.

Schneider had made all the calls from home. He knew that Himmler was also in Berlin and would summon him as soon as he set foot in his office. Before that meeting, he needed to be certain if Himmler was the only suspect or not.

He told Anna where he was going and told her to keep the door locked and not to answer the phone.

From Göring's house, he planned to go directly to police headquarters and face Himmler. He had thought out a storyline about Anna Weiss that just might keep Himmler happy. If it didn't then he still had Hitler's letter. But he guessed even that might not be enough against someone like Himmler. Especially if he thought Schneider was looking into matters that he shouldn't be. He knew he couldn't leave Anna alone in Berlin for very long; it was simply too dangerous for her. So, he told her that if all went well, he intended to take her with him to Prague and then to this camp at Auschwitz where the priest was being held. He waited outside his flat to listen for the key being turned in the lock behind him. It was the best he could do for now.

For once, the RAF had not visited the previous night, so Schneider found the roads no worse than on any other day. He followed the diversion signs around the destroyed streets, gradually working his way to the outskirts of the capital. In some streets the tram cars were still running, and he saw the Berliners making their way to work as normal. But he also saw the queues already starting to form outside the few shops that were open. Anything that could be bought was snapped up. Bartering had almost replaced currency in some parts of the city. Propaganda still preached the final victory, but the eyes of the citizens betrayed only a will to survive until the end. Gradually, the city and its people thinned out as he reached the suburbs. Here there was little evidence of the war as, by and large, the attacks had been concentrated on the centre and its factories. As if by magic, the last of the buildings disappeared and he was in the countryside that surrounded Göring's home.

He stopped at the gates and his identity was verified. He was expected. Schneider was interested to note that unlike the other leading Nazis, Göring was not guarded by the SS but by his own Luftwaffe troops. He drove up the long drive to Carinhall, named after Göring's dead first wife. It was described as a hunting lodge, but it was a palace. Rare paintings purloined from museums all over conquered Europe adorned the walls. Antique furnishings filled every room and corridor. But it had a feeling of vulgarity, of obscene decadence almost, of things being there just for the sake of being possessed rather than from any real appreciation of them. It was as if a glutton had just taken anything that caught his eye, merely to have it, as if this possession would endow him with the respect he so obviously craved. Instead, it engendered pity and revulsion. Clearly, Göring collected antiques with the same abandon that he used to collect his official titles – over a hundred of them.

Schneider was shown into what seemed to serve as a study. He was told the Reichsmarschall would be with him shortly. Schneider surveyed the room, his eyes passing from one priceless artefact to the next. Pictures and sculptures were everywhere. The thickest, most elaborately patterned drapes he had ever seen shaded the room from the autumn sunlight. The desk was in keeping with the rest of the furnishings. Massive, but clearly unused, its only adornment being two framed photographs, one of a woman and one of Hitler that Schneider noticed bore a personal hand-written greeting to Göring, a memento of happier times between them. A seat that was proportioned more like a throne stood behind the desk. Schneider knew nothing of antiques, but he guessed from the chair's intricate carving that it was probably priceless. The last thing it should be used for was to support Göring's backside.

Hanging on the wall behind the desk was a large painting of an elderly man. The eyes almost looked alive and seemed to follow him around the room. Schneider knew even less about art than he did about antiques, but he felt himself drawn to this painting. He had never seen anything so vibrant before. In some ways the figure seemed to have a life of its own, as if it was much more than a two-dimensional image. He recalled the picture of Hitler in Himmler's study. Now he could see how shallow it was in comparison to this masterpiece. He went for a closer look and stood returning the gaze. He had never seen such beauty before, such genius. He became lost in its every facet, oblivious to everything else around him.

'It's rather magnificent, don't you think? I acquired it only recently. It is one of the last self-portraits done by Rembrandt. Are you interested in fine art, Chief Investigator Schneider?'

Göring had entered through a recessed door, the construction of which was so perfect that it had been invisible when closed. He was bigger than Schneider had imagined he would be. But he wasn't just big, he was obese. He was bedecked in what seemed to be a Roman toga, but he walked with all the confidence of one whose dress sense was perfect and beyond the reproach of others. If Schneider hadn't have known who this man was, he would have thought him in need of psychiatric help. But such was his complete self-assurance that even as a stranger he would have somehow created respect.

He dispensed with both handshakes and the Nazi greeting and invited Schneider to take a seat. He fully occupied the throne, his buttocks spreading like lava to overflow the seat. The face was huge, ringed by heavy jowls. The feminine hands had rings on almost every finger. The eyes were unnaturally bright with large pupils. Schneider had seen such eyes before. Years ago, he had investigated and broken an illegal drug trafficking ring in Berlin. He remembered now the eyes of those addicts. They had the same unnatural look about them. Was it possible that the second man of the Reich was a drug addict?

'So, what can I do for you, Chief Investigator?'

Schneider decided on a frontal attack. He produced the letter from Hitler and as Göring was reading it he snapped, 'I am here to investigate the murder of Obergruppenführer Heydrich. What can you tell me about this?'

Göring could have reacted in many ways. Outrage, anger, fear or surprise. All would have told Schneider something. But instead of any of these, Göring just laughed. It was a full, deep laugh that befitted a man of this gargantuan build. Tears of mirth welled in his eyes. He threw the letter back towards Schneider as if it were an unpaid wine bill.

'My God, Schneider, but you're good. No wonder you've put so many behind bars. So, you want to see if I'm involved in killing Heydrich. Well, I won't pretend that I'm not glad to see that bastard dead. And given the chance, I would gladly have killed him myself. But I'm afraid that someone else has to take the credit here.'

Göring opened a drawer in his desk and took out a bowl filled with what appeared to be small stones. His eyes grew wider as he studied them. Then he started to run his fingers through them, letting them slip over and through his stubby fingers. Only the sparkling identified them as polished diamonds. The feel of them seemed to give him some kind of pleasure.

'Once, you know, I was the Führer's closest friend. He chose me as his successor. But then those fools let him start a war before we were ready. And what happens? We are being bled white in Russia, we have lost Africa, and at home we are being bombed back to the Stone Age. And in the middle of all this, he chooses such a man to replace me as his successor. A man more interested in his plans for the Jews than in successfully defending his country. And when I try to tell the Führer, what happens? I end up here with nothing to do. No, I am afraid you have the wrong man, Schneider.'

Schneider agreed. As Göring had been speaking, he had studied the face carefully. He was convinced that the man was a regular drug user, but not only that. He could see the despair, the resignation that this former giant had sunk into. He was a spent force, lost now in his reveries of what might have been and finding such comfort as he could in his diamonds and paintings. He wouldn't have been able to rouse himself for such an attack.

'If it wasn't you, Reichsmarschall, then who do you think I should speak to?'

'Schneider, you know the answer to that yourself. Go and find the proof against Himmler. But be careful if you value your life. That letter won't protect you. I suggest you go and speak to the people who killed the assassins. That might give you some ideas.'

'What ideas?'

Ponderously, Göring pulled himself to his feet. He moved round the desk to Schneider, his flowing silk robe making a soft hissing sound as it passed over the polished floor. He held his hand out to Schneider and showed him the perfect diamond lying in its large palm.

'This is a two-carat diamond worth more than you will ever earn, Schneider. But what is its true value?

Only those who have been graced with the ability to truly appreciate its inner beauty can truly value it. So it is with information. Some men have the ability to weigh the true value of information in much the same way. So, go and find out this information. It will show you the kind of man you are really dealing with.'

Despite further questioning, Schneider could get nothing more out of him, so he left. Göring had offered to make a plane available to him, but he had declined. With Hitler's letter he could get a plane anytime he needed one, so why make it easy for someone else to know his movements? He now knew his enemy. But what did Göring mean about Heydrich's plan for the Jews? It wasn't anything to do with Schneider, but something about it troubled him. He was no longer able to compartmentalise his mind. The faces of Jews he had known who had simply disappeared were starting to haunt his dreams more and more. Not only his dreams, but his waking mind as well. Where had all these people really gone? He would mention it to Anna when he got back. In the meantime, it was time to face Himmler.

Berlin

Rather than wait for a summons, Schneider went directly to Himmler's office and asked to see him. How long he had to wait would show how importantly Himmler took his investigation, or rather how he perceived the risk to himself. He was summoned in under two minutes. Clearly, the Reichsführer was concerned at what he had been doing. Schneider decided to keep him guessing, to see if he could glean anything else.

'So, Schneider, I hear you have been busy since we last spoke. Please let me have a full report on your progress.'

'There is very little to report so far, Reichsführer. I think I may have uncovered something, but it is too soon to say.'

Himmler stared at him, his fingers drumming out an impatient beat on the desk. 'Very little to report? I find that surprising. You have been very busy. Meeting with Frau Heydrich and the Reichsmarschall. Interviewing several of Heydrich's staff and examining his papers. Surely you must have seen by now that the SS report was as full as possible and that the murderers are now dead? But tell me what it is you think you have uncovered. I may be able to help you.'

The small eyes peered from behind the pince-nez with no hint of anxiety. But Himmler had already given Schneider more information than he imagined. Any and every conversation carries a risk that the speaker will reveal more than he intends. No matter how carefully he tries to avoid this happening, it is usually inevitable. Some word, some hesitation or gesture reveals more than intended, particularly to an expert like Schneider. Even someone like Himmler sometimes unwittingly said more than he meant to. So, what had Schneider learned? He now knew that both Heydrich's and Göring's houses were under surveillance. How else could Himmler know about these visits? If Schneider had been followed himself, then Himmler would undoubtedly have mentioned Anna Weiss. And the little pederast in Dachau had also kept his mouth shut for now. So, Schneider tried the story he had rehearsed all the way here.

He took on a slightly confused, almost worried frown. His eyes sought Himmler's for reassurance. There was hesitation in his voice.

'Very well, Reichsführer. As you will undoubtedly know, I have been ordered by the Führer himself to report to him. But I am not used to dealing with such matters and gladly will welcome your advice on how to proceed. I do not wish to cause the Führer unnecessary concern. You are right that the killers have been found and dealt with. My concern was to determine whether they had any help from inside Heydrich's own office.'

Schneider paused to watch for any reaction from Himmler. There was none, not even the blink of an eye.

'After careful checking, I am almost satisfied there was none. But there is one thing that still concerns me, and that is the idea that outsiders may have had access to his travel plans. Hence the reason for my visit to the Reichsmarschall. I went to the very top so that anyone who might be guilty would not be alerted. I wanted to know who in the Luftwaffe knew when Heydrich was going to Prague. The Reichsmarschall is checking that now, but I am almost sure the British were simply waiting for his next visit, no matter when that was to be. When I get the Reichsmarschall's report, I will confirm to the Führer that the SS report is correct. Is that acceptable to you, Reichsführer?'

'An excellent job, Schneider. By all means ensure there was no Luftwaffe involvement. Let me see your final report before it goes to the Führer. That will be all.'

Schneider was being dismissed as someone of no significance. And therefore of no danger. As far as Himmler was concerned, he was completely off target. It was just as Schneider had hoped. As he got to the door he paused as if remembering something else, something of little consequence.

Himmler looked up, a little annoyance now visible in the line above the eyes. He had more important things to deal with than this charade.

'There is one other thing, Reichsführer. One of Heydrich's secretaries dealt with all his travel arrangements. I have taken her away from her own duties to help me cross-reference these with the Luftwaffe report. I hope you do not mind?'

'Why should I mind what you do with a secretary? Who is she anyway?'

'Anna Weiss.'

For a moment, almost more imagined than real, something flickered in Himmler's eyes. Then it was gone. But now he was trapped. To show any interest in this particular secretary might have rekindled Schneider's investigation. So, he just had to accept it, for now at least.

'Let me have your report as soon as possible.'

He returned to the file he was reading. But as Schneider left, he noticed that the Reichsführer's left hand had curled into a fist, as if he wanted to crush something or someone.

Before leaving the building, Schneider paid a visit to his old unit. He found Hans Albert hard at work as ever, reading crime reports. He was clearly delighted to see his old boss but that rapidly faded when Schneider told him he was to be in charge of the squad until further notice. He added that he would be gone for some time but didn't elaborate.

Albert knew there was little point in asking his boss anything further, instead saying, 'If there is anything I can do to help, you know you only have to ask.'

Schneider knew what he meant. There were times when it was better if the Gestapo and the SD didn't know what the police were doing. He knew he could count on his long-suffering assistant for any covert help he needed.

He headed straight back to the flat. While he had been away, Anna had also been busy. She had spent a large part of the day cleaning and dusting, something that Schneider had always thought an unnecessary waste of time and energy. Until now, he had never noticed just how much dust had accumulated over everything in the tiny flat.

'I hope you don't mind. I couldn't just sit around and wait for you to come back or for the Gestapo to turn up instead. I would have gone mad. So, I found some brushes and tidied up a little.'

She had tied her hair back and her face was marked with grime. She had pulled on an old pair of shapeless overalls, which also bore full testimony to the battle that had raged against several years of cleaning indolence on his part. She looked every inch a cleaner, but all that Schneider saw was the most attractive woman he had ever seen. It was an alien, almost forgotten feeling. He couldn't recall the last time he had socialised with a woman, let alone had any sort of relationship with one. Now he knew what had been missing from his life. Yet he found himself lost for words, like some adolescent at his first school dance. He just stared at her. Anna misinterpreted his look.

'I'm sorry if I shouldn't have done it. I promise I won't touch anything again.'

Finally, he managed to get some words out. 'No. No. I'm the one who should be sorry for having you staying in such a pigsty. I never realised how filthy this place was until now. I'm sorry that I've put you to so much trouble.'

Suddenly both of them seemed to realise how

ludicrous the whole situation was. Here they were apologising to each other about nothing when at any moment they could find themselves arrested or worse. They both broke into gales of laughter, and the more they tried to stop the more they laughed. Somehow, they ended up supporting each other, Schneider's arms on hers. It felt so natural that instinctively, without thinking, he drew her towards him and let his arms surround her. She stopped laughing and found his eyes. Schneider may have been supremely confident in his professional role, but with women he had neither confidence nor experience. His arms slackened around her and fell to his side.

'I'm sorry. I don't know what I was thinking of. I—'

'Don't start that again or we'll never stop laughing. I don't think it's a good idea. You know my past and what that means in this country. I might not be around for very long, and I don't want you to get hurt. You have already done so much for me.'

Schneider wanted to say so much, to open his heart to another human being for the first time in his life. A torrent of words flooded his brain, but none came out. She was right. He had to keep a clear head. But his hands still held the memory of her body, and he knew that memory wouldn't easily go away. Nor did he want it to.

'Well, I suppose that means I'll just have to make sure you stay around for a long time.'

'I'd like that.'

Both knew something was possible between them, but not now. It was the wrong time in the wrong place. But places and times change. It gave both of them something to hope for, at least.

After Anna had washed and changed, Schneider surprised her and himself by suggesting they go out to eat. With rationing and the constant threat of air raids, it was an unusual suggestion, not least because most restaurants had long since closed. But Schneider said he knew just the place and it was close enough to walk. He ignored her obvious excitement and would give her no information about where they were going. He was pleased to see that she put on some lipstick and had somehow managed to get a pair of silk stockings. He himself had even found a coloured shirt and tie. He felt they made a handsome couple as they set out.

Schneider had another reason for the outing. It was an easy way to see if Himmler had put a tail on him. They strolled down the almost deserted street, stopping as if by chance to examine something, anything in a shop window. As Anna looked, Schneider surveyed the almost deserted street behind him, watching for any sudden movements into doorways, but there was none. In Nazi Germany, people had always tended to stay in the illusory safety of their own home. Now, there was just nowhere to go anyway. Several times Schneider checked behind him. If they were being followed, he couldn't see anyone.

They arrived at the restaurant. Its darkened windows were filthy, and it was clearly closed. So, Anna was surprised when Schneider banged on the rusting fire door and waited. She heard a bolt slip back and a finger of light fell on Schneider's face through the slit in the door. He said nothing. Quickly the light was cut off and she heard other bolts being pulled and finally a key turning in the lock. The door opened onto a rear hallway. Inside stood two of the biggest men she had ever seen. Not only were they physically huge but their scarred faces and broken noses gave them an air of genuine menace that even the Gestapo must have envied.

'Good evening, gentlemen,' Schneider said. 'I thought it was time I paid you a visit. Please do not be alarmed, it is entirely social. Do you have a table for me and my guest?'

It was obvious that Schneider had been recognised. One of the giants, whom Schneider seemed to know and called 'Gustav', led them without delay down the hallway. Gradually, lights appeared and the muted strains of a Strauss waltz filled the air. Another door opened and Anna learned that it was still possible to eat and drink well in war-torn Berlin provided you knew where to go and had the right credentials. Schneider clearly satisfied both tests. A man who was obviously the owner hurried over to them and showed them to a very discreet table in the far corner. A bottle of vintage champagne appeared.

'Chief Investigator Schneider. It is a pleasure to be able to welcome you to my humble establishment at long last.'

The man had all the charm of a second-hand car salesman. His sparse hair was plastered to his head and his smooth face, apart from the needle-thin moustache, reeked of expensive cologne. He wore a double-breasted dinner suit, which failed to hide the bulge of a rather large holster below his left arm. His eyes were everywhere, like two ocular snake tongues constantly searching the breeze for danger. Schneider spoke to Anna as if the man and his overpowering presence weren't there.

'It is, of course, completely illegal in a time of war to deal on the black market or to hoard food. Nevertheless, there are still those who do it. We are in such a place. But in such places, walls definitely do have ears, and sometimes things are heard which, to my mind, are far more important than a little contraband changing hands. And so I continue to let such places flourish. But I have never visited any of them until tonight, so I do not know what to order. Perhaps if we just wait and see what comes?'

The car salesman had blanched at the mention of information being passed to the police. His eyes grew even more searching, to see if any of his other customers had heard. It seemed that the table was secluded enough to have avoided this. Reassured, he took his cue from Schneider and left.

Anna was desperate to find out more about this place but knew Schneider would tell her in his own time. She was already starting to know him. So, she ate instead.

Over the next two hours, Schneider and Anna enjoyed the finest meal of their lives. Neither was a gourmet, and such cuisine was unknown to them. The first taste of foie gras was almost sexual in its intensity, and that set the scene for the rest of the evening. Unknown fish and meat of a taste and texture neither had experienced before followed. And through it all, the best French wines accompanied each dish. When they weren't eating, they passed the time simply looking at each other. Words seemed superfluous to them. A simple but exquisite chocolate mousse ended the meal. Only then did the owner reappear.

'I hope everything was to your satisfaction. May I offer you a cognac?'

Schneider seemed to have mellowed under the formidable effects of the food and drink. 'Indeed you can. I must say you seem to be doing even better than we thought. Perhaps there are matters that should be looked into here?'

'Come now, Chief Investigator. You know I am a poor man just managing to make ends meet in these difficult times. Look at how few now come here.'

They studied the other people in the room. Every table was taken. Most patrons were in uniform, field grey for the army, blue for the air force and black for the SS. No one appeared to be below the rank of colonel or its equivalent. That everyone in the room was breaking the law seemed to be of absolutely no consequence to anyone there.

Schneider nodded in sympathy. 'Perhaps you are right. But there is a matter that I think you can help me with. May we retire somewhere more private?'

He was away only a few minutes. When he came back, it seemed that something had pleased him, or a problem had been solved. Anna didn't ask. But she did ask who the owner was.

'Him? He is Berlin's best and worst kind of criminal. Worst because there is nothing he doesn't have his finger into. He is probably the richest man in the city if truth be told. No, that's not true. I met that man earlier today. Then he is the second richest man. And all of his wealth is quite illegal. Why, you may ask, don't the police do anything about this? Because he is also the best kind of criminal, in that any violence is always directed against other criminals, never the innocent public. And he provides a sort of service, I suppose. Over the years he has provided me with information I could not have got otherwise. He also provides other services.'

Schneider didn't explain what these were, but Anna knew that was what the meeting must have been about.

They returned to the flat – acutely aware of each other and the only bed in the next room. But they both knew what was required for now. Schneider told her that tomorrow they would set off for Prague. Business first. Once more he slept on the couch.

– 9 –

Prague

Schneider had used the Hitler letter to get rooms for
himself and Anna in the Hradčany palace overlooking
the old town. It was the centre of German government in the former Czechoslovakia, and it was also
Heydrich's destination on that last fateful day before
his killing. In any event, it would have been useless
to try to find a decent hotel at this stage of the war,
especially in an occupied country. He and Anna
had flown into the former capital of Czechoslovakia
that morning. A car had whisked them through
the old town and up to the imposing building that
now represented German authority. Without any
delay, Schneider summoned all the senior SS officers
in the palace. The rumour of his coming and his
authority meant they were all assembled in less than
ten minutes.

'You know my authority and why I am here. I expect,
as the Führer himself would expect, full and complete
co-operation from you all. The sooner I can resolve
this matter, the sooner I can return to my normal

police work. I hope to find the answer somewhere in the files relating to the hunt for the assassins.'

As he looked at their stone faces, he knew that any or all of them could be involved in the murder. But some instinct had already told him that the man he was looking for wasn't here. It was an instinct that he had always had and seldom let him down. There were other things he still needed to do, however.

His tone softened and he nodded in silent empathy with his audience.

'I know you have all tried your best to find something, anything that was overlooked. I know that the Führer has full confidence in all of you. But you are warriors, whereas I am only a humble police officer. I can't fight the enemies of the Reich the way that you do, but I can perhaps find things you may have overlooked through no fault of your own.'

One of the men seated in the front row stood up, clearly indicating he wished to ask a question. 'What do you hope to find in these files?'

Schneider could read behind the question. What this man was really asking was, what did he expect to find that might cause him any difficulty? He probably spoke for the whole audience.

'If I knew that, I would indeed be the great detective that some people seem to think I am. I don't know, but rest assured it will not reflect badly on anyone here.'

With these words of encouragement, he brought the meeting to a close. If only these self-servers knew he wasn't interested in them or anything in their files at all.

'I want offices for myself and my assistant to work in, and I want them ready for this afternoon. While that is being done, Heydrich's driver will take me on the same route that he took on the morning of the killing. And I want the details of every man involved in the hunt for the killers to be delivered to my assistant by five o'clock today.'

He told Anna to familiarise herself with Heydrich's office and staff until he returned. Her knowledge of Heydrich might throw up anything unusual here. He walked down to the courtyard to find a large Mercedes, a driver and an escort. Despite protests about his safety, he dismissed the escort. One spy was surely enough, even for Himmler. He took the front seat beside the driver. It was easier to speak to him that way.

The driver seemed nervous, which was normal, and therefore not suspicious. He stared straight ahead, awaiting Schneider's orders. He was another SS clone, but Schneider knew that he had to get him to think like a man again rather than a machine. So, he chatted to him.

'I just want you to drive along the route that Heydrich normally took and show me where the ambush took place. I have read your statement, but I want to see the locus for myself.'

Schneider asked him about Prague and whether he liked it here. He asked about his family and his home back in Germany, and this small talk seemed to allay the other man's suspicion, as much as any conversation with a police officer can. Not only was the driver aware of his reputation as a police officer but the Hitler letter was always somewhere in the background.

As they drove, Schneider studied the road and buildings along the route. He could have been in Germany. The architecture was essentially central European, which meant German. The city was undamaged by the war, and it was only the surly looks of the few bystanders that proved he was an alien, and an unwelcome one at that.

'Herr Chief Investigator, we are approaching the corner where the attack took place. Do you want me to slow down?'

'Did you slow down that day?'

'No more than any other day. As you see, it is a very sharp bend.'

'Drive as you did that day and then stop once you have passed the corner. I want to look at the scene on foot.'

The driver did as he was instructed and Schneider spent a good thirty minutes wandering around, checking angles, asking searching questions of the driver and generally acting the part of the great detective. It was all a sham. He knew he would find nothing to interest him there, but he had to keep up appearances for Himmler's sake. Occasionally, he held up his hands as if measuring some particular angles or distances.

He stomped back and forth, nodding and frowning in turn. Eventually, even Schneider thought he had done enough to convince the watching driver.

During the drive back he asked the only question that he actually needed to ask. It was the driver he was interested in, not the scene. The drive there had merely been a way of getting to talk to him, of relaxing him, without it seeming like an interrogation. He was getting the driver to recount the details of the attack and what had happened afterwards.

'So, who was the first person to arrive from the palace?'

'I can't remember, Chief Investigator. There was so much confusion with the shooting and the Obergruppenführer lying injured. I chased the attackers for maybe twenty or thirty metres and then came back to find out how seriously the Obergruppenführer was hit. I couldn't leave him alone and unprotected. Some Czechs were standing watching and some Czech police had also arrived. I head the sirens coming down from the palace and then the ambulance and other SS arrived. It was all so chaotic.'

'Take your time and relive the scene in your mind. Put yourself back there. You are standing over Heydrich. He is still conscious and speaking to you. You see people standing nearby. Close your eyes and see it as it was that day. Hear the noises of that day, and the smells of the explosion and the gunfire. Do you have it now?'

The driver furrowed his brow in concentration. Schneider could imagine his mind playing the sequence back like a movie. He must have thought about this a hundred times, maybe a thousand times. His head was nodding as he mentally ticked off each scene in turn. It was all as he had already told them before.

'Don't let the memory run itself. Pause and look around you. You are really back there, and you are reliving it now. See it as it actually happened, not as you remember it. Maybe you'll see something you didn't think important before.'

Schneider watched the man trying to do it. His voice was reassuring. There was no pressure, only gentle encouragement. The driver returned to his memory, the head now nodding more slowly as he took Schneider's advice. Then it stopped, as if he had found something that hadn't been there before. He shook his head, perhaps trying to deny it. His eyes sprung open. They were afraid. He looked away from Schneider's piercing glance.

Now was the time to ask the question.

'Who was the first person you saw from the palace?'

The driver was almost willing himself to forget what he had just seen in his mind's eye.

He couldn't be allowed to do that.

'You know my authority. I act on the Führer's behalf, no one else's. What did you just remember?'

'It just came to me. I was trying to think of the first German I saw coming from the palace, and I remember now. He didn't come from the palace; he came from the opposite direction. He arrived maybe five seconds before the first car. He just looked at us and then left. I don't know if he even knows I saw him, for I didn't see him again after that. I didn't put it in my report because I didn't recall it until now. Is it important?'

'No, I don't think so. He was probably only passing by and didn't want to get involved. I'm just trying to build up a full picture, that's all. Anyway, who was he?'

'It was Standartenführer Heizmann.'

Now Schneider knew why the driver had been afraid. He asked a few other questions of no import, for he already had the answer he needed. The first German there was Himmler's liaison officer in the Hradčany palace. Now why would he just happen to be on the spot when Heydrich was assassinated?

Schneider returned to the Hradčany and found that his office was now available. He told Anna to start gathering the files he had asked for. He had already warned her on the journey to Prague to assume that every room they were given would be bugged. They would act out their roles for Himmler's benefit, only discussing what they had really found when they took a walk in the courtyard. There was nothing more he could do until the files were available. He sent Anna back to continue her checking.

On a whim, he decided to take another drive. Schneider had never been a classical thinker. He could never explain how he arrived at his conclusions.

They came when they came. He had found, however, that if he just wandered around the scene of a crime, sometimes he would pick things up, almost on the subconscious level, that seemed to have eluded his conscious mind. So, he decided to visit the village of Lidice. The SS report had said that the assassins had received some help there. Maybe something there would give him another clue. He hadn't achieved his success in detecting crime by leaving anything unchecked. He called Heydrich's driver and told him to meet him again in the courtyard. He had found him a reasonable man and honest as well. Maybe he could extract something else, some other kernel of truth, from him on the drive. The car was waiting and this time he was pleased to note there was no escort, at least none that he could see.

'Where do you want to go now, sir?'

'There's a little village not far from Prague I want to see. Apparently, some of the inhabitants helped the assassins. I just want to see the place and maybe get the local police to let me speak to some of these people. We'll see when we get there.'

The driver seemed confused by Schneider's instruction. He just stood at the car staring blankly at him.

'What's the matter? Don't you know where it is? Go and ask if you're not sure. There's bound to be a map in the car, isn't there?'

'But . . . but don't you know what happened? It isn't there any more.'

Schneider didn't know what he was talking about. What wasn't there? The map? Maybe he had misjudged this man's intelligence. 'What's not there? What are you talking about?'

'The village, sir. It's . . . gone.'

Schneider could see there was something here that he didn't understand. He could almost sense the eyes watching him from the buildings that surrounded the courtyard. Here wasn't a good place to find out.

'Just take me to where the village was. Can you do that?'

'Yes, sir. I can do that. But I don't know what you expect to find there, sir. There's nothing left.'

During the drive, Schneider got the full story. It wasn't even a secret. Everyone in Prague knew what had happened to Lidice. Himmler had decided to destroy this small mining village as a reprisal for Heydrich's death. It was to serve as a warning to the resistance. Every man in the village had been shot. Every woman was sent to a concentration camp. As for the children, some of them had joined their mothers, while others had been deemed suitable for adoption by childless German couples. They would be stripped of their own nationality and recreated in the image of their German masters. In some ways this was even crueller than death itself to their parents. After the village was empty, it had been razed to the ground. Even its name had been removed from road signs.

The driver stopped at the outskirts, or at least what

would have been the outskirts. Schneider only knew he had arrived because the driver told him so. All that remained of the village was a dull ashen hue on the land. Every building had been flattened and then bulldozed into the earth. Every road and lane had been torn up. Every sign that humans had once lived here was gone. Schneider wandered over the wasteland. There was nothing to see. But then something glinted in the pale autumn sun. It was a doll's eye. Schneider put the small memento of someone's shattered childhood in his pocket. He thought his head might explode as unwanted and incessant thoughts finally forced their way into his conscious mind. He would never be able to go back now, even if he wanted to. He realised that the politics of a country couldn't be ignored, that it wasn't simply enough to know that evil was afoot in your own country and to identify that evil to yourself. He had hoped his revelations of the last few days would be enough. But now he saw clearly that knowledge, on its own, was never enough. Only action would do, and he had finally reached his road to Damascus.

It was starting to get dark as he returned to the car.

'Let's get the hell out of here. I've got some files to look at.'

Files that he intended to examine very closely indeed.

*

When he got back to the palace, he asked Anna to walk with him in the courtyard. He told her everything he

147

had seen at Lidice. He expected her to be shocked, or even to disbelieve him. She simply accepted it. Then he remembered whose secretary she had been. She must have seen this and much worse, even if only as cold facts typed on a sheet of paper. His admiration for her grew. To have seen so much and still remain the gentle person that stood before him. To know that your very blood marked you out for death and yet not to let that fill you with hate. Schneider knew that he had met someone special.

That evening was spent poring over the files that he had requested. From the original SS report he knew that the assassins had supposedly been found sheltering in a Prague church along with over a hundred members of the Czech resistance movement. The church had been surrounded but those inside had understandably declined to surrender to the SS. A long and protracted gun battle raged until all the people in the church had been killed. No prisoners were taken alive.

The first time Schneider had read this, he had imagined it was a case of the usual SS clumsiness and brutality. But hadn't Hitler himself ordered that the assassins were to be taken alive for interrogation? Surely every attempt must have been made to capture the assassins alive. The later public trial and execution would have served propaganda purposes very well. Now he looked more closely at who was involved in this action. He wanted to find out who was in command and what happened after the shooting stopped. It didn't take him long, and he wasn't surprised to find that Standartenführer Heizmann had been in command. It fitted the vague, almost subliminal theory that had started to take shape in his mind. He would pay Heizmann a visit in due course, when he had more evidence. He checked to see where Heizmann was stationed now. He found that he was now attached to a special unit in Russia. Could he go there? He knew he would if that was where the answer finally lay.

He turned his attention to those soldiers who were first into the church. He read and re-read their reports until he was satisfied he could see between the lines. All of them reported the gunfire from the church decreasing as more and more of those inside were shot. This, coupled with their limited ammunition, made their position hopeless. Eventually, the shooting stopped altogether. The Germans waited for some time before entering. As expected, they found everyone dead. There had been over 120 people in the church. Was it possible that no one had only been wounded? Schneider knew that somebody must have been left alive. Maybe they were summarily executed by the SS, but this was unlikely. The ordinary troops knew who was in the church. They knew how badly they were wanted alive. They wouldn't have killed anyone, at least not without orders to do so. Schneider dug out the autopsy reports on the assassins and read them again. Two had clearly died from bullet wounds inflicted during the siege of the church. But the third one had committed suicide by shooting himself in the head. Maybe it was true. But Schneider intended to put his theory to the test. He quickly jotted down the names of the soldiers who claimed to have entered the church first. He would have to find out where they were now. Only they could give him the next part of the jigsaw.

Unfortunately for Schneider, Standartenführer Heizmann was way ahead of him. He knew exactly where these soldiers were. The Reichsführer himself had briefed him and given him some very specific orders. He had never failed his Reichsführer before and didn't see any reason to fail now. In any event, he enjoyed his special type of work.

*

Autumn was passing into winter. B. saw that the time was getting closer. He sent another message to Himmler, this time through a clerk in the Swedish embassy who had come to his attention – a man whose taste for the good things in life far exceeded his salary and was open to compromise. Carefully, he placed the copy in the thin but growing file. His hand shook a little as he locked the safe, whether from the cold or from something else he didn't know. He would show the file to his superior when he thought the time was right.

– 10 –

Berlin

Schneider threw down the papers in disbelief. He had gone to the SS personnel office to establish the current whereabouts of the four soldiers he was looking for. He had thought it would be a simple task, but the young clerk had arrogantly refused him access to the personnel records. He produced his letter but this time it didn't work its instant magic. The young man was clearly impressed and showed the first traces of fear in his refusal to allow Schneider access. Nevertheless, he still refused, for a greater fear ruled here. Schneider was told to wait while the matter was checked with the Reichsführer. He toyed with the idea of forcing his way past the guards to look for himself. Surely the letter would protect him. But this wasn't the time; he didn't have nearly enough to go on yet. The day would come when he might have to challenge Himmler directly, but that day had still to arrive. So, he waited.

The clerk returned, his confidence in his position also partially restored. He asked Schneider to follow him, but instead of taking him to the records office, he took him to a small private room which contained nothing but a small desk with a phone on it. He picked up the receiver and held it towards Schneider as if it might bite.

'The Reichsführer.'

Schneider didn't have time to think what this meant. 'Herr Reichsführer. What can I do for you?'

Himmler went straight to the point. 'Schneider, I understand that you have asked to see certain records. Why?'

It might have been almost more imagined than real, but Schneider thought that for the first time Himmler sounded a bit concerned, almost rattled.

'Certainly, Herr Reichsführer. These men were involved in the action against Heydrich's killers. There are some matters concerning the priests in the church I wish to check with them. I think we may have discovered how his movements were known.'

His use of the 'we' had been deliberate flattery. If Himmler thought he was still in control of the investigation, so much the better. He waited while Himmler weighed up what he had been told. Was he still dealing with a simple police officer intent on finding nonexistent evidence or was there now a threat? He decided, and Schneider could almost feel the relief over the phone.

'I see. You must do as you think fit. But may I repeat that I do not expect you to find anything new, nor to take much longer in finalising this matter. Put me back on to the clerk and I will give the necessary authorisation.'

The call had told Schneider a lot. Once again, he had gleaned things that Himmler had not intended to reveal. First, these files must have been marked as requiring Himmler's personal authorisation before anyone was permitted to see them. Unusual for such low-ranking staff. Second, Himmler had been worried about what might be discovered from these men. Schneider wondered how Himmler would have reacted if he had simply told him the truth. He would have enjoyed shocking some reaction into such a soulless man. Instead, he had spun him the yarn about the priests. Thank God he had always been good at making up stories on the spur of the moment. More importantly, the call also told him that if Himmler was prepared to drop everything to take a call about these files, then they must contain something so vital to Himmler that Schneider's life would mean nothing to him. It was a thought he was to bitterly recall later. He had just made a terrible miscalculation, and people would die because of it.

*

Schneider had not been allowed to remove the files from SS headquarters. It was clear that the clerk held Himmler's words spoken directly to him over the phone as having much more power than a piece of paper. Perhaps he was right. Schneider had no power himself, only the vicarious effect of the Führer's signature. And that could be withdrawn at any time. Himmler, on the other hand, had the whole of the SS at his disposal. That was real, tangible power, and he couldn't blame the clerk at all. But it didn't matter, for he could extract all the information he needed right there.

The first file was that of Sergeant Jürgen Becker. He had joined the SS in 1936 and had been attached to a Waffen-SS division during the early days of the attack on Russia. He had suffered frostbite in January 1942 and had been assigned to the SS garrison in Prague. Following the Heydrich assassination, he had been transferred back to active duty on the southern front in Russia.

Schneider groaned. He could end up spending the rest of his days traversing conquered Europe trying to speak to these men. Surely one of them must still be in Germany? Then he remembered what was at stake and why he was doing this. He still didn't have a clear vision of what he expected to find, he only knew that something was driving him on. Maybe it was only the dead soldier in the courtyard, but Schneider intuitively knew there was something much bigger, much more important than merely assuaging his own guilt. To find the answer he would travel to the ends of the Earth if need be. He noted the details of Sergeant Becker in his notebook and turned to the next file.

Corporal Martin Sammer would not be able to

help Schneider. He had been killed by partisans two weeks ago. The third man was dead as well. He had also been shot two weeks ago, but this time by his own people. He had been convicted of treason by an SS court martial and executed. The file gave no details of what the treasonable act had been. Schneider didn't know enough about the SS to know if this was normal or not. Maybe Himmler refused to acknowledge that any of his men could fall short of the perfection he demanded, but it seemed a little strange that the file contained no details at all. All he could do was turn to the fourth file.

Private Hans Müller was still alive, at least according to his file. He had joined the SS in 1939 and had served both at SS headquarters here in Berlin and then in Prague. Following the assassination, he had been moved to Paris. As far as his file showed, he was still there. At last, someone who was still alive and within reach. Schneider decided to visit him first. And Paris was much more appealing than the eastern front.

He had never been to Paris but knew it was the city of romance. He wondered where the old Schneider had gone who had never thought of such things. He told himself he would need Anna with him as a secretary; but even as the thought occurred, he knew it was a lie. He wanted her there simply to be with her. Guilt washed over him as he realised what he was thinking. In the midst of all this horror, he was thinking of romance. But was that so bad? In the final analysis, wasn't love the only remedy to what was happening in his country? It was the only thought he could find to console himself with. Maybe later he would find out if it was true or not.

Paris

Paris is Paris. It didn't matter that it had been occupied by the hated Boche for over two years now. People adapt, and Parisians adapt better than most. They treated the Germans in the same infuriating superior manner that had long been tolerated by countless visitors to Paris. The German soldiers, mostly simple country boys, were as cowed as every other visitor. So, the city carried on as always. The street cafés and bistros charged their inflated prices to French and German alike. The shops boomed as the more discerning German officers bought up every ounce of French perfume and lingerie that could be had. The shopkeepers shrugged their Gallic shrug and merely increased their prices. Business was business – let others fight the war.

Schneider and Anna flew into Orly airport early the next morning. He had arranged for a car to be waiting for his arrival. The driver was the usual SS spy, but by now Schneider was used to them. They took in the sites as they drove to SS headquarters. He hadn't warned them of his arrival as he wanted to surprise Hans Müller. The spontaneous memory is often the most truthful. He didn't mind if it would take some time to find Müller. It was true what people said about Paris. He felt different somehow, as if his body was in the grip of some mild electrical stimulation. He sensed much more about the woman beside him, his mind attuned to her every movement, every gesture. He was enjoying Anna's company more and more.

They arrived at the large hotel that now served as SS headquarters. Schneider quickly got to the officer in charge and the letter did the rest. Hans Müller would be traced and brought to him as soon as possible. He could have waited there for him. He should have waited there for him. He looked at his watch, which showed it was almost midday. A warning bell at the back of his mind was ringing. For the first time that he could remember, he ignored it. Schneider said that after lunch would do.

The previous night, after Anna had gone to bed, he had glanced at an old guide to Paris. He knew what he was looking for. He had found the entry about a famous restaurant in Paris and intended to surprise Anna by taking her there. His own gastronomic taste-buds had been awakened by the recent visit to the expensive restaurant in Berlin. He gave the driver the address in the Quai de la Tournelle. The restaurant was situated near Notre Dame Cathedral, and the driver could have been a tourist guide. It seemed that even the SS were affected by whatever was in the Paris air. He took them the scenic route over the Seine, pointing out various famous landmarks as they went. The autumn sun shone on them in the open car and reflected off the painted glass of the cathedral. Life was all around them in the streets, the cafés, at the market stalls. Schneider was starting to understand the attraction of this great city for lovers. Here, people just lived as they wished. Schneider had never felt so good in his life before. He even managed to forget about the investigation, at least for a minute at a time. Anna was laughing, her auburn hair billowing in the wind. It was all he could do to stop himself reaching for her. As if she understood, she reached out and took his hand. She squeezed it tight. There would be another time for them, perhaps even in Paris. Both knew it was no more than a wild hope, but it was hope and hope alone that nurtured the human spirit when nothing else remained.

It simply hadn't occurred to Schneider that he should reserve a table. He was surprised when the maître d' curtly told him that without a booking, a table for lunch was impossible. The little man preened his moustache and looked at Schneider as if he were an imbecile. To expect a table in La Tour d'Argent without booking. Pah! But what could you expect of Germans? Schneider would normally not have let something so unimportant upset him. He would just have gone somewhere else. But he had seen the dining room beyond. Half the tables were unoccupied. The other half were taken with a mixture of very well-groomed

Frenchmen, who must have been doing very well out of the German occupation, and high-ranking army officers and their French girlfriends. He looked at Anna's face and saw resignation and just a little disappointment. It was that which decided him.

His hand shot out and grabbed the waiter by his lapel. Schneider heard buttons popping. He pulled the little man closer, his eyes no longer reflecting the arrogance of a few seconds ago.

'I'm going to take that table by the window. The empty one. The one that gives the best view of the cathedral. Now, do you want to show me to it, or will I drag you there?'

No one behaved like this in La Tour d'Argent, not even the highest-ranking German officers. Either this man was extremely important or deranged. The maître d' decided to let others find out which. He straightened his crumpled jacket and led Schneider and a shocked Anna to the table. All eyes were on them as Schneider's 'whispered' threat to the officious little man had reverberated around the room. Schneider ignored the stares and ushered Anna into the seat by the window. The man hurried off and had a brief but much more discreet conversation with a man sitting at a corner table. He rose and came over to Schneider. As he passed the other tables en route, he smiled and simpered at their occupants, apologising for this disruption to their meals. He would soon have this problem sorted.

'Good afternoon. I am the proprietor of this restaurant. I do not think we have had the pleasure of meeting before.'

'My name is Schneider. I have just flown here from Berlin, and I would like some lunch, please.'

'Alas, that will not be possible. You have not reserved a table, and I do not think you would find it . . . eh . . . comfortable here. I do not think the food would be to your liking. I can recommend an establishment you might find more to your requirements as you are leaving.'

All the while, the proprietor was smiling his oily smile, his hand stroking the equally greasy hair plastered to his head. Schneider smiled back.

'I do have a table. This one. And I'll tell you if the food is to my liking after I've had it. Now, are you going to bring me a menu, or do I have to go into the kitchen to see what's cooking for myself?'

The proprietor was calm. Occasionally, and once only, Germans made this mistake. Since the armistice, some of them thought they owned Paris. But he had his own protection. He glanced at another guest who, with an exaggerated sigh, put down his fork and joined him at Schneider's table.

'This . . . ah . . . gentleman will not listen to reason, I'm afraid. And he has taken the general's table. Perhaps you could help, Manfred?'

Manfred drew himself up to his full five feet eight inches and inflated his chest like a pigeon. His eyes

160

narrowed as his hand shot into his jacket and produced a card.

'Gestapo. You have made a big mistake, my friend. Your papers.'

Schneider had never liked the Gestapo. They simply weren't good police officers. So, he decided to have a little game with this one. Let's see just how stupid he really was. He produced his normal police identification and waited. The man fell straight into the trap.

'Your authority does not extend outside Berlin. How dare you disturb my lunch like this? I'll see to it that—'

Schneider cut him off. Even the dullest policeman should have wondered what a detective from Berlin was doing in Paris and why he felt confident enough to behave in the way he was. 'You'll send me to a concentration camp? I think not. If anyone is going there, you are.'

Leisurely, Schneider produced the letter. He saw the eyes widen as it was read. Then the panic. Manfred sprang to attention.

'My apologies. I did not realise that—'

Schneider cut him off again. 'Tell this man to get us menus now. Oh, and I'm sure you'll manage to explain to the general that his table isn't available today. I'll consider your travel arrangements to somewhere out east over lunch.'

Manfred ushered the proprietor away, explaining in hissing tones what had happened. It took all of

Schneider's willpower not to burst out laughing at the change in the man. Anna had buried her face in a handkerchief to hide her own amusement. After that, the service was all that it should be in one of the most famous restaurants in France. Schneider put himself and Anna into the waiter's hands. He knew they would now get the best of everything. Besides, he didn't know the first thing about French food.

They dined on quenelles de brochet, the famous canard Tour d'Argent and finally crêpes Suzette. They drank Montrachet with the fish and Château Latour with the duck. Neither of them thought that such wines could ever be surpassed. They were wrong. They had never tasted Château d'Yquem before. The bill would have been astronomical if there had been a bill. Schneider told the proprietor to send it to the Führer. It was a small price for having offended such as Schneider. He personally saw them out and then took to his bed to recover.

Anna had found the whole episode greatly entertaining. Schneider had tried to keep up the pretence of being some Nazi ogre who at any moment could close the restaurant and whisk them all off to a concentration camp. The more wine they drank, the more it proved impossible. Eventually, they became oblivious of their surroundings, even of the view and the food. They were only aware of each other. Schneider had forgotten all about Hans Müller. He had forgotten all about everything.

All dreams must end and finally, reluctantly, they came back to the present. The car and driver were still waiting outside, and only then did Schneider realise that three hours had passed. Typically, he apologised to the driver for having kept him waiting so long. The effect of the wine was also wearing off and Schneider was looking forward to meeting Hans Müller. He knew exactly what he wanted to ask him.

They drove back across the Seine to SS headquarters. Schneider went directly to the interview rooms where he expected to find Müller waiting. Instead, he found the officer he had spoken to that morning. Instinctively, he knew something was very wrong.

'I'm afraid something terrible has happened, Herr Schneider. Private Müller was shot dead shortly after you arrived in Paris.'

Schneider asked the questions, even though he knew the answers. 'I suppose it is presumed he was the victim of the French resistance. I also suppose that no one has been apprehended.'

In fact, they were statements, not questions, and the officer merely nodded in confirmation. There was nothing more for Schneider to do in Paris. Himmler had killed the witness, and his assassin would be long gone by now. Schneider made his goodbyes there and then. While he had been eating and drinking, while he had been playing games with the Gestapo, Müller had been killed. It could only have been to stop Schneider getting to him. It was only an outside chance that he would have been able to help Schneider anyway. Yet now he was dead. Himmler wasn't a man to gamble even on outside chances. Schneider now realised with sudden clarity the miscalculation he had made only yesterday when he thought his life was in danger. It wasn't his life, it was the witnesses' lives. Whatever information they may have had, it died with them. That was what was so important. Schneider now knew if he ever got that information himself then he too would be a target. And so would Anna. But he knew he couldn't stop now.

One witness was still alive. At least, he had been yesterday. Schneider wondered how quickly he could get to the Russian front from Paris.

– 11 –

The Russian front

The very name conjured up unimaginable horrors for the average German, but unlike most imagined horrors, the reality was even worse. Those in the German military with any influence at all had spent the last year trying to be posted anywhere except the Russian front. In the second year since Hitler had launched Operation Barbarossa against the Soviet Union, Germany's losses were growing at astronomical rates. With well over a million casualties, there were those who felt that the war was already lost. Others still hoped that the current offensive in the Caucasus could at least produce enough success to force Stalin to sue for peace. The fanatics, and they were growing fewer with every passing day, still believed in the final victory preached by their Führer.

Schneider fell into none of these categories. He had given the Russian front almost no thought at all until yesterday. Now in the cramped confines of the plane carrying him and Anna back to Germany from Paris, he was trying to make sense of a map. Leaving Paris had been difficult, what with so many feelings now forever associated with it. How could one have feelings of joy and of intense failure at the same time? These emotions fought for space with anger at that failure, and fear that the joy might never be rediscovered. It had taken him some time to drag his mind back to the map and the decisions he now needed to make.

He couldn't believe the distances that German soldiers had already covered in their drive eastwards. At first glance it looked so impressive that it was almost possible to believe that Germany hadn't already won the war. Almost, for the thought was utterly extinguished when your eyes travelled further east on the map and became aware of the vast area of Russia still untouched by the war. He remembered what his old history master had said at school, that it was impossible for Napoleon or for anyone to conquer Russia. It was simply too big and too cold. And somehow, in this vastness, in the fog and confusion of war, Schneider intended to find one insignificant German soldier. He knew if he didn't find him before Himmler did, then it would be too late. Himmler already had a head start. Maybe it was already too late. Perhaps, deep down, he was actually hoping it was, to save him such a journey.

He had the pilot radio ahead to Berlin while they were on route. He required another plane immediately after landing. He didn't specify where this plane was to fly to because he still didn't know himself. His authority was already known at Berlin and, as he now expected, there was no argument. He then radioed Wehrmacht high command in Zossen, just outside Berlin. He wanted to know the current whereabouts of the SS division that Sergeant Becker belonged to. He had no means of convincing Zossen as to his authority except the power of his voice. He demanded and got the duty officer. He gave him his now familiar prescription about state security and working on the direct orders of the Führer. He read out the letter word for word. He told him if there was any delay, he would have him court martialled when he landed in Berlin. All had no effect. The duty officer was a stickler for regulation. Until he saw the letter, he would take no action. So, Schneider told him to radio the Führer's headquarters in East Prussia to confirm his authority. If he couldn't speak to the Führer, then he could speak to Bormann. He heard the hesitation, the perceptible weakening of the military arrogance that is apparent in that caste's dealings with anyone who isn't a superior officer. But it still wasn't enough. The young officer still needed sight of the actual letter. He would have to wait until he got to Berlin and could produce the actual authority. So, Schneider played his trump card.

'This matter cannot wait. If you will not radio the Führer, I will. You will hear from him very shortly. I do not think it will be the eastern front for you after this. I think you'll be looking at a firing squad this afternoon for high treason. Your name, please.'

Schneider waited one second, two seconds. He called to the pilot. 'Get me the direct link to the Führer's headquarters at once.'

The pilot looked at him as if he had gone mad. What was he talking about? Schneider listened to the breathing on the radio. It was growing quicker.

'Wait. Please wait. It is clear that you have the necessary authority. I will ensure the information is waiting for you when you arrive at the Berlin airfield.'

'Thank you. I will ensure the Führer hears of your assistance in this matter.'

It was going to take another hour. Schneider could do nothing else but wait. He had radioed the army rather than the SS in the small hope it would keep Himmler in the dark about his immediate plans. But he knew Himmler didn't wait for others. He always struck first.

Schneider had already told Anna of his plans. The Russian front was no place for a woman. So, once more, she would stay in his flat until he returned. If anyone asked, she was working under his direct orders. She could give no further information about it or where he was. That should be enough to keep her safe for now. Both knew there was nowhere else for her to go anyway.

As they approached Berlin, they could see the palls of smoke that hung over the city, clear evidence of a visit from the RAF the night before. It was a crisp clear autumn day and from this altitude Schneider could see entire blocks of houses that had been flattened as if by some giant hand. Everywhere there were holes appearing in the very fabric of the Reich capital. It reminded Schneider of a quilt burned by cigarettes. Eventually, these holes would join up until there was no quilt any more. But this wasn't reported by Goebbels' propaganda. It was simply ignored, and it was defeatism to mention it. If overheard, such talk could result in despatch to a concentration camp. These thoughts ran through Schneider's head as the plane made its final approach. This investigation had opened his eyes to the real nature of the Nazi regime. It had changed him. He didn't know what he would do when it was over, but of two things he was now sure. He couldn't go back to being a police officer in such a society. And he wanted Germany, his Germany, defeated.

The plane landed smoothly and taxied to one of the smaller terminals used by the Nazi elite. The pilot told him that his next plane was already waiting there. As he descended the steps, a young man stepped forward. He said he came from Zossen and had something for him. He needed, however, to verify Schneider's authority. Schneider couldn't help but smile. Even now, the duty officer was playing it by the book. With a sudden flash of insight, Schneider realised it was this very attitude that had carried the army to near total victory, but in the end would condemn them to absolute defeat. He produced his letter. The officer at Zossen had been as good as his word. Schneider tucked the sealed envelope into his pocket. His next plane, a Junkers Ju 88, sat only yards away. He went back to Anna, now waiting in the car sent to collect her. He wanted to hold her, for he knew it might be the last time. But the pilot was too close to even say anything. He had to act normally.

'I am leaving now for Prague. Please complete the checking of the files in my absence. I expect to return in a few days.'

It would do no harm to let the driver, Himmler's spy, think he was returning to Prague. Anything that delayed Himmler in the race between them was a bonus. She knew why he had to appear so distant.

'Of course, Chief Investigator. I hope you have a pleasant flight.'

With that, she was gone. Schneider hurried to the plane and told the pilot to take off and head towards Prague. He would give him his real course in the air. The plane was given immediate clearance and he was airborne again in under five minutes. He tried to see the car and Anna from the small porthole, but it was already too dark. To take his mind off what he was feeling, he pulled the envelope containing Jürgen Becker's whereabouts from his pocket. The note inside was short. It merely said that his division was currently based on the southern front on the Don River at somewhere called Stalingrad. Schneider had never heard of it.

He told the pilot that there had been a change of

plan and that he should now head towards southern Russia. He would give him more exact details when they were closer. He left the pilot to radio the flight change and went back to his map of Russia. He was amazed to find that Stalingrad was over a thousand miles from Berlin. He looked at the names en route: Warsaw, Kiev, Kharkov, Rostov and finally, miles from anywhere, as if it had sprung out of the very earth itself, Stalingrad. He recalled the newspapers reporting that the German army had captured this city fairly recently, with only some minor pockets of resistance to be mopped up. There had been a time when he might have accepted that as true. Now he knew better. Goebbels had been promising the decisive victory in Russia since the invasion. Who knew what the true situation was at Stalingrad? The pilot might. He had been in Russia for a long time.

The pilot was just coming off the radio after logging the change of flight plan. 'I have a direct route to Kharkov, where we must refuel. Can you tell me where we are going after that? Even with your special clearance there might be problems because we are getting close to the front line.'

'Yes. I want to go to Stalingrad.'

The plane suddenly lurched as the pilot's hands involuntarily gripped the joystick tighter. He looked as scared as any man Schneider had ever seen. Hope rose momentarily when he thought it was a joke, but Schneider's face told him otherwise.

'You cannot be serious, Chief Investigator. Do you not know what is happening there?'

'I'm sorry, I don't. Please enlighten me.'

The pilot told him of the war in the east. It was a war unlike any other. He had been on the eastern front since the start of the attack on Russia on 22 June 1941. He had witnessed the stunning early successes when almost the entire Russian air force was destroyed in the first three days, when city after city fell. He had seen the millions of Russian prisoners, and seen them for what they were: under-nourished, under-equipped peasants. The war would be over by Christmas. Yet no matter how far they advanced, no matter how many prisoners were taken, there was always further to go and more Russians to fight.

Then came the winter before Moscow. An army equipped for a short summer war was plunged into temperatures of forty degrees below freezing. It was here that Germans learned why some of the northern mythologies envisage hell as a place of freezing cold rather than one of burning heat. It was hell on earth for the German soldier. His thin uniform offered no protection against a wind that blew straight from Siberia. His boots stiffened and cracked, to be followed by his skin. Eyeballs literally froze. Men, who had been talking to a comrade one minute, dropped dead the next. An army literally petrified as its engines and weapons froze, along with its men's spirits. Frostbite was so common that only those cases requiring instant amputation could be dealt with. And amputation in such temperatures meant certain death. Food was so short that men began eating anything they could find: horses, cats, even rats. It was rumoured that some had even resorted to cannibalism. In such dire straits, withdrawal was the only option. But the Führer denied them this. Stand and fight, to the last man, to the last bullet if necessary. Dig in and wait for the spring and the final victory.

Exhausted beyond reason, they dug into the iron-hard ground already covered in snow and the bones of fallen comrades. They stood fast before Moscow. It was a feat of endurance beyond the understanding of anyone who wasn't there. Over a million men, without food, shelter or medical supplies, tried to survive in an arctic wilderness. Then the unthinkable happened. The Russians counter-attacked. In those conditions, only the fresh Siberian troops kept in reserve for just this eventuality could have managed it. The German line broke. They took one last look at Moscow's towers, turned their backs and headed west. Some thought the retreat might not end until they reached Berlin itself. Others were less optimistic and spoke of Paris, with the whole of the Reich being consumed by the Russian monster. Somehow, Hitler rallied his army even then. He ordered them to stand and fight. Ruthless SS squads executed thousands on the spot for cowardice. Gradually, the retreat slowed and finally stopped. Hundreds of thousands fought and died. But the new line held. Even the Siberians needed rest, and a torpor spread over both sides as they faced each other from their frozen trenches. Both sides knew that spring would come. What would Stalin and Hitler do then?

'I dropped supplies every day to those men. I was one of the lucky ones. I was in a warm aircraft with only Russian shells to bother me. Somehow, I survived. Should I thank God for this miracle? Isn't he the same God who watched over a million freezing to death? It was too much for me. I think I became insane, for the next thing I knew I was in a hospital in Poland. By the time I got out, they wouldn't let me fly in the combat zone any more, so I deliver mail instead. Or people like you.'

Schneider had listened to the pilot in awe. He had no idea. No German back home had. He didn't know what to say.

'I'm sorry.'

'Why are you sorry? You didn't start the war, did you? But I hope that people back home find out what is happening here and find a way to end it. Because if they don't, the Russian front is going to end up somewhere around Paris at this rate.'

'But isn't the war going better now? We are almost over the Volga, aren't we? Surely even the Russians can't fight for ever.'

'Can't they? I'll tell you what happened this year then. After the thaw came, Hitler decided that rather

174

than attack Moscow for a second time, we would attack the oil fields to the south. It was just like 1941 all over again. We advanced hundreds of miles and captured thousands of Russians, but still they kept on fighting. We reached Stalingrad, but the Russians hung on to the outskirts. We all thought they must be crazy to fight just for a name. But it was us who were mad. It was all just part of their plan. Last month, they attacked on our flank and now the entire Sixth Army is cut off in Stalingrad. The only way in or out of the place is by plane.'

'When you say cut off, you mean just for now surely?'

'Only if you believe in fairies and Goebbels. I'll tell you now, that army is a goner. And after that, so is all of Germany.'

Schneider thought the pilot must be exaggerating. And he had just committed a court martial offence with his defeatist utterance. To do that to a stranger was risky. To do that to someone acting for the Führer was madness. Maybe they had let him out of the hospital too soon.

'I don't think you should be making remarks like that. They could get you into serious trouble, although not with me. But I want to be very clear. Are you saying that since last month it would have been almost impossible for anyone to get into Stalingrad unless he had a special authority like mine?'

'That's exactly what I'm saying. Although why

anyone would want to go there, I don't know. So, should we forget about going there?'

Hope and expectation shone in the now obviously unstable eyes. But all Schneider could think of was that if Stalingrad was cut off, then maybe Himmler hadn't been able to get to the witness. There was only one way to find out. 'I'm afraid not. I want us to refuel immediately in Kharkov and then we head for Stalingrad.'

*

The refuelling had been carried out eventually. Fuel was at critical levels, and every ounce was being used in the hopeless effort to keep the besieged troops supplied from the air. Even with Hitler's letter, Schneider had great difficulty in finding enough fuel for the plane. He learned that Göring had assured the Führer that his Luftwaffe could keep Stalingrad supplied with everything it needed. It was another of his vain promises, and now the men inside the doomed city were paying the penalty. The officer in charge of Kharkov airbase had given him the simple arithmetic: if every plane in the Luftwaffe had been employed in supplying the beleaguered troops, it still would not be enough. There were simply not enough planes in the whole of Germany to supply Stalingrad. And the planes they did have were getting fewer every day as they ran the gamut of Russian anti-aircraft fire. But even if there were enough planes, the fuel to power them was almost gone. The Russians had destroyed all their oil wells in the region. All fuel had to be transported by truck or train from Germany. And that in itself used up a considerable quantity of the very fuel so desperately needed. It was the immutable law of diminishing returns. Germany had already lost this battle.

Was he crazy to risk the flight? He stood every chance of being shot down over the Russian lines. If he made it in, he still had to make it back out and face the same risk again. The makeshift runway in Stalingrad, if it could be called a runway, was under constant shelling. It was periodically repaired by filling the shell craters with anything that could be found and then allowing the weather to freeze the repair into the rest of the surface. His plane could be damaged and then he would be trapped. And to top it all, his pilot was unstable.

Any sane man would have simply decided not to go. So, why was he going? Schneider couldn't be sure that the soldier he was looking for was still alive. Even if by some miracle he was, it was a long shot that he would be able to tell Schneider what he needed to know. But it was the last lead he had – the only lead. He knew if he hesitated for even a fraction of a second, if he allowed his mind to fully comprehend the risk he was running, he would order the pilot to turn round now. Then there was Anna. Could he go back to her without at least having tried? Could he ever hope for anything between them after that? He knew what he would have said in her shoes. You had the chance, the only chance to do something, to change something, but you didn't take it.

There was really no decision to make, after all. He told the pilot to get the plane refuelled as quickly as possible and give him a direct flight plan to Stalingrad. He was airborne again less than twenty minutes later. After they had cleared Kharkov, the pilot gave him a choice. His hand played effortlessly with the plane's controls as he gave Schneider the hard facts.

'There are only two ways of getting to Stalingrad in one piece. Either we exceed the altitude limit for this plane and hope we are high enough to escape most of the anti-aircraft fire, or we do just the opposite and fly as low and as fast as possible, hoping to fly under the Russian fire. What do you think we should do?'

Schneider knew next to nothing about planes and flying. 'I presume there are risks to either course, apart from the Russians, that is?'

'Oh yes, there are risks all right. If we take the high road, there is a chance that the engines might fail through lack of oxygen. If that happens, we crash. If we take the low road, and I misjudge our height by even a whisker, we crash.'

The pilot had offered both choices in a matter-of-fact voice, as if he was asking Schneider to choose between two suits. Neither choice seemed appealing. Schneider knew he had to rely on the pilot, no matter his apparent mental state. Presumably he wanted to live as well.

'I'll leave it to you to decide.'

'All right, the low road it is then. You might want to shut your eyes. But whatever you do, don't distract me in any way. At the height I'll be flying, the slightest miscalculation will be our last. So, I need to concentrate on one thing and one thing only: keeping us as near to the ground as possible without actually hitting it. I'll tell you when we are getting near. It'll be another hour or so yet . . . A prayer wouldn't do any harm nearer the time.'

Schneider watched the Russian countryside unfold beneath the plane. It was flat and unremarkable. Occasionally, they passed over a village, but he couldn't see if it was still inhabited or not. The first snows of the winter had already blanketed the countryside, giving a warning of the temperatures to come. Although the German army was now better equipped than the year before, it was still suffering losses to the weather. These could only grow in the months to come.

Schneider heard the engine note change as the plane started to nose downwards. The pilot beckoned him forward.

'I've started our descent. I'll take us as low as I dare before we cross the front line. Then we'll see what we'll see. You might want to strap yourself well in back there.'

Schneider took the seat beside the pilot. 'If we're

going down, I think I'd like to see it for myself. I'll sit here with you.'

'That's fine with me. But remember, no distractions. The run over the Russian lines will last about twenty minutes, if we make it that is. I'll tell you when we're clear. We'll be there in about two minutes.'

The plane had been descending sharply and Schneider could see the German front line fast approaching. The troops changed from being insects to men and he could even make out some of the upturned faces. He had never been so low in a plane before and, without the disguise of altitude, was suddenly aware of the speed they were covering the ground at. He realised the pilot had not been exaggerating and that the slightest mistake at these speeds could only be fatal. As if it wasn't going fast enough, the pilot pushed the throttles again to get every last ounce of speed out of the screaming engines. The plane bucked and leapt as it was buffeted by its own downdraft. They could have been no more than fifty feet above the ground when suddenly the last German faces disappeared. Seconds later, Russian faces appeared, and they were pointing rifles at the plane. Schneider could see the muzzle flashes and instinctively pulled back from the window.

'You don't need to bother about them. By the time they've aimed we're already past. It's the anti-aircraft guns we've got to worry about. If they can get them depressed quickly enough, they might get lucky.'

Schneider glanced at the pilot. His whole being was concentrated directly ahead. Every two seconds or so, his eyes flitted for the merest fraction of time to the altimeter. Schneider's eyes followed. The needle was bouncing at forty feet. Incredibly, he felt the plane sink lower as the pilot trimmed another five feet or so from their height. He returned to the window. If he reached out, he thought he could almost touch the Russians below. He saw their mouths working in hatred, saw the upstretched clenched fists. Then the shells started exploding above the plane. It writhed and twisted like something possessed as the pilot struggled to keep them from ploughing into the earth, now closer than ever. It was like the ultimate ride at a funfair, but this one was real. Fear gripped him as never before. His fate was now completely out of his own control. The scream of the engines pounded him almost senseless, and he was sure he could smell smoke in the cockpit. They weren't going to make it, after all. Despite himself, a scream escaped Schneider's clenched teeth. Then he realised the pilot was also screaming, but in pain. Shrapnel from one of the exploding shells had shattered his side window, driving a shard of glass deep into his shoulder.

'Quickly! Grab the stick in front of you and pull it up. I can't hold it.'

Schneider did as he was told and suddenly the plane shot upwards, almost vertically. In his panic he let the control column go and the plane just as suddenly was plummeting back towards the earth.

'Don't let go, for God's sake. Just hold it steady. That's it, easy, small movements. We're almost there. Do you see it?'

Schneider looked to the front. The plane was now flying much higher, and he could see what seemed to be the ruins of a town only a few miles ahead. Miraculously, the plane's sudden up-and-down motion seemed to have thrown the Russian gunners off, and they reached the comparative safety of the German lines around Stalingrad without any further mishap.

The pilot was bleeding badly and he desperately directed Schneider to make a turn to the right. Suddenly, there was a flat patch of land ahead that was cleared of snow. The emergency airstrip. But the pilot was almost unconscious, and Schneider knew there was no way he could land this plane.

'You've got to stay awake to land this thing. Tell me what you want me to do.'

There was no response. The pilot's head had slumped onto his chest. Schneider knew there was no alternative. He leaned over and jabbed his thumb viciously into the pilot's neck. He was rewarded with a groan and the eyes opened.

'Now, quickly, it's our last chance. You'll have to land this plane.'

The pilot took a moment to realise where he was. Then he remembered and something came back into his eyes. He pulled himself forward and took the controls.

'Above your head, the landing gear lever. Pull it down.'

Schneider searched the panel above his head and found it clearly marked. He pulled on the lever and was rewarded with a thump as the wheels lowered.

'Quickly, the flaps. Set them at maximum.'

Schneider had no idea where these were. It was a scenario from some hellish nightmare, to be alone in a plane with an almost unconscious pilot. He could have given up then, just let death happen. But he refused to. He had things to live for. He forced his mind back from the abyss of its panic. He remembered how the pilot had landed for refuelling. It was there, just behind the throttle controls. He pulled the lever as far back as it would go. The plane's engines had almost stalled with the added drag of the lowered wheels, and Schneider engaged the flaps just in time. With the last of his strength, the pilot managed to aim at the runway and cut power. The plane's wheels hit the Russian earth hard as the pilot lost consciousness. The plane leapt back into the air once, twice, and then finally settled. Schneider managed to switch off the engines as the pilot slumped over the control column. Slowly the plane lost momentum and came to a halt. Schneider had reached Stalingrad.

Stalingrad, November 1942

Schneider was almost overcome by his first impressions. After the plane had stopped and he realised he wasn't going to die, at least not yet, his heart and breathing started to return to something approaching a normal rate. The pilot was by now deeply unconscious, and Schneider did the best he could to staunch the blood pumping from the gaping wound on his shoulder. It seemed to be taking a long time for help to arrive and through the already frosting window, Schneider could see nothing but snow and more snow. His eyes were already starting to hurt as they peered over this sea of unending whiteness. He scrubbed the almost opaque windows, but they continued to frost over faster than he thought possible. He could only imagine what temperature outside the plane could produce such an effect. Then just as his eyes were almost screwed closed, he detected another colour and saw movement in this desolation. There was no ambulance, no doctor, not even a medical orderly. Just two gaunt, sunken-eyed figures who shuffled towards the plane, their hands and necks thrust deep into the pitifully thin coats that were their only protection against the wind and snow. As they were approaching, Schneider had thought they must be Russian prisoners of war. He was wrong. These were the soldiers of the once glorious all-conquering German Sixth Army, now approaching the fourth month of the battle of Stalingrad.

They greeted him without salutes or even the least interest in who he was. Schneider wondered how he should deal with such men, but it wasn't a problem. They clearly had another overriding, all-consuming priority as their eyes devoured the inside of the plane, apparently searching for something. When they saw it contained only Schneider and the injured pilot, they reluctantly turned their attention to him. He asked them to get the pilot to the hospital and to tell him where he could find German headquarters. The nearer man hawked and spat, a bright green stain despoiling the virginal snow, the sound deeply unpleasant from his water-filled lungs.

'That's a good one . . . hospital. We'll take him to the old tractor works over there. There's a medical orderly there who might have time to look at him, provided he doesn't bleed to death first.'

They were completely indifferent to the pilot's fate. Germany had abandoned them, so why should they care about anyone else? Schneider realised they had been searching the plane for food. He felt suddenly guilty, for he could have brought bread and other supplies in the empty plane. He had had thoughts only for his own investigation. But he knew his guilt was misplaced. What difference were a few loaves going to make here?

He followed the two men as they pulled the pilot out of the cockpit and laid him on an old cart abandoned near the plane's final stopping point. They wheeled him across to the tractor works. There was nothing more that Schneider could do. If the pilot lived, maybe he would be able to fly them out. If he died, then Schneider's only hope was that another pilot was somewhere in this city. He couldn't think about that now. He knew that if he did, Anna and the life he had perhaps lost with her would fill his mind. It was more than he would be able to bear, so he forced the thought into a recess of his mind. He would face that demon only when he needed to.

With a silent prayer for both of them, Schneider left the pilot to his fate. He walked along what appeared to have been the main road and studied the people passing by. They told him a lot about life here. No one showed the slightest interest in him or anyone else on the road. There was only one thing to do here: stay alive. Every waking second had to be devoted to that task. Every ounce of heat had to be preserved, every scrap of food hoarded. A passer-by was only of interest when he died. His boots and clothing might help the living to stay alive just a little longer. But no clothing could protect from the cold of that Stalingrad winter.

Already Schneider's face was completely numb. Pain stabbed into his knee and ankle joints, bizarrely feeling like a burn rather than the cold. His mind was starting to slow down, and he knew now how easy it must be for a man to succumb to a freezing death. It was painless and infinitely more appealing than trying to carry on here. His admiration and pity for the wretches who passed him grew in equal proportion.

He saw an army captain, who at least was trying to maintain some semblance of being a soldier. He half nodded, half saluted in Schneider's direction. Schneider asked where headquarters were and the captain told him that Stalingrad was now split into several pockets, each with its own command.

'Where can I find the commanding general, then?'

'That is not far. I am attached to the staff there myself. Please come with me.'

As they walked, Schneider surveyed his surroundings and spoke with the captain. Although the city had only been completely cut off for few weeks, it was already in a desperate situation. Fighting was street to street, under incessant shellfire. And all the time the slow but relentless Russian advance compressed the area of the city they still controlled. The men trapped at Stalingrad knew they had been abandoned and that only death or Russian imprisonment now awaited them. In the meantime, they would endure unimaginable cold, starvation and pain until the end came. Some of the braver of them had already taken their own lives by the simple remedy of exposing themselves to the ever-vigilant Russian snipers.

Every building was pock-marked with the effects of daily shelling. Not a window remained intact, and scarcely a roof. The street was covered in fallen masonry and glass. Schneider's nostrils were clogged with that cloying, almost tangible odour that comes from burning oil and rubber. But there was something more. A sickly-sweet stench. It was the first time he had smelled death in such abundance and so closely. Long ago they had given up trying to bury the dead in Stalingrad. The expenditure of precious energy in trying to open the iron-hard ground was too much. Now the dead lay piled liked heaps of misshapen timbers. Most had been stripped of their boots and outer clothing by those stubbornly clinging to precarious life. Even in this deep freeze, putrefaction still advanced, though slowly. That was what Schneider was now gagging on.

It wasn't just his sense of smell. Stalingrad seemed to overwhelm all the physical senses. Nothing was left untouched by what was happening around him. Eyes only saw the horror, but his ears heard the sounds of men suffering and dying, the sounds of lost souls abandoned to their fate. He heard the heavy cannon fire and the sudden whoosh of shells overhead. An explosion threw him backwards. Patiently, his companion waited, still upright and unmoved. He was an old hand at life in Stalingrad. He knew when to duck and when to save energy. But perhaps the worst sound of all was the solitary crack of the sniper's rifle that signalled the sudden end to another life. Schneider wondered how anyone could live in such conditions. Even as he asked himself the question, he knew the answer. These men were already dead. Only their base instincts for self-preservation refused to accept the fact.

The captain led him into what appeared to be the ruins of the town hall. He followed him down to the dank basement which now served as Sixth Army headquarters. Desks were set up everywhere. Telephones were constantly ringing. Soldiers hurried from one to the other, still trying to maintain the semblance of command and control in their ever-shrinking world. Others carried files and sheaves of papers. It looked almost normal. If he hadn't seen outside first, Schneider might even have believed there was still some hope for this army and its men.

The captain had disappeared to attend to his own duties, having promised Schneider that someone would see him shortly. Only now did Schneider realise that the captain had never asked his name nor why he was there. He hadn't even asked about how things were in Germany. Like everyone else in Stalingrad, he had absolutely no interest in Schneider. But his not asking about home? Schneider now knew the answer only too well. It was too painful to ask about somewhere you knew you would never see again.

Another captain approached. He was as indifferent to Schneider as his predecessor. 'Yes, what can I do for you?'

'I want to see the commanding officer. It is a matter of urgency.'

'And who might you be?'

Schneider produced his letter. Even here, where men were far beyond his control, the words of Adolf Hitler still commanded complete obedience.

'Please follow me.'

Schneider followed his guide thorough a warren of corridors all equally packed and busy. He passed through other checks on his authority and eventually reached a room with a closed door. His guide knocked and ushered him in. The room's occupant would have looked like a mild-mannered schoolteacher if he hadn't been wearing the uniform of a German general. He looked at Schneider in a weary, almost apologetic way.

'I am General Friedrich Paulus, commander of the Sixth Army. I understand you are here on the Führer's direct orders. Please tell me how I may assist you.'

The man seemed so calm and in control, as if he didn't realise the extent of the disaster facing him and his men. For a moment, Schneider considered that maybe he didn't. Could this man still believe that he was going to be rescued, that the talk of wonder weapons was true? But that was impossible, for this was an experienced war general. He knew exactly what was happening and, more importantly, that he couldn't do anything about it. Except for one thing. Surrender. And that was impossible because the Führer said so. So, this quiet, introverted man stood by while hundreds of the men who looked to him for leadership suffered and died every day. He was like some modern-day Pontius Pilate. Schneider found himself disliking the man immediately.

'You know the extent of my authority. I have come to find one man on a matter that does not concern you. I require to find this man immediately. Here are his details. Also, my pilot was injured bringing me here. Find out if he is able to fly or find me an alternative pilot. I intend to leave here as soon as possible.'

A full general is not used to being spoken to in such brusque tones, but Paulus accepted it. Perhaps, thought Schneider, this was why he also accepted so readily the Führer's instructions not to surrender. This man was not a leader, only someone disguised as one.

Paulus studied the details that Schneider had passed to him and picked up the phone. 'Where is the SS division now?'

He waited a few seconds, his eyes staring blankly ahead as he listened to the response.

'Yes, I know it. Is it possible to get a message to them?' After a brief pause, he said, 'I see. Can you get the pilot brought here and treated if he is able to be moved? And if the plane is still intact, have it refuelled and ready for departure.'

Paulus replaced the phone. He looked distracted, as if he had another more pressing matter to deal with. Schneider knew all this wreck of a man had to do was to wait while his army died around him. There was nothing else for him to do here.

'I'm afraid the SS division's phone lines are cut. It happens all the time, as you can probably imagine. I cannot tell you how long it will take to get them functioning again. I'm sorry.'

Paulus started to shuffle the mess of papers on his desk as a sign of dismissal, but Schneider hadn't come this far to be stopped by a phone line. He knew that Himmler wouldn't be.

'I will go there myself. Get someone to guide me there.'

Life flashed briefly in the general's dead eyes. 'But they are on the front line itself. If you think it is bad here, it is as nothing compared to the front line. I cannot permit it.'

'You forget yourself. I have full authority to do as I see fit. Or do you disagree?'

Paulus shrugged. They were all going to die anyway. 'Of course not. If you choose to kill yourself, that is your privilege. I will find someone to escort you there.'

*

A veteran of Stalingrad had been found to lead Schneider. Karl was twenty-one years old, it transpired, but looked at least forty. He was dressed in a manner that would only have passed muster among the blind. He wore the remains of his German army uniform, but this was covered by two Russian greatcoats, one of which clearly bore the exit holes of bullets on its blood-stained back. He had wrapped two or three Russian scarves around his neck and wore a thick woollen balaclava on his head. His hands were encased in fingerless gloves, and his feet in the bright yellow felt boots favoured by the Russians for their suppleness and warmth. It was clear that military dress code and the looting of the dead had their own rules here, and Schneider was already finding out what these were. He was now dressed in a woollen jacket covered with a heavy coat. He had gloves, a hat and thick boots on, and still he shivered, like someone diseased. He found it difficult to talk through his constantly chattering teeth. He had been in Stalingrad for less than an hour but slowly, relentlessly, he was starting to freeze to death.

His guide exhibited all the respect for him that he had already learned was the norm here. 'I don't suppose you've ever been near a front line before. Well, I don't have time to tell you everything, but I'll give you three golden rules to follow if you want to be alive in ten minutes' time. If I move, you move right behind me. Keep your head below the trench parapet at all times. It takes the Siberians less than a second to aim and fire. And lastly, if the Ruskies attack, run like fuck.'

Schneider could tell this man was a professional. He wasn't annoyed at the words. He was happy to take the advice.

'I understand. Ready when you are.'

They had been walking through what was left of Stalingrad. As they approached the front, the buildings showed more and more signs of damage. In parts the landscape looked almost lunar. Schneider was aware that the noise of firing and explosions was growing louder. He heard barked commands, and as they turned the shattered corner of a building, they found a party of Russian soldiers. It was Schneider's first sight of these *Untermenschen*, as Goebbels insisted on calling them. They must have been discovered seconds earlier hidden deep in the building. The four of them looked almost starving even by Stalingrad standards. They could have been trapped behind the German lines for weeks. Now, dragged out to face the blinding white snow fields, their eyes were screwed shut in agony. They muttered in Russian, their hands held out as if begging. But to Schneider they looked no different from the Germans around them. They were young men forced to fight a war they didn't want either. At least their war was over for now. Soon they would be freed when Stalingrad fell.

'Where do you keep the prisoners?' Schneider asked.

Karl looked at him as if he had asked him the way to the opera. 'Prisoners? That's a good one, when we can't even feed ourselves. Watch.'

Casually, without hurry, the sergeant who had been doing all the shouting pulled his pistol. He walked up to each of the squinting men, put the pistol to the back of his head and blew his brains out. As soon as the last man had hit the ground, the sergeant and the two other German soldiers started pulling open the coats, looking for anything to wear or eat. Karl almost joined them until Schneider physically pulled him back. If this was war on the eastern front, Schneider wanted no part of it. The police officer in him told him he had just witnessed murder, but what could he do? He told his guide to lead on.

'Do you see that wall on the corner there? Behind that we are in range of the snipers. So, we keep as close to it as possible. It's about twenty metres to the next bit of shelter. How fast can you run?'

'Fast enough to stay right behind you.'

'Let's see, then.'

Karl peered round the wall. One eye and for less than half a second. He jerked back and a bullet cracked against the wall where his head had just been. He looked at Schneider to see his reaction. Schneider tried as best he could to look confident. He knew he failed miserably.

'We'll give them a couple of minutes because now they'll be waiting for us. But some fool will soon give them another target somewhere else. So, when I say go, be ready.'

Already Schneider felt his heart racing. Incredibly,

he was pouring sweat and freezing at the same time. He breathed deeply, trying to control himself. He sensed Karl coiling himself, ready for the dash. He moved slightly away from the wall and crouched like a sprinter waiting for the gun, in every sense of the word. Schneider followed suit. Suddenly, Karl was gone. It happened so quickly that Schneider was still crouched. One second he was there, the next just gone. Too late now, he rushed after him. He could see him already halfway along the wall, hunched low with his legs working like pistons. Schneider tried his best to emulate him, but the gap kept growing. How long had he been running for? It felt like ten seconds already, and he could imagine every sniper turning in his direction and every rifle being trained on him. But it had only been less than two seconds and already he was approaching the safety of another ruined building. He saw Karl hurl himself through an opening and prepared to follow suit.

The bullet caught his shoulder and knocked him off balance. He knew that if he fell in the open, he was finished. Scrabbling boots fought desperately to maintain traction. Somehow, he managed to keep his feet on the treacherously icy surface and half fell, half leapt into the building. Even as he did so, he heard a bullet pass his ear like an angry wasp. He collapsed gasping in the freezing air as his heart hammered at an impossible speed in his aching chest, but he had made it.

He lay winded, more thankful than he had ever

been to be alive, until he remembered his shoulder. He struggled to his feet and pulled off his coat, frantically searching his arm and shoulder for the wound. Despite the cold, his jacket and shirt followed the coat. He had already seen the medical facilities in Stalingrad. Any wound might mean death. There was none. The bullet had somehow passed through his thick coat, tearing its shoulder almost off, but no skin was broken. His coat was ruined but it was a small price to pay. He sank back to the ground in relief. Karl was watching him while casually rolling a cigarette.

'You needn't look so relieved. You haven't made it yet. Now, let's get down this tunnel here. It will take us to the front-line trench.'

Schneider scrambled down the increasingly narrow tunnel. In places it had been shored up with bits of timber that creaked and groaned as they brushed past. Schneider had always been prone to claustrophobia, and when the light flickered for the umpteenth time and then died, he felt his chest tighten. Irrational thoughts of being buried alive, of being gnawed at by rats, burst uninvited into his mind. He stopped crawling, his body refusing to obey his panicking brain. Sweat poured off him even more than before, if that was possible. His throat contracted. Sparks danced before his open eyes. He had to get out before it was too late. Involuntarily, his hands were starting to claw at the earth and supports when the lights came back on. His panic started to subside.

'It's all right. It happens all the time. Keep going, we're nearly there. And remember what I said about keeping your head down.'

They emerged back into daylight. Schneider saw they were at the end of a long trench. If he kept bent over then his head remained below the parapet. But a moment's forgetfulness, the need to ease the constant strain on the back, would result in death. He saw the bodies of two men who had clearly made that mistake lying in a corner. The small entrance wound drilled neatly between the eyes belied the gaping exit wounds to the rear of their skulls. The Geneva Convention had no place on the Russian front. Both sides' snipers regularly used dum-dum bullets. Already the bodies were stripped, their eyes staring in silent accusation at their desecrators.

The living in the trench were dressed as eclectically as Karl. There were eight men that Schneider could see. Eight men to defend a trench that must have been over sixty metres long. He didn't have to be a general to know that if the Russians attacked here in any strength, this line would snap as easily as a dry twig in an autumn wind. All the time, shells were flying over or exploding nearby, but the eight men ignored them. One man kept a constant watch through a periscope. The other seven just lay with their backs against the trench wall. Waiting, just waiting. They were broken men, the flame of fanaticism long extinguished from their exhausted glances at him.

He moved slowly along the trench, muttering the name 'Jürgen Becker' as he passed each man. Only the fifth man reacted.

'I'm Becker. Who are you and what do you want?'

At least he was still alive. Schneider beckoned towards the tunnel.

'I am Police Chief Investigator Rolf Schneider and I've come all the way from Berlin to find you.'

Becker seemed less than impressed. 'Well, congratulations, now you've found me. So, I'll say again, what do you want?'

The other men were now looking at him, but he had no choice in such a situation.

'To talk to you about Heydrich's assassination in Prague. You were one of the men who got the killers, weren't you?'

The eyes took on a surprised, slightly wary look. 'Yes, I was. But I can't talk about these matters without authorisation.'

Schneider proffered the letter. Absently he noticed the envelope was now crumpled and stained with Stalingrad mud. 'I think you'll find I have all the authorisation I need.'

The eyes looked distinctly alarmed after reading the letter. Schneider suddenly realised he could simply vanish here if Becker so desired. He had to act quickly.

'I don't think we can talk here. I want you to come back to headquarters with me.'

'Back to Germany?'

He heard the faint ring of hope in Becker's voice. Schneider had meant Paulus's building, but maybe this was something he could use.

'Perhaps. That will depend on how co-operative you are. Shall we go?'

Schneider told Karl this man was coming back with them. Becker made a very hasty farewell to his comrades. He had to reassure them he was going voluntarily. Schneider had seen the suspicion in their eyes replaced by envy. Anything was better than the front line at Stalingrad.

The journey back through the tunnel didn't seem so terrifying the second time around. The lights held out and they reached the building where, only minutes earlier, Schneider had almost been the victim of a sniper. This time it was Becker.

As they emerged from the tunnel, Schneider heard a shout and Becker landed almost on top of him. Karl was shouting and firing his machine pistol. By the time Schneider had got to his feet, Karl was back beside them.

'Jesus Christ, but that was close. Some bastard was waiting there and took a pot shot just as your friend here was getting out of the tunnel. I just caught the movement out of the side of my eye, otherwise he would be dead. These fucking Russians are getting everywhere.'

'How do you know it was a Russian?'

'Well, who else would it be? You don't think it was one of our own trying to kill us now? I know things are desperate, but we at least wait for people to die before we start robbing them.'

'Maybe you're right. Let's get the hell out of here. The sooner we're away from the snipers, the better.'

But Schneider knew it was a German. Why wait for the second man to emerge and then shoot at him? Because he himself was the target. Schneider was certain the man he had just glimpsed disappearing was wearing a black coat, an SS coat. He knew it was one of Himmler's assassins. Even here, in Stalingrad, he had tried to stop him talking to Becker. Schneider had to get Becker out quickly.

After Becker's near escape, the journey back was uneventful. All three of them arrived at headquarters out of breath, but alive. Now Schneider might start to get to the truth. He got an office by the simple expedient of throwing its rather indolent-looking occupant out. He told Becker he was investigating the circumstances surrounding Heydrich's death. In particular, he told him that he had formed the view that the assassins had help from the priests in the cathedral where they had been killed. He wanted to check exactly who had been doing what when Becker and the others finally entered the church.

Becker eyed him suspiciously. 'Why now? It can't matter now, can it? And why risk your life coming here to ask me?'

Schneider knew they were all reasonable questions, questions that any man might have asked. Except for one thing. This was Stalingrad, and he was holding the only ticket out.

'The reason I need to know these answers does not concern you. All you need to focus on is remembering what happened and keeping in mind that if I am not satisfied with your answers then you'll stay here to die with these other poor bastards. Is that what you want?'

Only a lunatic would want to stay there, so Becker started to remember.

'It all seems so long ago now. But I will do my best to help. We had the church surrounded. I think it was more than two days before the shooting from inside stopped. I was told to take a squad inside to see what was happening. We got in through the sacristy and could see just about all the church from there. Most of them seemed dead, or at least so badly wounded that they couldn't fire any longer. So, we entered very carefully. We would have shot anyone who offered the slightest threat. But no one did. Then we found one of them alive with only a minor injury. He had been creased on the head by a bullet. He was only semi-conscious and his weapon was lying about three feet away from him. He couldn't threaten anybody. But he was shot anyway. They said he had a grenade in his jacket, but I didn't see any. After that we just collected the weapons together and went back to our barracks. It's all just as I told them at the time.'

'Yes, I know. But I want to ask you some other questions now. Who said he had a grenade?'

'Standartenführer Heizmann.'

'But he wasn't in the church with you, was he? How did he know?'

Becker looked confused at the question. 'But he was in the church. He must have come in just as we left the sacristy. He was just behind us when he shouted something about him having a grenade and shot the man.'

'That was not in your report, was it? Your report simply said that all of them were dead or dying when you got into the church, didn't it? Why did you lie?'

'It wasn't a lie. They were all dead by the time we left. It's just that Standartenführer Heizmann told us it would be better if we didn't say anything about him being there. He said he was there on the direct instructions of the Reichsführer, who wanted his presence kept out of the reports.'

'Did he say why?'

'No. And I didn't ask someone like him his reasons.'

'And then he just left. Is there anything else your report missed out?'

Becker seemed to hesitate as if weighing up the risks to himself.

'Remember my authority comes from the Führer himself. Better than that, I can get you out of Stalingrad.'

That was the clincher. The escape from Stalingrad won out over whatever apprehension he had. Becker had decided which path to follow.

'Just before Heizmann shot him, the man said

something. He sort of regained consciousness for a moment and seemed almost to recognise Heizmann. But he couldn't have, could he?'

Schneider felt a tingle of anticipation. 'Go on.'

'He said, "Why did he let this happen? We were supposed to get away. Tell him." And then Heizmann shot him.'

Becker had no idea who 'he' was. It was obvious to Schneider that Becker had simply presumed 'he' must be someone in the Czech resistance. It was not so outlandish an assumption for him to make in the circumstances.

Schneider questioned him a little longer, but it soon became clear this was all he could tell him.

'Have I helped with the investigation? Are you going to take me back to Germany?'

Schneider knew he didn't want to spend a second longer in Stalingrad than he needed to. He could share Becker's desperation. But Himmler would know and put two and two together. So, he had to leave him. But this man, this SS man who had fought all over Europe, who had seen and carried out horrors beyond Schneider's imagination, was looking at him like an orphaned puppy in a stray dogs' home. Compassion welled up in Schneider, even for such a man. Maybe there was one way.

'I am going to tell you something that you may find difficult to believe. If I take you out of here, you will be killed.'

Becker blinked at him stupidly. 'If I stay here, I'll definitely be killed. At least I stand a chance somewhere else.'

'I'm afraid you don't understand. All of your squad from Prague are dead. They have all been murdered to ensure their silence. If you go back to Germany, you will be killed also.'

'But who would want us killed? It doesn't . . .' Then the penny dropped. Becker knew who was after him. And against such an enemy, there was no defence. 'So, I suppose I'm better off here then. Just waiting for the Russians.'

'Remember that shot at you earlier. Who knows which side it came from? Even here someone might be ordered to kill you, but I think that would have happened by now if it was going to happen. It's more likely that your death or capture here serves the same purpose. Your silence. But who would know if you died or not? Thousands must be missing or presumed dead here. When the Russians capture the rest, I don't think they'll be sending a list of names to Germany, do you?'

'But how does that help me?'

'If you disappear, if you leave here without anyone knowing, you stand a chance at least. Is there anyone who could help you?'

Becker saw this was his only chance. He thought for a moment. 'You will have to refuel in Kharkov, won't you? I have some friends there who should be able to fix me up with new papers. I can become someone else who is also missing. I don't have any close family. Things like that can wait until after the war anyway.'

Schneider knew that Becker would disappear. To do anything else would mean death, and clearly the man was desperate to live.

'I'll drop you in Kharkov. Assuming, that is, our pilot is still alive and the plane still serviceable.'

He found the pilot was still alive. His shoulder had been stitched but no bones were broken. He declared himself fit to fly. Schneider knew he would have done so even if he had lost an arm. No one wanted to stay here. The plane had survived and had even been refuelled. They were ready to make the run back over the Russian lines.

'How many men can this plane carry?' Schneider asked the pilot.

'It's designed to carry four. Why?'

'Get the medical orderly to find a couple of the most seriously wounded men, not officers, who have children back in Germany. Tell him to load them onto the plane.'

'But that will slow us down over the Russian lines.'

'That's a risk we're both going to take. But it's going to be dark soon. Isn't it safer then?'

'I suppose if we wait until night and then fly high, we might make it.'

'That's agreed, then.'

Schneider oversaw the loading of the sick. He made

sure the men were who they claimed to be. Twice he was offered bribes by senior officers to take them instead. He ignored their pleadings. When the plane was loaded, he told Becker to climb in. The pilot was already making his pre-flight checks and paid no attention to Becker joining the wounded men. Schneider sat in the empty bombardier's seat. He tried to block out his feelings for those who had to stay behind in this hell, but he couldn't stop the overwhelming guilt of his leaving while others remained to die a terrible death. But he also knew his remaining and dying here would serve even less purpose. So, he had taken his place on the plane. He hadn't said goodbye to Paulus.

The plane took off and climbed. He saw the odd flash in the darkness but, miraculously, no one seemed to be firing at them. They passed back into German territory and two hours later landed at Kharkov. Becker disappeared into the night without a backward glance. Schneider never learned what became of him. After refuelling they flew on, reaching Berlin as the first light of dawn broke.

— 13 —

Berlin, November 1942

Schneider headed straight to his flat. He could see that there had been another heavy air raid the night before and he wanted to know that Anna was safe from that, as well as from anything else. The place had been transformed during his short absence. Now it had all the warmth of a home, somewhere a man would want to come back to. Schneider was a man of habit and usually found it intolerable when anyone moved his belongings in the office. For some reason, here, he liked it.

Without a word, they rushed into each other's arms as if it were the most natural thing in the world. He held her silently, just feeling the pleasure of being near her again. They didn't kiss nor did they speak about his trip, for both knew that walls could have ears, particularly if Himmler was listening. Reluctantly, he finally let her go and then went through the masquerade of mouthing the usual pleasantries to each other that any eavesdropper might expect between boss and secretary. He gestured to her coat and said he felt like a walk to ease his back after the journey. Perhaps she would like to accompany him? She put on her coat, and they strolled through the awakening streets. As they walked, he told her everything about Stalingrad. She had nothing to tell him in return. No one had disturbed her stay. She asked him what he planned to do now.

'First of all, I need to find a reason for speaking to Standartenführer Heizmann. I'll think of something, but eventually Himmler is going to suspect what I'm doing. But if I can get Heydrich's papers by then, maybe I'll be able to use them to protect us. So, I need to speak to this priest of yours as well. And when I'm doing that, perhaps I can also find out something more about this gold and where it was coming from. I still don't know why Himmler was so keen to keep that from me. I know it was coming from somewhere in the east, and I'm sure one of the places mentioned was this Auschwitz camp where your priest is.'

'Is the gold really so important?'

'Himmler seemed to think so. I don't know, but there's something about it that seemed more to me that just stealing.'

'Well, before you cure all the ills of the world, let's go back to the flat and get some hot food inside you. When was the last time you had something decent to eat?'

Schneider was surprised to find he couldn't remember. In Stalingrad, food had never entered his head.

They returned to the flat and after eating all that was put before him, Schneider went to bed. He hadn't slept for more than two days, and the memory of Stalingrad was starting to fade. His nervous system was returning to normal and he was exhausted.

He was awakened by Anna pulling furiously at his shoulder. To Schneider it seemed he had only just closed his eyes.

'Wake up. Wake up, for God's sake. The SS are here. They're banging on the door.'

Schneider slowly became aware of his surroundings. Normally, he was one of those individuals who make the transition from being asleep to being awake instantaneously, with complete awareness. But the strain of the last few days had caught up with him. He became aware of the hammering on his door. It was growing steadily louder. If he didn't open it quickly, they would break it in.

'Hurry, Anna. Into the kitchen and stay there.'

He pulled a dressing gown on and ran to the door.

'All right, I'm coming. Just a moment.'

He checked Anna was safely hidden and turned the key.

'What is the meaning of this? Don't you know I was asleep?'

The two po-faced SS men showed nothing to indicate whether they knew this or not. They had been sent on an errand and they would complete it. One of them flicked out his ID while the other tried to see past Schneider into the apartment. Deliberately, Schneider spread himself as he casually examined the open wallet in front of him. The wallet was withdrawn even before he had started to read the card, but both of them knew such formalities were unnecessary. 'The Reichsführer wishes to see you immediately.'

It could mean anything or nothing.

'Presumably, you'll allow me the courtesy of dressing first. I'll be downstairs in five minutes.'

He didn't wait for an answer, nor did he invite them in. He splashed his face with cold water, dressed quickly and scribbled a note to Anna. She cautiously opened the kitchen door, but he gestured her back inside. His note told her to wait for him until this evening. If he didn't return by then, she must try to get out of Germany. He resisted the almost overwhelming desire to see her again for what might be the last time, laid the note on the dining table and left.

He travelled in the usual silence to SS headquarters and was led directly to Himmler's office. Without any delay he was ushered in. The room and its occupant were both as Schneider had last seen them. It was as if Himmler hadn't moved since then. This time, however, there was no pretend display of power with a file. The veneer of calm control that was Himmler's hallmark had cracked. He lurched to his feet as Schneider entered and launched straight into a frenzied tirade, as if he was finally managing to relieve himself of a pressure that had been relentlessly building.

'Schneider, I have brought you here to find out exactly what you think you are doing. We agreed, did we not, that there was nothing more for you to find in this investigation. Yet now I am informed that you have been to Stalingrad of all places. Both myself and the Führer require this investigation to be completed immediately. So, kindly tell me why you risked your life and those of others on this absurd journey to Stalingrad.'

Schneider was composed and assured in his explanation.

'I am sorry, Reichsführer, if I have displeased you. As I told you at our last meeting, I suspected there may have been a conspiracy involved in the killing of Heydrich. I believed it was somehow controlled through the Catholic Church. As you know, several priests in Prague have been implicated in the killing. My fear is that this is just part of a wider conspiracy involving the church and may threaten the lives of other leaders in the Reich. It is my duty to ensure no harm comes to the Führer – or you.'

Himmler looked almost confused. As well he might, because despite appearances, Schneider was making the story up as he went.

'Your motives are laudable, Schneider, I'll give you that. But who could help you in Stalingrad?'

'I wanted to check if any of the priests had said anything when the church was stormed. I believe it is crucial to this investigation. So, I discovered the only man left alive who had been in the first party into the church was now in Stalingrad. Of course, I didn't realise quite what it was like there, or I would have reconsidered my actions. In any event, it was a fruitless trip. The man I was looking for seems to have been lost.'

'Who was this?'

Schneider watched the reaction very carefully as he said the name. 'Sergeant Jürgen Becker.'

The name clearly registered with Himmler. It was all he could do to stop his relief showing, so he took off his glasses and cleaned them, as if it was a matter of no importance.

'So, this, ah . . . Becker has been lost in action, has he? And there is no one else to help you who was in the church?'

Now it was Himmler's turn to watch Schneider's every reaction.

'I am afraid not, Reichsführer. There were only four men involved, and Becker was the last of them.'

Himmler studied his face for a few seconds more, but Schneider managed to maintain his look of professional disappointment. Himmler nodded. The police officer in front of him had clearly never learned about Heizmann's involvement.

'So, there is nothing more to be done. I will expect your report within the next few days and then you can return to your normal duties of apprehending criminals.'

'As you wish, Reichsführer. There is, however, one other person I would like to speak to first. It is a very minor matter. But I believe he may have spoken to some of the terrorists from Lidice before they were executed. I want to see if any of them had any connection to the church. It is the last possible link I have uncovered.'

It was thin, very thin, but it was the best he could think of on the spur of the moment.

Himmler looked weary again. Would this policeman never stop his searching? At least he was way off the mark. 'And who is this man?'

'Oh, you know him very well, Reichsführer. He is your liaison officer in Prague, Standartenführer Heizmann.'

Schneider was pleased to see the hand ball involuntarily into a fist. The basilisk eyes blinked once and then twice, but that was all. The face remained its inscrutable self.

'I am at a loss as to how he could help. I think you should conclude your investigation now.'

'I will be guided by you, Reichsführer, naturally. However, my report would then be incomplete, and I would have no alternative but to mention this. I do not wish the Führer to be misinformed.'

He had finally done it. There had been no alternative but to challenge Himmler directly. He knew Himmler wouldn't accept such a report going to Hitler. He also knew that from now on Himmler would check even more closely what he was doing. Time was beginning to run out. He hardly dared to draw breath as he awaited Himmler's reaction. He knew that he could well be dead in a few minutes or simply disappear into some camp. He had tried as best he could to prepare himself for whatever was to come, but he wasn't prepared for what Himmler had to say to him.

'Continue if you must, Schneider. However, in that case I think there is a matter that we should address now. It is something that perhaps we should have dealt with at the outset of your investigation. I have always been uncomfortable with someone outside the SS interviewing SS members. As you know, we have our own system of justice in the SS, and our own courts. I have accordingly decided to award you the rank of SS Standartenführer. I think it is only appropriate and a just reward for your efforts.'

Schneider was stunned. His mind was working like a machine, frantically trying to discern the hidden plot behind Himmler's offer. He tried to gain time.

'But I thought the Führer wanted someone outside the SS to carry out this investigation?'

'That is so, and you will still be entirely independent. The rank is more honorary than anything else. It just means that you will not look so out of place. I have taken the liberty of having a uniform prepared for you. You can collect it before you leave. I hope that in future you will wear it when you come here. It makes everything seem so much tidier, don't you think?'

Schneider could have protested, could have tried to use Hitler's letter. But he decided to accept it. Maybe it would even have some benefit.

He muttered some words of thanks. He had just worked out what was really behind this 'honour'. Now he was under Himmler's jurisdiction and was subject to the SS justice Himmler had just mentioned. It would be a very neat way of getting rid of him.

*

The two goons who had brought him here had disappeared, so he decided to walk back to the flat. He knew Himmler hadn't thought up his plan on the spur of the moment. The prepared uniform he now carried home with him attested to its preparation. It was just another safeguard Himmler had put in place. At any moment he could find himself hauled up before an SS court on some trumped-up charge, and that would be the end of him. For the hundredth time he thought about what he was doing and wondered if it was really worth it. For the hundredth time he got the same answer.

When he got back to the flat, he told Anna what had happened. They had squeezed into the bathroom, with the bath tap running to defeat any microphone. At first, she thought it was ludicrous and insisted that he try on his new uniform. For a fleeting moment they were just two people laughing together at the absurdity of their lives. But when he explained about the special SS courts, she also saw Himmler's plan.

They went out to the nearby park to discuss what they should do. He could simply conclude the investigation and return to being a police officer. That would satisfy Himmler. Maybe she could get a job back in Berlin and, assuming nobody ever found out about her Jewish blood, they could be together. But if her secret was discovered, she would die, and he could too. In any event, Heydrich's papers were somewhere. They probably also held the details of Anna's race. If someone other than Schneider found them, that would be the end. And both of them knew Himmler would never stop searching for those papers.

But now there was another more personal reason. Schneider wanted to get Himmler. He knew he was dealing with a cold-blooded murderer, a man who was probably responsible for thousands of deaths. He could do nothing about this as a police officer. Only Heydrich's papers offered an answer. And there was also Lina Heydrich. Schneider had given his word to her that he would track down her husband's killers. He wouldn't break his word if he could avoid it.

He told Anna what needed to be done. They agreed to fly to Poland tomorrow, go to this camp at Auschwitz and find the priest. If he could help them to find Heydrich's files, they would have their weapon. If he couldn't, Schneider would speak to Heizmann. If that turned up blank then there was nothing else. Nothing else at all.

– 14 –

Poland, December 1942

Schneider and his authority had become so well known at Tempelhof airport that his instructions to have a plane standing by for him had been followed without comment. He and Anna had driven themselves to the airport and boarded the waiting plane just as the first grey light of dawn was breaking over the control tower.

It had been another night of heavy air raids, and they had spent most of it in one of the overcrowded U-Bahn stations that doubled as air raid shelters during the night. The Berliners had become hardened to the constant bombardment and faced it with their typical stoicism and humour. Some told risqué jokes about Göring and the Luftwaffe. Others sang to anyone who would listen. Children found these nocturnal outings an adventure, and were forever awakening those who tried to sleep. Food and water was shared. New friendships were forged, new lovers found and lost. Discussions raged over almost every topic except one. There was no talk of the war itself. Somewhere deep in their collective psyche, this wretched mass of humanity knew the unthinkable, the unstateable: that the war was already lost.

Schneider and Anna had huddled together, trying to keep themselves to themselves. Occasionally, a child clambered over their legs, only to be quickly snatched away by an apologetic parent. Even here, Schneider was known as a police officer, and police officers worked for the SS, for the Nazi state, so it was better to keep your distance. For once, this suited both of them as they needed no company but their own. At about five a.m. the all-clear had finally sounded and they had trooped back up to the street, everyone wondering what they would find this time. Schneider studied the faces as they climbed the stairs to the world above, their inner thoughts etched in lines of worry. Would everything be gone, everything they had worked their whole lives for? And yet there was still determination there, something in most of their eyes that said things must get better. Why? Because these same eyes strayed to the children mirroring the fear that all parents feel. What will become of them in the future if it doesn't?

The air raid had been concentrated on another part of the city, and Schneider's street was untouched. He and Anna snatched a couple of hours' sleep before rising again for the journey to the airport. Like everyone else in Berlin, they needed the rest that the constant bombing now never allowed enough of, and they were both asleep before the plane took off on the short flight to Warsaw.

After three years of German rule, Poland was relatively safe for them to travel around in, and Schneider had ordered a car to be waiting without a driver. Warsaw seemed no better or worse than any German city in the fourth year of war. The damage inflicted by the German blitzkrieg in 1939 was still obvious, but the essentials of life had long since been restored. People looked hungry and tired, but life went on. Poles ignored their German masters and were ignored in return. At least there was no night bombing here.

Schneider had checked the whereabouts of Auschwitz prior to leaving Berlin. He discovered it was situated near the Polish town of Oświęcim, not far from Krakow. He had obtained a map of Poland and showed Anna the route: the main road south to Krakow, then south-west to Oświęcim and the camp. It was about 300 kilometres in all, and he expected to be there by the afternoon. But he hadn't counted on Anna's navigation. Within minutes of leaving the airfield, they were hopelessly lost. Road signs were few and far between, and they somehow ended up in the centre of Warsaw. Fortunately, the war and petrol shortages meant they were one of the few cars on the road and eventually Schneider spotted a sign to Krakow.

He relaxed into his driving now; he was on the right road. He hadn't done much driving in the last few years, and he had missed it. He recalled a vague plan to buy a sports car and tour Europe when he retired. Life had seemed so simple then. Even now, he intended to make the most of this opportunity and was looking forward to seeing Poland as it passed by. But no sooner had they started on the road when suddenly, without any warning, they came to a brick wall that appeared to totally block it off. It was as if a part of the city had simply been cut off from the rest. There was no alternative but to drive alongside the wall. But it simply went on and on. It twisted and followed a route that blocked every road that might have run through it. It was one of the strangest sights he had ever seen. Schneider asked Anna if she had any idea what this wall was, but she had none. There was no alternative but to drive on. Eventually the wall must end, even if it was outside Warsaw.

The streets that ran along the wall were absolutely deserted, and it appeared they were driving in a ghost city. Not even a cat or dog disturbed the stillness. Somehow, the silence imbued the unadorned ever-present wall with a feeling of some brooding but unseen evil. And then, at last, when he had almost given up hope of the wall ever ending, Schneider saw the opening. It was guarded by SS troops who were in the process of overseeing the loading of people onto trucks. These people were streaming through the opening from the other side of the wall. Before he could drive any closer, the car was stopped by one of the SS soldiers. Self-importantly, he gestured that they should turn around. Schneider had no intention of spending the rest of his life driving around a wall. He stopped the engine and climbed out. The SS sentry immediately unshouldered his rifle and pointed it at him.

'Get back in the car and leave at once, otherwise you will be arrested.'

Schneider could see that the people coming through the wall were starving. Men, women and children, young and old alike, displayed the gaunt and bony faces of hunger. Their filthy, ill-fitting clothes hung on emaciated bodies. Their eyes were perpetually downcast, afraid to even look at the SS soldiers.

'I will not tell you again. Leave here immediately.' As if to reinforce his earlier threat, the sentry ostentatiously cocked his rifle.

'I will leave as soon as you tell me where I can find the road to Krakow.'

Schneider presumed his fluent German would be enough to relax the soldier. It wasn't.

'You are under arrest for refusing to obey my orders.'

Now, he could see two other soldiers approaching, led by a young officer. Perhaps he was the person to speak to. Schneider started to explain the misunderstanding, but the officer totally ignored him and spoke to the sentry.

'What is happening here?'

'This man refuses to leave so I have arrested him, Herr Obersturmführer.'

The lieutenant glared at Schneider. Then he saw Anna. 'So, you were out for a drive with your Polish plaything and thought you would come to see today's shipment to impress her. Well, I hope she is worth it. I shall deal with her myself. When will you Polacks learn to do as you are told?'

Maybe it was what he said about Anna, Schneider didn't know, but he felt a hot rage surging through him. 'I think you have just made the biggest mistake of your short life, lieutenant. I am going to reach into my jacket and show you my authority. Then we will continue this conversation.'

Slowly and very deliberately, Schneider produced his letter. It had its usual effect and the crash of the lieutenant's boots slamming together as he came to attention resonated across the square. The others took their cue from him and followed suit.

'We will deal with your ill manners shortly. First of all, tell me what is happening here?'

Like every good police officer the world over, Schneider sensed when there was something unusual happening. If they were so keen to keep people away, it was worth asking the question. Behind the lieutenant's growing fear, there was now surprise on his face. He had presumed that someone with Schneider's authority must know everything already.

'It is today's quota, sir.'

'Quota?'

'Yes, sir. The Jews who are going to Auschwitz.'

Schneider now noticed the faded dirty Stars of David on everyone coming through the wall. This wall must be to keep the Jews separated from the rest of the population of Warsaw. He knew that before the war Warsaw had one of the biggest Jewish populations in Europe. Could you really cut a city the size of Warsaw in half, sever roads and streets and separate one people from another? Yet the proof that such a task was possible was in front of him. And why were they going to Auschwitz? What was that place?

'So, this wall encloses the Jews? How many go to Auschwitz?'

'Yes, sir, this is the Warsaw ghetto. We built it two years ago to keep them separate. It's easier to organise the transports that way. But there's not many of the Yids left. Most of them have already gone to Treblinka or Auschwitz. I think there are about fifty thousand left. They'll be gone within the next month and then the city will be free of Jews.'

Schneider almost asked what happened to them in these places but stopped himself just in time. He couldn't show too much ignorance without arousing suspicion. And deep down he had the most awful feeling about what he was seeing here. He remembered the rumours about what was happening in the east. He had to get to Auschwitz without further delay. His intention to humiliate the boy before him vanished.

What would be the purpose now? Quickly he got directions to Krakow and left them to their grim task. When he got back into the car, he saw that Anna had been crying. She had seen the stars of David; she had seen what was happening to her people.

'I should be out there with them instead of denying who I really am. I don't deserve to live, not any more.'

Schneider could think of no words to comfort her, so he just drove as fast as he could. To Auschwitz.

Auschwitz, later that day

They had driven the whole way in silence. Gradually, Anna's sobs had softened and died. But he knew he didn't have the words to speak to her about what they had just witnessed. She was in her own private hell, and he couldn't help her. Mercifully, she fell asleep after a while.

The road to Krakow was devoid of other users, save for the occasional German military vehicle. Apart from them, there was nothing to tell him Poland was not as it always had been. He saw farmers working in their fields and, in Krakow itself, shops and markets were open. The juddering of the car over the cobbled streets of the old town woke Anna. He saw a café that was open and stopped. They both needed something to eat and drink, and it would be a chance for Anna to compose herself. The only food on offer was potato soup and bread. Schneider ordered for both of them.

The soup was good, but the bread had that almost sawdust-like taste he had become accustomed to since the war started. Anna mechanically fed herself and the silence grew between them.

Schneider finally tried to reach her. 'I know what you are thinking, but what good would it do for you to have been in that queue? If you really want to help your people, let's complete what we set out to do.'

She looked at him with sorrow. 'You don't understand. I have spent all my adult life denying who and what I am. I didn't really know who I was until I saw them. And still I deny who I am. I don't want to die any more than you do. But I don't even have enough courage to admit who I am. So, how can you rely on someone like me? I'll only let you down.' Tears welled up in her reddened eyes.

'Would someone without courage have taken those files to the priest week after week? Would they be here now trying to find him again? I'll tell you what someone without courage would do. They would try to get to Switzerland, and with this letter I could take you there if you want. Do you want me to do that?'

'Would you do that for me?'

'You know I'd do anything for you.'

'And after we got to Switzerland, you would come back here, to finish this off?'

'You know that as well.'

'Then so would I. So, let's finish it off before we think of a future, any future.'

Her eyes had dried. There was even a hint of the old Anna in them.

'Let's drink to courage, then.'

He raised his cup of weak tea to her. She smiled. It felt so good to see her smile again.

'I can't forget what I saw today, but maybe you're right. Courage might be found in many disguises. And I think it's now time for you to assume yours, don't you?'

Before leaving Berlin, Anna had suggested that he take his new SS uniform with him. She told him that she had often seen the effect that such a uniform has. Even with his magic letter, the uniform could still prove valuable. Maybe in a camp like Auschwitz, where it was the only recognised symbol of authority, it might be necessary to convince a prisoner that he could help them. Schneider didn't like the idea, but equally he could see the merits of her argument. Reluctantly, he had packed it in his case.

'I don't know if I can.'

'Do you think if you had been wearing it in Warsaw, that guard would have spoken to you the way he did? You might have been shot for nothing. In Auschwitz, it might be even worse. You're the one who told me we have to finish this off. If wearing that uniform helps us, why not?'

Schneider was forced to agree. He got his case from the car and used the small café toilet to transform himself. When he emerged, the change on the faces of the owner and the other customers was immediate. He could almost feel the fear that now emanated from the owner. Maybe Anna was right. He paid the bill, much to the man's surprise, and set off for Auschwitz. The town of Oświęcim was signposted, and he knew the camp was close by.

Oświęcim was a nondescript little town, and the road to it was narrow, potholed and unkempt. The further Schneider drove along this road, the more he wondered about the camp. The road was clearly poorly maintained and there was nothing to suggest it was heavily used. Could all the Warsaw Jews have been brought here over such a road? Maybe the guard had been exaggerating about the numbers, and the camp was nothing more than a small labour camp. Schneider had certainly never come across the name of Auschwitz in any police report or other official document he had seen. But he knew with a growing insight that lots of things had never been included in official reports. Then again, he had never noticed the glaring omissions, and he wondered now why that was. He still didn't have an answer that he could face.

He drove through streets that bore all the hall-marks of poverty. Windows were cracked or boarded up and litter blew everywhere. A few figures trudged aimlessly, wrapped as best they could against the wind. He stopped in what passed for the town centre when he saw some German soldiers on a street corner. His uniform clearly worked, and they were relieved to discover he only wanted directions to the camp. They hurriedly complied and sent Schneider on his way. He left the depressing town and drove over relentlessly flat fields, now brown and barren in the winter cold. He spotted the camp over this landscape while still some distance away. It was huge, seeming to extend forever in row upon row of equally spaced huts. Again he wondered how a road like this could service such a place, but then the answer to this puzzle appeared before him. Auschwitz was at the centre of a rail network. He could see several tracks converging and then disappearing into the camp through the large gates that appeared to be the only entrance. The tracks gleamed like polished silver in the setting sun, a testimony to their constant use. The light caught a sign over the gates which he was able to read as he drew nearer: *Arbeit Macht Frei*. Work sets you free. It was an unusual slogan, and Schneider reasoned he was arriving at some kind of labour camp where the prisoners were enjoined to work hard in return for the promise of eventual freedom. But he couldn't see any factories or other evidence of production to suggest what was made here. The only sign of manufacture were four large chimneys that gave off heavy black smoke into the darkening sky.

He stopped at the guard post and identified himself to the somewhat surprised guard. He eyed Schneider suspiciously, and Anna even more so. It was obvious they didn't get many unexpected visitors here.

Schneider stuck his police identification out of the window.

'I have come to see the commandant. Tell me where his office is.'

The guard moved directly in front of the car. 'I regret that no one may enter here without the necessary pass. Do you have such a pass?'

Schneider climbed out of the car to ensure the guard saw his SS uniform and rank. It made no apparent difference; the guard remained unmoved. As always, Schneider's mind was constantly analysing all the information it received. Something was happening here that was highly secret if an SS Standartenführer was not to be admitted. Perhaps this was the location of the wonder weapons that Hitler kept promising? But where was the factory, then? Underground, as a defence against bombing? Then he remembered the ragged line of Jews he had seen that morning in Warsaw. What work could thousands of unskilled Jews do here? Why would Anna's priest be sent here unless it was a concentration camp, in which case his uniform should have been enough to get him inside. A tingle from nowhere caused him to shudder. He suddenly sensed that something unlike anything he had ever experienced before was happening behind these gates. He produced his letter and demanded that he be admitted. The guard read it once, then a second time and, finally, a third. He looked at Schneider in confusion. Then he started to read the letter again. Schneider leaned forward and snatched it from him.

'Open these gates now, otherwise I'll open them myself.'

'Herr Standartenführer, I do not know what to do. Your letter . . . but you do not have a pass for this camp. I must telephone for instructions.'

It was the first time the letter had not brought instant obedience. But there could be no higher authority. He had to show here and now that he would be denied nothing in this camp if he demanded it, whatever was going on behind these gates.

'YOU WILL OPEN UP NOW.'

His voice carried absolute conviction, and his eyes bored into the guard. His hand edged towards his pistol. His other hand still held the letter, thrust out in front of him, the source of his absolute authority. The guard looked again at the signature on that letter, backed down and swung open the gates.

Schneider drove through, following the guard's stuttered directions to the commandant's office. Even in the twilight, Schneider could see the well-kept roads and paths that wound between the houses. Some children were still playing football. It could have been a small village anywhere in Germany. It all spoke of a large German staff who lived here with their families and tried to carry on as if they were still in the Fatherland.

He followed the signs to the office block where he knew the commandant would be waiting. The guard had been reaching for the phone even as Schneider drove off. He parked the car just as the door opened and a man came hurrying down the steps. Schneider told Anna to wait in the car and climbed out. Even as the commandant was snapping out a salute, Schneider was almost overcome by the smell. A thick, almost greasy stench, like you might expect to find in a rendering plant, pervaded the whole atmosphere. His face must have signalled his disgust because the commandant nodded sympathetically.

'I know. It's terrible the first time you smell it, but you get used to it in time. I almost don't notice it at all now.'

Hauptsturmführer Rudolf Höss, the commandant of Auschwitz, had been there for over two years, more than enough time for his olfactory sensitivities to be dulled. He extended his hand, shook Schneider's warmly and invited him into his office. At least the smell was almost tolerable there.

It was one of the tidiest offices that Schneider had seen. Every file on the desk was arranged in geometric precision. The pen stood at right angles to the inkwell, which was precisely placed at the very top of the desk. Even the shining apples in the fruit bowl seemed to have been individually positioned. It was the room of a man with a fixation for order. Schneider thought such a man should be able to find the priest for him quickly, even in a camp this size. After the usual pleasantries about his journey, they got down to business.

'What can I do for you, Standartenführer?'

'I am looking for a prisoner I understand is in this camp. I need to speak to him urgently on a matter of the utmost importance to the Reich. I realise it is late and your staff may have gone, but I need to see this man immediately. Do you wish to see my authority?'

'The guard has already advised me of it. Perhaps if you had let me know you were coming, I could have prevented the ... ah ... misunderstanding. Nevertheless, I would like to see it for myself. I believe it is important to be clear on such matters.'

Schneider passed him the letter. He read it very carefully, twice over. He was clearly a very careful man. For a moment his fingers caressed the signature on the letter as if it was some kind of holy relic.

'Very impressive. Do not worry about my staff. For a matter of such importance, I will be happy to find this man for you myself. And I will be happy to offer you accommodation here overnight. The roads in Poland are not the easiest to negotiate in the dark. If you give me the prisoner's name and the approximate date he arrived here, I can start to check if he is still with us. We process so many now, he may already be gone.'

Schneider didn't know what he meant by 'process'. His instincts told him not to show any ignorance, otherwise his host might clam up on him. First of all, he had to find out if the priest was alive.

'He is a Catholic priest, a Rolf Stein. He was brought here about four months ago.'

233

Höss looked concerned. 'Four months is a very long time here. Unless he was a special category prisoner, or is very tough, I fear he may already be gone. But I will check. Give me thirty minutes or so and I will know for definite. Would you like to go to the guesthouse now to freshen up? My wife and I would be delighted if you would dine with us tonight. It is not often we get company here.'

Schneider accepted the invitation. To do otherwise would have been unusual. In any event, he found himself repulsed and fascinated by Höss in almost equal measures. Perhaps at dinner he could find out why.

Schneider rejoined Anna in the car and drove the short distance to the guest block. As they drove, he told her what Höss had said. An elderly soldier, too old for active service, showed them to their adequate rooms. They washed off the grime of their journey, but nothing could get rid of the smell in their nostrils. Schneider decided to keep on his SS uniform. It seemed the only way to dress in such a place. He dusted it off as best he could and checked himself in the mirror. He would never get used to it. They walked back through the darkness to the commandant's office. The chimney now glowed a dull red at its smoking orifice. Clearly it worked non-stop, polluting the air twenty-four hours a day. Schneider introduced Anna as his secretary. The tension was almost palpable as they waited for Höss to reveal the results of his search.

'Sometimes I think that our every action is governed

by fate. I believe my being given this command is such an example. In all humility I do not believe that anyone else could have carried out the task as efficiently as I. Another example is your coming here today and getting the search done for Stein immediately. If you had left it until tomorrow, you would have been too late. He was due for processing this very night, but I have now arranged for him to be brought here first. I do not need to tell you I was surprised that he is still here. He really must be a tough one to have survived so long.'

Schneider was so relieved that this man was still alive, he allowed himself a question. 'What will happen to him after we have finished with him?'

'He will go back to be processed, of course. By the way, please do not say anything to him about that tonight. It's better if they don't know what's going to happen to them.'

If the priest was not to be warned about this 'processing', clearly it was something unpleasant. Höss thought Schneider must know what it was and an awkward silence descended. Schneider knew that to show any lack of knowledge about what was happening here would only raise suspicions. So, he relied on his years of police interrogation experience. When you know nothing, say nothing, and let the other man talk. But this wasn't an interrogation, and he didn't know how long he could get away with it. He was saved by a knock at the door. A guard had brought Father Stein.

'In light of the nature of my investigation, I must ask to see this man alone. I am sure you understand. In any event, he may feel more willingness to speak if we are alone.'

'I understand. My position here means I am constantly aware of the need for secrecy.'

Höss rose and said he would take Anna over to his house to introduce her to his wife. When Schneider was finished with the priest, he could follow. Höss hoped he wouldn't be too long as his wife was making something special. Schneider was amazed that this man could behave so normally in such a place. When he saw the priest, he knew Höss's actions were beyond his comprehension, beyond sanity. Schneider was now in no doubt what 'processing' ultimately meant, even if he was unclear what exactly was involved.

What can you offer a man with less than two hours to live? What levers can you pull to bend him to your will? Schneider didn't have an answer, didn't know what he could offer him. Life? He doubted if he would be believed. Even the paper had a limit to its powers. Money? It was meaningless to this man. There had to be something. Then the man's eyes gave him the answer. They were fixed not on Schneider nor his uniform but on an apple lying on the desk. Schneider picked it up. The man's eyes followed as if attached by an invisible string.

'Would you like this?'

A nervous nod.

Schneider passed the piece of fruit over and it was devoured, core, pips and all, in less than ten seconds.

'Would you like another?'

The same nervous nod.

'First of all, I want to ask you something. Is that all right?'

The priest nodded. Schneider pushed the entire bowl of fruit towards him. He waited until another apple had been devoured. The eyes never left the fruit, even when Schneider started speaking.

'First of all, please don't be confused by this uniform. I am here to help you if I can. My name is Rolf Schneider and I am a police officer, not a member of the SS. I have come here to see you for two reasons. First, I promised Lina Heydrich that I would get to the truth of her husband's death, and I think you can help me to find that truth. Second, I am here with someone you know, Anna Weiss. It was Anna who told me about you, and what you have hidden. But since I have been here, I know there is now a third even more important reason. There is something happening here that I think the world needs to know about. I want you to tell me.'

He waited to see what reaction he got. Nothing. The eyes were still fastened on the fruit, the old tooth-less jaws chewing another apple. Schneider pulled a chair out and asked the priest if he would like to sit down. He sank into the chair, his jaws never missing a beat. Instinctively, Schneider decided to come straight to the point.

'I need Heydrich's papers. Will you tell me where they are?'

The eyes finally lifted from the fruit, the initial pangs of starvation satiated. Schneider noticed now, behind the superficial glaze of starvation, a depth to the eyes that spoke of great humanity and knowledge. But that must have been from another time and place. Humanity and knowledge had not allowed the priest to survive here. Cunning and a will to survive at all costs were all that mattered here.

'What did Anna tell you of my relationship with Heydrich?'

Schneider only knew the little that Anna herself knew. The priest was watching him carefully, studying his face, searching for any attempt at deception.

'She could tell me very little, only that she delivered papers to you in a church, as Heydrich requested. She told me nothing of how you knew Heydrich. Maybe she doesn't know herself.'

'Oh, she knows all right, but maybe it didn't seem important. Let me ask you something else, then. Where did she give me the papers?'

'I've already told you. In the church.'

The priest's studying of his face intensified. Clearly, he saw this answer as crucial.

Schneider tried to remember everything Anna had told him. So much had happened since then. What was it the priest was wanting him to say? She had only gone to the church and handed over the papers.

Nothing else. Desperately, he tried to reconstruct the scene in his mind's eye. How do you hand over papers? You just hand them over. There is nothing to it. But you wouldn't do it where others could see you. Where in a church was private? Then he remembered.

'It was in the confession box. She pretended she was going to confession.'

The priest nodded. He relaxed a fraction, but he still wasn't certain. 'If she is here, let me see her.'

He went back to his eating. Schneider picked up the phone on the desk and pushed the button marked 'House'. In a few seconds, Höss answered.

'Can you send my secretary over? There are some notes I want her to take.'

While he waited, Schneider let the priest finish the last of the apples. The man was close to death from starvation. He ate as if Schneider wasn't there, reaching for the next apple as soon as he had finished the last one. And he stank, the reek of someone unwashed for months. It rivalled the chimney in its intensity, but the man seemed unaware of it himself. The last apple disappeared, and the eyes searched the desk to confirm there were no more. Only then did they return to Schneider.

'Do you want me to tell you how I met Heydrich? Even now, I think it might have been God's plan, for I was a simple priest, nothing more. One night some people came to my door. I had never seen them before. They were not parishioners of mine, not

239

even Catholics; they were Jews, who told me that the Gestapo was chasing them. They asked me for shelter, a man, a woman and two children. They were desperate, almost crazed with terror. I will never forget the fear in those two young children's innocent eyes. What could I do? What would our Saviour have done? I offered them sanctuary in the church and refused to let the Gestapo in. They threatened me, but in those times they were still wary of the Church, so they went away. I knew that they would return and take the family eventually. So, I gave them what little money I had and sent them to a friend of mine who I knew would help them. The Gestapo had been so confident that these people had nowhere to run that they didn't even leave a guard behind. You can imagine their reaction when they came back the next day with orders to arrest me as well as the family. I told them they were gone, but they searched anyway.'

His mind went back to that small victory and a smile touched his bloodless lips.

'Eventually, I was taken to Heydrich. They threatened me with all sorts of punishment and concentration camps, but I refused to give them any information. They beat me lightly, almost in a half-hearted manner, as if my vocation still offered some protection. But I knew that in the end it would offer none. I expected to die in a camp. But then Heydrich intervened. He had heard about this difficult priest who was refusing to tell his thugs where the Jewish family had gone.

He spoke to me for a long time. He told me about the horrors I would face. He bribed me with money for my church. He told me I owed this family nothing, they weren't even Christian. I think he was surprised when I told him that was all the more reason to help them. I had given them my sacred word, and there was nothing he could do to make me break that oath. He seemed to think about this for a long time, as if it was something he couldn't quite understand. Then he asked me, "If you give your word, your sworn word, you would never break it?" I told him I could not conceive of such dishonesty, and he laughed. He said, "I think you are the first truly honest man I have met."

'After that I was returned to a cell, but I wasn't questioned any further. I even got a meal. The next day Heydrich saw me again. He put his proposal to me. If I would give him my word to safeguard certain papers for him, he would stop the hunt for this family and release me back to my parish. He would make funds available to me to help the poor and the sick in my parish. I didn't know what to do. But then I thought if I didn't keep these papers then someone else would, and that wouldn't help the sick. I asked him what these papers were, and he said they were only of value to him, but my knowing their contents could only lead to my death. It was better if I knew nothing. So, I agreed. He even told me where they could be safely hidden, where no one would look. He told me no one would suspect a nobody like me. I wasn't offended; it was just his cruel logic.'

It was an incredible story, and Schneider was totally enthralled. One of the most powerful men in Germany and an insignificant priest striking a deal that could change the world. The priest had stopped as if once more weighing the deal in his mind.

'Often I have considered if I did the right thing that day. Well, God will be my judge on that. I hope the family survived, and I did help others in need. But the papers I received showed the depths of evil that this country had sunk to. For I read the papers. We are drowning in evil, and it won't be cleansed from us until Nazi Germany lies broken in the gutter of total defeat.'

He stopped again, the agony of remembering that day etched on his ravaged face.

'And that is all. That is how I ended up with those papers.'

Anna arrived just at that moment and, incredibly, as soon as the door was shut, she ran and embraced the old man. She kissed him on his filthy hair, and he muttered some words in Latin while making the sign of the cross over her. For a reason he still couldn't quite grasp, Schneider found it profoundly moving.

'I never hoped to see you again, child. Am I hallucinating?'

'No, Father, it is really me. And this man is here to help you. Can you tell him what he needs to know? Are the papers still safe?'

'I believe they are. At least, they were when I was brought here. But they contain many evil things that could be used to cause great harm in this already unhappy world.'

He paused, considering. Then he looked directly at Schneider.

'How can I know that you will use them for good?'

'There's nothing I can do except give you my word. The same word I gave to Lina Heydrich. I don't know the nature of your relationship with Heydrich, but she at least is innocent of anything he might have done.'

The old priest seemed to drift away. Then the eyes cleared.

'Yes, she is innocent. But Reinhard? I pray for his soul every day. He gave me these things because he took my word, sworn on the gospel of our Saviour, that I would keep them safe. I was a simple priest, no threat to him. In return, he helped many in my parish. If anything happened to him, he wanted me to get the papers to the Vatican. He thought the Pope was the only man in Europe who could use them for good and against those who had destroyed him. It was to be the bitterest of revenges, for he was a Nazi through and through, but his vanity outweighed his loyalty to his cause. If he couldn't rule, then his killers would not be allowed to rule either. Quite Dante-esque, don't you think? But it was one of his few misjudgements, for he was expecting other men to act as he would. The Holy Father could never use what was in those papers. They would have been suppressed in the deepest vaults of the Vatican. When Heydrich died, I didn't know what to do. I kept the papers, trying to think of some way I could use them for good. Then I was brought here.'

'Did they know you had the papers?'

'No. I wasn't arrested because of them. I spoke out in a sermon against this government and its evil. The Church is weaker now, and her priests are expected to remain silent, so I was arrested. My protector had gone, and I was sent here. Since then, I have tried as best I could to carry on living as a priest. Life still exists here, and at least I have not been tortured as so many others have. In this realm of evil, men need the word of God more than outside.'

Schneider could think of no greater torture than being brought here, but the old man seemed just to accept it. Schneider was awed at the depths of his faith. He had never known that faith could be so sustaining. Perhaps there was something beyond this life, after all. But he had to focus on the present.

'Will you tell me where they are?'

'I gave him my word and I have kept it. Till now. But maybe God will forgive me, along with all the other wrongs of my life.'

'Father, I . . .'

'Heydrich took my word as an honest man. Can I do less to you? Look to the altar of God, my son. Stand before the altar of God and let the light of the sun guide you.'

It took Schneider a second or two to realise what he had been told. Then he remembered the altar in the church he attended as a child. The priest there had shown him. But Schneider had misunderstood what he had just been told.

'Thank you, Father. I think I can get you out of here, but for how long I don't know.'

'It's too late for me, my son. I'm already a dead man. Let God take me in his own time.'

Schneider sensed arguing with the old man was pointless. There was nowhere he would be safe. But he could warn him of how short his time was. 'Father, if I don't do something, that will be tonight. Höss told me.'

'Let it be so, then. I can pray with the others and hope for God's eternal mercy for myself. It's better this way. If I am gone, no one else can ask me about the papers.'

Anna begged him to let Schneider help him. But he was adamant.

'Before you leave this place, my son, ask Höss to show you what happens here. It will help you with what needs to be done.'

Anna was almost hysterical, pleading with him to change his mind. He gathered her in his arms and stroked her hair like a child. He whispered in her ear and eventually her sobs subsided. She looked at him and nodded. He let her go and blessed both of them. Schneider called the guard in, and the old priest left the office to meet his fate and his God. It was one of the bravest things Schneider had ever seen. His hand wiped away the tears that had unknowingly run down his cheeks.

*

After what had happened, the meal with the Höss family was almost unbearable. Fortunately, Höss did not require conversationalists, only listeners, and Schneider and Anna fitted the bill perfectly that night. He spoke at length about the ultimate German victory, his children and his love of animals. He never once mentioned the camp, nor his work there, and they realised it was banned from the dinner table. It was very *petit bourgeois*, to leave the rigours of the daily grind outside, but to Höss his job was no different to any other. Frau Höss did her best to be a charming hostess, but her efforts were totally wasted on the guests. They both knew this was Father Stein's last night on Earth and that, as they sat eating, he was probably dying less than half a mile away. Eventually, they feigned exhaustion from their journey. They assured Höss that the meeting with the prisoner had been useful and that the accommodation was fine. Schneider told him they would be leaving tomorrow and wondered if Höss could show him round first. Höss was clearly delighted to do so. Somebody with direct access to the Führer could report on what a splendid job he was doing. It was arranged that Schneider should come to his office after breakfast and he would give him the complete tour.

As they walked back, Anna asked if she could join them.

'I don't think that's a good idea. I don't know what is happening here, but it must be something awful. I don't think you should see it, whatever it is. And you know your people are here. Could you manage to keep a hard Aryan face before Höss? Anything else would only make him suspicious.'

Anna agreed quite readily. Schneider was surprised, then he realised she had only offered for his sake, so that he wouldn't have to face it alone.

*

Schneider ate an excellent breakfast of fresh rolls and genuine coffee. The camp clearly had its own bakery, and Höss one of the few people in Poland with access to coffee beans. Schneider's sense of guilt at such a breakfast was overcome by the smell of strong, fresh coffee. He rationalised it would do no good just to waste it but salved his conscience by restricting himself to two cups only. He knew his shame about drinking coffee was as nothing to what had happened last night, but he couldn't revisit that yet, not now, not with the unknown horrors he had to face today. He told Anna he would be as quick as he could, and in the meantime she could arrange a flight back to Berlin that afternoon. He intended to find Heydrich's papers

247

that very night if they were still there. Only then would he know if he had any chance at all.

Höss was waiting in his office. It was impossible to tell if he had done any work since last night, as the desk remained its pristine self.

'Good morning, Standartenführer. I trust you slept well and that you are perhaps becoming a little more accustomed to the . . . ah . . . aroma?'

Schneider was surprised to find it was true. Although the stench in the air was as strong as ever, he had almost forgotten about it until Höss reminded him.

'Is there anything in particular you would like to see?'

'I would like to see the whole process if possible. I have heard so much about it all in general terms, but, of course, the devil is in the detail.'

Schneider would play the part of the important visitor from Berlin, checking on Höss's work and reporting back to the Führer in glowing terms. A little flattery always helped with someone like Höss.

'Very well, then. The next shipment is due in thirty minutes. We can follow it through the entire process. It will take about two hours. Do you have enough time?'

Schneider assured him he had as much time as he needed. Although it was now well into winter, the sky was a clear blue. Höss suggested they walk to the unloading area and he could point out some of the camp's features as they walked.

'There are really two camps here. The one we are walking through is the original camp where most of the processing work is done. The other camp – we call it Birkenau because there used to be a birch wood there – is where most of the factories are located. A lot of them are now underground because of the threat of air raids. Our production of rubber and gasoline is growing each month. Would you like to see these also?'

Schneider remembered his thoughts as he was driving up to the camp. So, there were underground factories here, but they didn't contain wonder weapons. He didn't need to see an underground factory.

'I do not think I have time for that. Perhaps if we just look at the original camp.'

'Very well. When I came here, the camp was much smaller than it is now. I have greatly expanded its capacity and hope to expand it still further. At any one time there is somewhere between 100,000 and 150,000 here, yet I run the whole thing with less than 3,000 staff. How have I managed to achieve this miracle of production? It is really quite simple. It is all down to making sure everything runs smoothly and efficiently, with no hold-ups permitted. And that must start from the moment of arrival.'

They had reached the railway station. Schneider could see some SS guards, warmly wrapped in their black greatcoats, chatting and smoking. Their large dogs fretted and pulled against the chains holding them. Two officers stood separately, laughing together. It could have been a railway station anywhere in Germany, except for the huddle of other men in dirty striped uniforms. About fifty of them stood near the SS men, with heads bowed and hands stuffed under their arms. There was no talk or laughter among them. Apart from their shivering in the cold, they could have been statues. All of them, SS and prisoners alike, were clearly waiting for a train to arrive.

As if on cue, a whistle sounded, and reluctantly the guards crushed out their cigarettes. The prisoners split up and lined the entire platform. The guards and their dogs followed and took up positions behind them. Schneider had that gift peculiar to great police officers of taking in almost every detail of a scene. He noticed one of the officers move off and take up position on a slightly raised section at the end of the platform. He could sense the anticipation in the air. The train whistle sounded again, louder and closer.

'I don't often come here myself now. There's no need because they are all so skilled at it. I think you will be amazed at just how quickly we can deal with over a thousand people.'

Höss was beaming with pride. Schneider again felt that sense of dread that had followed him ever since he arrived here. He had never been superstitious, but he felt that every stone of this place was somehow infused with malevolence. The train was now in sight, slowing as it approached. The brakes squealed as it finally stopped and the engine let out a long sigh, as if of relief. At least twenty cars were attached to the engine. Schneider saw these seemed to be cattle cars, an unusual form of transport for people. Even as the train was grinding to a halt, the prisoners on the platform were rushing forward and opening the bolts on the outside. They pulled the large, sliding doors open and then all hell broke out. The SS guards surged forward, blowing whistles and shouting. Their dogs added to this cacophony, barking and snapping at all around them. The prisoners themselves were gesticulating furiously to those inside the cars to get out as quickly as possible. To Schneider, it seemed a scene of chaos. Höss must have noticed his doubts and immediately strove to allay them.

'Do not think this is poorly organised, Herr Standartenführer. It is designed to be like this. If they do not have time to think, they follow our orders much more readily. The constant movement and noise keeps them disorientated and afraid, so they follow our orders like sheep. And the prisoners who help them to move along keep reassuring them all will be well if they just keep moving. That was my own refinement. Most people have a touching faith in their own race's moral superiority. The Jews are no different in that regard. So, when their own people tell them everything is all right, they believe them.'

Schneider watched as the trucks spilled out their sea of humanity onto the platform. Old and young, male and female, the healthy and the sick all tumbled out together. Schneider could see the fit trying to help the less able, children trying to support aged grandparents. All of them, from the oldest to the youngest child, bore the yellow Star of David. Some of the adults clutched battered suitcases to themselves that no doubt held all their worldly goods. The platform was now almost filled, and Schneider could see that Höss was right. There was no argument, no disobedience. There was little noise at all apart from the odd cry for water or the name of a family member who seemed to be missing.

'Where do these people come from?'

'They come from all over Europe. But this particular train is from Berlin itself. These are some of our own Jews.'

Schneider realised that these people had been locked inside the cars without food, water or any sanitary facilities. And once locked, the cars were not opened until they got to their destination. He could see that some of the cars had been jammed so tightly that there was not even enough room for people to lie down. It was so inhumane, so barbaric, that it defied description, or any attempt at understanding, yet Schneider had to appear unconcerned by what he was seeing. He was an SS Standartenführer, after all, with the personal trust of the Führer.

'How long would the journey have taken? The war must make it difficult.'

'From Berlin? Not so long, maybe two or three days only. Some of the ones from France can take up to a week.'

Höss said this dispassionately. The horror of human beings being sealed into one of these trucks for a week without food and water didn't seem to even cross his mind.

The last of the new arrivals had by now descended onto the platform. Many were so weak that they had difficulty in even standing, but there was no respite from the constant orders. The guards and their viciously biting dogs immediately had the column moving towards the SS officer at the end of the platform. As soon as this pitiful column moved off, some of the prisoners climbed into the cattle cars and started throwing out those who hadn't survived the journey. Every car yielded up victims, and soon there was a pile of bodies lying on the platform. One of the SS guards started counting them, carefully writing his tally on a clipboard. Schneider realised it didn't matter how many died on the journey provided the numbers added up. His sense of foreboding climbed even higher.

The slow-moving column reached the end of the platform. The SS officer started to indicate right or left as he split the column in two with a wave of his hand. Schneider couldn't tell on what basis this selection was being made, and he turned to Höss quizzically.

'He's one of the camp doctors. He's separating those

fit enough to work from those who are too weak. Let us go down and you can get a better look.'

It was the last thing he wanted to do, to get any nearer to this scene of absolute misery and suffering, but the old priest had asked him to do it, to see everything here. He nodded to Höss.

As they approached, Schneider could see that the column on the right was mainly made up of men, whereas the one on the left was mainly women and children. He presumed the right column was those fit for work, and Höss confirmed this. For some reason, the prisoners seemed to favour the right column. He could see men trying to pull themselves up straight, trying to puff out their chests and walk faster, showing they were fit for work. Even very old men tried. But the keen eye of the SS doctor wasn't often deceived. Only young men with no obvious weakness went to the right. Some of the fitter-looking women also went to the right. If they had children and refused to be separated from them, then they were allowed to go with them to the left. Nothing was allowed to hold up the inexorable progression of the column. Thirty minutes after the train had arrived, its living occupants had already passed the first stage of 'processing'.

Schneider was still trying to rationalise what he was seeing. Those on the right were clearly the workers. They must be better fed, and this was why so many wanted to be in that line. But he knew this made no sense. If they wanted workers, why transport them the way they did, with so many dying? In any event, the selection could have been made in Berlin so that only workers came east. He sensed the real horror was yet to come, when he discovered what happens to those in the left column. Schneider wondered how any man, let alone a detective, could ever have guessed or suspected what was happening to the Jews in Germany. It was a question that was troubling him more and more. He knew the answer but still couldn't accept it. Could a whole race simply turn a blind eye to what they knew was happening? Could every individual in that race say it wasn't my responsibility? At least now he had a chance to try to redeem himself. What would the rest of his race say after the war? Would they try to blame it all on the likes of Himmler and Höss? Would the rest of the world listen? Would God?

'The ones on the right go to the factories now?'

'Yes. They will work there until they are useless and then they too are processed. You don't want to see the factory, so we will follow those on the left, where you will see the next stage. I think you will be very impressed by this part.'

The workers' column set off first for the longer walk to the Birkenau camp. Goodbyes were hurled between the columns as families that had been separated shouted their final endearments to each other. None of them could have any idea when they would see these loved ones again. It was a moment when hysteria could easily have broken out and led to disorder.

But Schneider was close enough now to hear the prisoners from the platform keeping this in check with promises of finding out where fathers and mothers or husbands, wives and children were. They told the waiting prisoners in the left-hand column that it was only for now, that soon they would all be together again. One woman refused to be calmed and broke away screaming, trying to reach her husband who was already disappearing. One of the SS soldiers dealt her a vicious blow with his rifle that sent her sprawling. Two prisoners hurriedly picked up the stunned woman and carried her back into line. Blood dripped from the jagged wound on her forehead, and she murmured softly to herself in Yiddish.

The guards now told the remaining column to move. A barbed-wire gate was opened, and they started into the camp proper. At first, Schneider thought his ears were playing tricks on him. He heard music – a Brahms lullaby, to be precise – and it was growing louder. Höss looked at him with an amused smile on his face.

'Don't be alarmed, you're not imagining it. You really are hearing music. You know that half the great orchestras of Europe were made up almost entirely of Jews? So, we have quite a few professional musicians here. I thought it would be a good idea if they played to the prisoners. It all helps to keep them calm. Surely, somewhere with an orchestra playing cannot be so bad, eh?'

The music grew louder, and Schneider saw about ten musicians assembled near the cluster of buildings they were approaching. The 'orchestra' was made up of violins and cellos with a conductor, and all of them were in the striped suits of the prisoner. Constantly, during the march here, the prisoners who had been on the platform hurried back and forth along the line reassuring them, telling them everything was going to be fine. Such was the speed of the operation, the reassurance, the music, that Schneider almost believed it himself. He could see hope spreading onto a few faces as they recognised the melody. But there was something very sinister here. Again, he felt fingers of horror running up his spine. He just knew something unspeakable was about to happen, and his every instinct told him to get away from this place as fast as he could. He mastered the urge and stayed. The column had been halted and told to rest. About the first 250 prisoners were then sectioned off and ordered to continue forward.

'Do you like it?'

Höss was indicating a sign over the building they had almost reached. It said 'Bath House'. Schneider had no idea what it meant. He even lost his pretence of knowledge.

'I'm sorry. I don't understand.'

Höss was clearly disappointed. 'Oh, I thought my idea would have been known to you. But perhaps not, so let me explain. Put yourself into their position. You have just come on a long journey. You are tired, hungry and frightened. You have heard some rumours about what is to happen to you here. But by now you are a little reassured: the other prisoners, the music, the barracks you can see to live in. You know we Germans demand cleanliness and so you must bathe. At the same time, your clothes will be fumigated. Then you can go to your barracks and meet the others. Of course you believe it, or at least want to believe it. Just watch.'

Schneider and Höss followed the prisoners inside the bath house and observed from the doorway. A feeling of dread grew in Schneider's mind. He still didn't understand, but he couldn't ask anything else. He just watched.

The prisoners were led into what appeared to be changing rooms. The old prisoners encouraged them to strip quickly but to remember where they had hung their clothes on the numbered pegs for afterwards. Everything had to be hung up for fumigation. They themselves were going for showers, which would also disinfect them. Parents should help children to undress. The sooner they were showered, the sooner they could get to their barracks. There was even talk of hot food. The people started to undress, slowly at first, but then with gathering momentum as the prisoners kept up their litany of reassurance. There was no segregation of the sexes, and women tried in vain to retain some semblance of modesty. Soon everyone was naked, and the prisoners led them into an adjoining room. It was fully tiled and had shower heads coming out of the ceiling. More and more were led in. The prisoners had all moved out of the shower room and now they started pushing more in, cramming in as many as could be forced inside. Children were handed in, to be passed over the heads of the packed adults. All the time the words of reassurance continued, right up to the moment the door was closed and bolted from the outside.

One of the SS guards who had remained at the entrance stepped outside. He gestured up to the roof and Schneider heard footsteps above his head. There was a grating sound of metal on metal, as if something was being unscrewed. He waited, his sense of horror growing by the second, but nothing else happened. Schneider looked at the prisoners who had remained outside, the old hands who had escorted the new arrivals here. All of them had their eyes closed, rocking back and forward. Their lips moved silently. He realised they were praying in that way peculiar to the Jewish religion. He heard more sounds above his head and then the grating again, but now faster. The SS man outside seemed to get a message from the roof. He came back inside and reported to Höss.

'That's it, sir. You can watch now if you wish.'

Schneider heard a sound like nothing he had ever heard before, nor ever wished to hear again in his life. It started as a low moaning, a keening, that rose through the whole human scale of pitch and volume until it reached its crescendo in an ear-splitting shriek of pure agony.

Schneider didn't know how much more he could take. Even in the Polish winter chill, sweat was cascading down his back and face. Blood was rushing in his ears, and spots danced before his eyes. He tasted his morning coffee in his throat and his head began to swim. All his instincts told him to rush to the door and get away from this. Then he heard the words of an old priest who had died yesterday. He couldn't abandon him now. Somehow, he forced the vomit back down his throat, and slowly his head and eyes cleared. Höss was watching him closely.

'Don't be concerned, Standartenführer. It often affects people like this the first time they see it. If you want to leave, I will understand.'

Schneider wanted to pull out his pistol and put a bullet through his smug face. But he knew someone else would just take Höss's place. Nazi Germany had no shortage of such people. He took a deep breath before speaking.

'Thank you, but I am fine now. It was just the noise. It took me by surprise.'

'Yes, it's amazing, isn't it? It's only when they realise what is going to happen that they start to scream like this. That's why we get them here the way we do, in ignorance of their fate. Would you like to see what is happening?'

Who would want to look at such a monstrosity?

But the priest had told him he must be a witness to everything that was happening here. He nodded.

Höss led him over to the door, where there was a small glass peephole. He stepped aside for Schneider. If he had hesitated for even a fraction of a second, he would not have been able to do it. Through the door he could hear the screams that had now taken on an almost inhuman, bellowing timbre. Someone was banging furiously at the door, an unrelenting drum-roll of madness. He could hear voices shouting names, prayers and blasphemies. But worst of all, this close to the door, he could hear the children. He stepped forward and put his eye to the glass.

He could see nothing. Then the hand that had been splayed across the peephole was jerked away. Schneider saw hell on earth. People already doomed who refused to accept their fate clawed and battered their own families beneath them as they strove to find air. Most of the very young and the old were already dead or unconscious. But the rest still sought life. Incredibly, a human pyramid was forming in the centre of the room as the still living clawed their way up its faecal, slippery slopes, trying to find air. It was an illusion, for there was no air in that sealed room. Even as he watched, those at the top crumpled and toppled down. The noise had now also almost stopped. Death was among them. He stepped back, desperately trying to remember every horror. He wanted the world to know what he had seen here today. His mind flashed back to the Hieronymus Bosch picture of hell he had seen as a child. Bosch had no idea of what hell truly was. *Or looked like.*

'All in all, it takes about twenty minutes to be sure they are all dead. So, we'll give them another ten minutes, shall we? I've brought a flask of coffee if you would like some.'

Höss could have been watching an example of double entry book-keeping for all the emotion he showed. He was just doing his job. Such minds were way beyond Schneider's understanding, but Höss's reaction had at least given him the cold determination to see this through. He declined the coffee and said he would stay and watch everything. Höss chatted on as they waited.

'You know, we tried all sorts of ways until we came up with this. There was shooting to begin with, but it took so long and the men who did the shootings started to suffer nightmares. So, we tried carbon monoxide from engine exhausts. But it took too long and some of them survived. They were completely brain-damaged, but we still had to shoot them, so it was back to square one. Then somebody remembered Zyklon B. It's easy to mass produce and is very effective. So, that's what we use now.'

Schneider had to be careful. Höss obviously expected him to know what this Zyklon B was. 'I was never very good at science at school. Can you tell me exactly how this Zyklon B works?'

'I'd be happy to. It is essentially a cyanide-based product used in the extermination of rats. It comes as pellets and turns to gas when it is exposed to heat. So, it is easy to handle and to use. We just open a vent in the roof and pour the pellets in. Their own body heat does the rest. It is that simple, and our men do not get distressed like with the shootings.'

'But it is not instantaneous. Those inside stay alive for a while?'

'Well, everything can't be perfect. But there is no danger. The door is strong enough. They would never be able to break out.'

Schneider realised he and Höss were speaking two different languages. It was more than that: they came from two different worlds of morality. It was pointless to go on. Höss checked his watch and nodded to the guard. He threw a switch, and Schneider heard a pump start somewhere.

'It only takes a minute to pump out what is left of the gas. Then we can open up and you can see the next stage.'

Schneider would have sworn on his life that nothing could have been worse than what he had just witnessed. He was wrong. The prisoners, who stayed alive by lying to their own people to get them inside the gas chamber, now sprang into action again. They attacked the pyramid inside the death chamber with hooks, pulling the bodies apart and out. The eyes of the dead stared at them in silent rebuke. If there was a

God, surely he would punish this? But God did nothing as the women with long hair were thrown to one side. One of the prisoners quickly shaved the heads, pushing the hair into sacks. Again, Höss was on hand to explain.

'We use the hair to make socks for our U-boat crews. Apparently, it's one of the few things that doesn't rot on their long voyages.'

Other prisoners checked every mouth, using pliers to rip out any gold teeth or fillings. The continuous tinkle of these hitting the steel collecting buckets was a sound that Schneider would never forget for the rest of his life. The men worked like dervishes; already half the gas chamber was empty. It made no difference to them if it was a man, woman or child. The hook pulled them out, their mouths were quickly searched and then they were thrown to one side. How could men behave like this to anyone, never mind their own people? But Schneider knew he couldn't judge them. Only those in this situation could decide between death and living such as this. He prayed he would never have to make such a choice.

He saw that after the mouths were examined, other prisoners searched the more intimate parts of the bodies for hidden jewels. Incredibly, Schneider saw diamonds, pearls and other precious stones start to appear. He could take no more. He walked back through the changing room where still other prisoners were collecting and sorting the clothes and belongings of the victims. Nothing was going to waste. He walked outside, Höss at his back.

'The prisoners who do this for you – what happens to them?'

'Oh, we keep them alive for a month or so. But then they start to be affected as well. So, one day we just add them in and then start with a new bunch.'

'What happens to the bodies? How do you dispose of so many corpses?'

Schneider already knew the answer. It hung in every breath he breathed.

'We now have four crematoria working flat out. I have installed a lift to take the bodies directly from here to the fire. It is most effective and speeds up our rate considerably.'

'How many do you process here in a day?'

'Oh, that depends on trains, and all the crematoria working efficiently. On a good day we can deal with ten thousand or so.'

'I suppose you use your own gasoline from the factory to run them?'

Höss seemed to find the question amusing. His face took on an air of superiority.

'I was told it was impossible to burn so many bodies, that the fuel needed would be too much. But I already knew how to solve this. Once the crematoria are up to temperature, we keep them fuelled with the fat of the dead themselves. Human fat makes an excellent fuel.'

There was nothing more for Schneider to say. He

thanked Höss for the tour. He assured him he would take word back to Germany of the job he was doing here. He didn't ask him the question he most wanted to ask, for he already knew half the answer. With Heydrich's papers, he would get the other half.

He thought about lying to Anna about what he had seen today but knew he couldn't. He would tell her everything. She deserved to know what she was fighting against as well.

$$- 15 -$$

Berlin, December 1942

Himmler had received another message. He ordered that he wasn't to be disturbed, not even for the Führer himself. He needed peace to think. He sat staring at the piece of paper on his desk. The message was short, consisting of twelve words, but those words spoke volumes for Himmler's future.

H.

Fall of Stalingrad inevitable. Peace proposals likely. Must act now. Confirm date.

B.

As was his habit when he had to make a difficult decision, he walked to his window. Christmas was approaching and even a world war couldn't stop that. The streets were busy with shoppers trying to find something, anything, that could make a gift or, better still, a Christmas dinner. Unable to make his mind up about the message, he let it wander to what Christmas meant to him. A Christian celebration he abhorred but went along with for the sake of his child. But he knew that before it had been stolen by the Christians, it had been celebrated through the long dark winter nights, deep in the Teutoberg Forest, when his German fore-fathers renewed the eternal links to their native sacred soil, and cast the runes to see what the future held. That was his religion, a German religion.

He had been trying for years to reintroduce these mysteries into the SS. At Wewelsburg castle, he had gathered the SS elite around him to remember their true heritage. In the huge dining room, these modern-day knights assembled at the round table set above the crypt where his own remains were to be laid in final rest. He knew some thought him eccentric, but he knew better, for deep in every German soul the pure fire of the old religion still smouldered. Didn't almost every German of every denomination still retain that belief in prophesy, in that peculiar New Year ritual of plunging molten lead into water to see your future shaped? He wondered what the molten lead would foretell for him this year, for still he couldn't decide on the message.

He returned to his desk and the message lying there. He read it again, seeking any clue, any hidden nuance, that might guide him in the most difficult decision he had ever been asked to make. For the hundredth time he considered the alternatives. If he did nothing, he was safe, for no one could decipher the messages except him. But he knew that Germany was now doomed to lose this war, and what would happen to him then? The camps in the east would be used to damn him. So, his safety could only last for a year or two at most. Yet if he acted, what then? If his plan failed, he would die a most horrible death. Perhaps that could be avoided. A cyanide capsule would need to be his constant companion until the matter was settled one way or another. And if the plan succeeded? Peace, a new beginning maybe, without the spectre of the camps to haunt him. At least it gave him a chance. It was enough. But for the plan to have any chance, he had to find exactly the right date, and that would be almost impossible to predict.

Laughter from the street outside disturbed his analysis. Even now, the spirit of the coming Christmas gave hope to people. Then it came to him, the one possibility. He picked up the phone and asked for his arch enemy, Martin Bormann.

*

At the same time as Himmler was musing over his decision, Schneider was pondering an equally difficult problem. He and Anna had arrived back in Berlin. The flat was still undamaged by the air raids but that hardly mattered now. After what he had seen in Auschwitz, only one thing mattered to him. His whole life, his whole being, had been irrevocably altered by that experience. His past was gone, his future of no concern. The most outstanding of Germany's police officers no longer existed. Instead, there was a driven man, a zealot, who had only one purpose in life.

On the flight back that morning, he had explained what he planned to do to Anna. She had immediately seen the flaw that his new-found fanaticism had obscured. He had planned to go to the church that very night and find Heydrich's papers. If they were gone, then so was his whole plan. He told Anna he couldn't look beyond that for now, but he had another contingency that he wouldn't share with her. He hoped he wouldn't have to use it, for it would make his time with her even shorter and he now cherished the days and hours they had left together.

'If you find them, what are you going to do with them?'

'Read them, of course. And then use them.'

'No, I mean after you have read them. Where will you keep them safe? As soon as it becomes known you have them, Himmler will stop at nothing to find them. So, where can you keep them safe after you've taken them from the church?'

Schneider really hadn't thought about that. He was surprised at himself, for normally he thought of every eventuality. He knew his anger had been blinding him and he tried to think clearly, like the Schneider of old. But all he could think of was that room in Auschwitz and the sound of gold teeth landing in a metal bucket. That anger would never leave him.

'You're right. It's just that I want to do something right now, and those papers are our only hope.'

Then Anna came up with an answer. He still couldn't believe he hadn't thought of it himself. He had given her the solution, after all.

They went to the nearby park and, in its privacy, carefully refined each step of their plan. When it was as good as it could be, Schneider went to police headquarters. He needed to check a file, and he didn't trust the phones at all now. He was in and out in less than ten minutes. His research had produced neither good nor bad news. He had been checking on Rolf Stein's replacement as parish priest. He had hoped to find some evidence of anti-Nazi sentiment, but instead he found nothing. But the file also showed that at least the man wasn't a puppet of the Gestapo, nor an informer. That meant nothing these days. He could still easily be a Nazi supporter, even if he was a Catholic priest. They would just have to cross that bridge when they came to it.

He returned to the flat and they waited for darkness to fall. In December, it didn't take long. They set off for the church, Schneider hiding his SS uniform beneath a raincoat. He still couldn't be certain they weren't being followed, and there was no point in alerting any watcher that he was up to something unusual. The church was in darkness, as they had expected, as only morning masses took place there now. Schneider removed his raincoat and straightened the black uniform. Satisfied, he thumped on the door of the priest's house until it was opened. He had to play his part well if the plan was to succeed. He had rehearsed it a hundred times in his mind.

'I need access to your church immediately on a matter of state security.'

He bellowed the order out, making no attempt to explain or even to offer his name. He hoped the black uniform would be enough. He thought the priest's reactions might also give him a clue as to where his sympathies lay.

'Of course, of course. But first I need to know who you are.'

So, he wasn't so easily cowed, after all. Schneider thrust his police papers at the priest. He studied them for a moment and then returned them to Schneider.

'If I have understood these papers correctly, you are a police officer, yet you are dressed in an SS uniform. That's somewhat unusual, isn't it?'

It wasn't going as Schneider had planned it at all. The priest's deadpan face gave nothing away about what he was really thinking. He couldn't take a chance and trust him, not tonight of all nights.

'You dare to question me? Do you know that only yesterday I had your predecessor executed for treason? I can just as easily do the same to you. Are you also an enemy of the state?'

The priest backed down. Maybe he sensed that Schneider was telling the truth about his predecessor having been executed. Maybe he was a Nazi. Schneider didn't care which.

'Please forgive me. In these times, it is better to be careful. I am not an enemy of the state. I am loyal to our Führer. I will get the keys immediately and take you there myself.'

'Thank you, but that will not be necessary. I want you to remain here. My assistant will remain with you. After we have gone, if you ever mention this to anyone, or even mention my existence, you will be arrested and taken to a concentration camp. Do I make myself clear?'

'I assure you there is no need for threats. I am a loyal citizen.'

Anna followed the priest inside the house. She would make sure he didn't telephone anyone until they were finished. Schneider took the keys and let himself into the church. It was the first time he had been inside a church for years, but the smells of his childhood came back to him. The candles and the incense combined into a unique fragrance peculiar to Catholic churches. The church was in darkness, save for a small red light that glowed in the distance. He knew that every Catholic church kept such a candle glowing near the Eucharist, usually kept by the altar. He used a small torch to find his way there. He couldn't risk a light, with the air raid wardens on constant patrol. He played the dim light over the altar. It wasn't large and seemed to be made from marble. It was covered with a white cloth that reached halfway down its sides. Two candlesticks and a crucifix were its only adornments. Schneider moved the candlesticks to the centre of the altar and lifted the cloth away from the sides. Then he got down on his knees and followed his dim light over the marble surface. It was plain, and he could see it was made up of four slabs, joined at each corner with cement. A cross had been carved in the centre of each slab, and some words of Latin inscribed below.

The old priest had told him the papers were inside the altar. Schneider knew that Catholic altars were hollow, to allow the placing of religious relics inside before the altar was consecrated. It was the ideal hiding place for the papers. He only needed to find the opening.

Carefully he searched, his fingers feeling for any crack. But the object was completely intact. Even if the old priest had had the strength to move the top slab, it would have been impossible for him to do so as it was also cemented in place, and there was nothing to show it had ever been opened since. So, the papers could not be inside.

Why had the old priest misled him? Had he been lying? Schneider was sure he hadn't been. Was he confused after all he had been through? Maybe, but Schneider had seen a clear intelligence in the old eyes. So, if not in the altar, where were the papers?

Schneider slumped down against the altar and went over the words of the old priest.

Stand before the altar of God and let the light of the sun guide you.

Schneider suddenly realised he had only assumed the priest meant that the papers were in the altar. But had he meant something quite different? Schneider knew his only option was to follow precisely what the priest had said. He got up and walked around the altar until he was facing down the centre aisle of the church. So, where was the light of the sun?

The church, like most buildings in Germany in the fourth year of war, was unheated and Schneider's breath was testament to how cold it was. His fingers were becoming so numb he could barely feel the torch in his hand. He scanned the roof with the small torch, keenly aware of the blackout, and the risk he was taking if any light escaped. But he had to take that risk if he was going to find the papers, and now would be his only chance.

He could see the roof was solid and there were no windows at either end of the church. The only sunlight would come from the row of small windows high on the side walls of the church. Schneider studied the windows for a few minutes, imagining the sun shining through them. Would that sunlight somehow show him where the papers were hidden?

But the sunlight would have streamed through all the windows and there would be no particular direction or focus to it. As the sun moved across the sky, the light in the church would move with it. So, if he was on the right track, he needed an exact time for the priest's instructions to make any sense.

He shone the torch again over the pews and empty confession boxes. How could the papers be hidden somewhere there? But they were the only places the sunlight would have fallen on. It made no sense.

But then he remembered there was another light in the church, the little red light beside the tabernacle that holds the Eucharist, which Catholics believe has been consecrated and transformed into the body of Christ. Schneider felt a tingle of realisation. Christ was the *son* of God. Was this what the priest meant?

He hurried across to the tabernacle. A quick examination revealed a simple glass-encased electric light secured to the church wall by a metal stand. He tugged at it a few times, but it was solid. It was not the secret lever he had hoped for, that would magically open a hidden chamber where the papers would be.

Schneider was crushed. He would have to go back to Anna and tell her it was all over. He had failed. Why had the old priest not been specific? With sudden insight, he realised that even on the night he would be gassed to death, the priest still had an absolute and unshakeable faith in God. He could not be 100 per cent certain he could trust Schneider, so he had trusted God instead. He trusted God would help Schneider to solve the puzzle, *if that was God's will.* Schneider was stunned. There was no God; the priest had deluded himself and, in doing so, he had ended any chance of Schneider finding the papers. He knew that eventually Himmler would hear of his meeting in Auschwitz. He wouldn't know why they had met, but a man like Himmler leaves nothing to chance. That church must hold something of value that Himmler needed to find. He would tear the church apart to find it, brick by brick if need be.

But maybe God did intervene. Or maybe it was just Schneider's keen analytical mind. For whatever reason, a voice in his head reminded him he should stand *before* the altar of God. He had, but now realised he had been facing the wrong way. A priest standing before an altar faces the altar. There would be no sunlight there, only the little red light. And the light was only to *guide* him. It was not the answer in itself. But guide him to what? The only place could be the tabernacle, just below the light.

He pulled aside the little curtain that covered the front. As he expected, from his years as an altar boy, it was locked. But the key was in the lock. With a trembling hand, he turned the key and opened the tabernacle. It contained only a small chalice holding the consecrated hosts that would be used for communion. Despite long since ceasing to be a believer, he still hesitated before daring to remove the chalice. Vaguely he recalled the Jesuit boast of having a child for two years, and the child being theirs for the rest of his life. It had obviously worked in his case. He looked up at the large crucifix on the wall and its broken Jesus figure hanging on it.

'If you do exist, if you care, then help me now.'

He waited for a sign, a divine intervention, but nothing happened. He hadn't expected it to.

He regathered his resolve and took the chalice out and set it on the altar. The tabernacle was dark and empty, but he now knew he was on the right track. He felt inside the smooth wooden walls of the tabernacle and his fingers encountered a small, raised area at the rear. He held his breath and pushed. There was a click as the rear wall opened an inch. He shone his torch in and saw some envelopes, the top one marked 'Top Secret – For the Eyes of the Führer Only'. He had done it. In that moment he realised that his contingency plan could now be discarded. He knew he would now live for a little longer, for the contingency plan would have meant his death. If he hadn't found the papers, he had planned to meet Himmler one last time and shoot him dead. It would have been a small recompense for Auschwitz.

He looked back up at the crucified Christ. Was it a miracle? He didn't know, but for the first time in years he fell to his knees and thanked God.

He went back and collected Anna, keeping the envelopes tucked in his tunic. He reiterated his warning to the priest about telling anyone of this visit, then set off. There was no time for reading the papers just now. They could do that if they won.

*

Heinrich Himmler detested Martin Bormann with a vengeance. Since Hess's deranged flight to Scotland, he had become the Führer's *éminence grise*. Even Himmler found it impossible to speak to the Führer without going through Bormann first. Not that he would ever refuse Himmler access. At least not yet. But as Bormann's power and megalomania grew, who knew what he might attempt? Himmler would take pleasure in dealing with him at his leisure afterwards. As a pretext for the call, he had given Bormann some figures about SS replacement regiments to pass on to the Führer. He wouldn't need to disturb him himself, but he knew the Führer was anxious to get as many new fighting men onto the Russian front as soon as possible. Then, as if it was an almost forgotten afterthought, he had asked his question. The great Reichsführer SS seemed almost embarrassed to be asking. With everything that was happening in the east, he knew it must be far from all their minds. But Bormann knew as well as he did what wives were like about Christmas. So, if he knew, could he tell him?

Bormann had many faults, perhaps more than most of the other leading Nazis, but he was a devoted family man. He understood Christmas and children, and he knew that Himmler spent little enough time with his only child as it was. So, he told him what he wanted to know. He told him Hitler's Christmas arrangements, the one time when all the leading Nazis could be guaranteed to be together. Now Himmler knew where they would be. He thanked Bormann and told him he was in his debt. Then he started composing his reply to B. The date would be Christmas Eve.

Stuttgart, the next day

Schneider had thought long and hard about driving. On the road, it was more difficult for Himmler to know where they were and, more importantly, where they were going. But the distance was too great and, with the growing number of air raids starting to destroy roads throughout Germany, it was just too much of a gamble. In any event, he would be carrying the papers, and time was vital. He had used his letter again and arranged for a plane. They drove to the airport, where he told the waiting pilot to fly them to Stuttgart. Maybe Himmler wouldn't realise their ultimate destination until it was too late. Schneider kept the box holding the papers clutched tightly to him throughout the short flight, which seemed to last a lifetime. Every change in the engine note, every change of direction, caused his hands to grasp the box even tighter. He had never felt so helpless in all his life. He could see the pilot speaking into his radio. At any moment he expected to be told the plane was being ordered to land. Or worse, to see fighters on their wing forcing them to comply. His fears proved to be groundless, and the plane landed without incident. The car he had ordered was waiting for him.

Before the war, the Black Forest had been one of Germany's greatest tourist attractions. It was the fairy-tale Germany of the picture postcard kind. Enchanting villages, good food and wine, and simple country folk made it a haven for holidaymakers. Since the war, all that had changed. The young men were at the front, and those left behind had enough difficulty in feeding themselves, let alone tourists.

Schneider recalled a vague memory of a short trip there with his parents, when he had spent long days hiking with them. It was the closest he had ever been to his father. He hadn't thought of that trip again until now, and it brought back bittersweet memories of that time of innocence. He remembered he had wanted that holiday to last for ever. Now, instead of that youthful purity, his mind was filled with Auschwitz and all he had seen there. He could never go back to what he had been only weeks before, never mind the days of his youth. Those days were gone for good, and he didn't intend to spend any more time here than he needed to.

He headed south on the Schwarzwaldhochstrasse. In winter it was almost deserted, its icy, treacherous curves discouraging to all but the bravest driver. It was the most difficult and least likely route he could have chosen, and accordingly the safest for them. He had told the pilot after they had landed that he was going to Strasbourg. That should buy him a little time while Himmler tried to work out who he wanted to see there.

The roads demanded his fullest concentration and Anna sat silently beside him, Heydrich's box at her feet. It was as if they were both afraid to let it out of their sight for even a second. He drove steadily but carefully and soon he saw the sign for Freiburg. He avoided the city and kept going south. He was only too aware that he was bound to be challenged eventually, but he still had the letter. To his right, the vineyards of the Alsace passed by on the other side of the Rhine. The vines had been cut back after the autumn harvest and now were little more than row upon row of wooden stumps. Yet Schneider knew that with the coming of the spring these stumps would miraculously put forth fresh shoots and grow again until, come the autumn, they were once more clothed in bunches of ripe fruit ready for picking. For a brief moment it gave him a lift about his own future. Maybe there was a chance of a new life for them, but he knew he couldn't think beyond the next hour, never mind the next wine harvest.

The road was a little busier now, mainly with military vehicles. He saw they were being driven by old men, well into their fifties. Every able-bodied man was fighting far away from Germany's borders. Only the old or infirm remained in the country. And the SS. He saw the checkpoint up ahead. It was only about a mile to his goal, which he could now see clearly just beyond the road block. For the second time in twenty-four hours he said a silent prayer.

The heavily armed SS men waved his car to a stop. They were alert and kept their machine pistols pointed at the car. Schneider told himself this was standard procedure. He couldn't afford to be paranoid now. He didn't wait for the usual demand for his papers. He stepped out of the car so that they could see his uniform. They came to attention, but not too smartly. A uniform could be stolen; a man might not be what he appeared. Especially here. So, they kept their weapons ready. Schneider felt his heart racing as he tried to dominate the men with his eyes. Deliberately, he moved his hands to his hips in a gesture of arrogance. It also hid the tremble he was starting to imagine there. The next minute or so would decide his and Anna's future, and what was to happen to the papers. He could see his goal now only yards away. He had to get it absolutely right. He didn't wait for them to speak.

'I am Standartenführer Schneider. Where is the officer in command here?'

'He is in the guard house, Herr Standartenführer.'

Schneider set off at a rapid pace. One of the guards followed him. They hadn't seen his papers yet. He entered the small but cosy room. A warm fire burned in the hearth. The officer in charge was reading some papers. He was young with straw-coloured hair and had the clear innocent face of a child. It was an illusion, of course, for children do not become SS officers. But at least Schneider greatly outranked him. He kept up the act he had started outside.

'Is there anyone else here but you?'

Schneider's voice carried so much authority that the officer involuntarily sprung to his feet.

'No, sir.'

'Excellent. Dismiss the guard. I need to speak to you on a matter of the utmost importance and secrecy.'

The young officer was starting to regain his wits. The guard still had his weapon pointed at Schneider.

'Herr Standartenführer, I have no idea who you are. Please may I see your papers first?'

'Do as I say. If you delay me in this matter, you will answer to the Führer himself. Dismiss the guard.'

Schneider threw down his letter as he was barking out his order. The young officer read it and the guard was dismissed. Schneider tucked the letter back in his pocket and waited until they were alone.

'What I am about to tell you will cost you your life if you repeat it. Do you understand me?'

It was clear he had the officer's undivided attention.

'I am on a mission for the Führer, as you now know. What you do not know is the nature of that mission. Suffice to say, the Führer suspects treason at the highest level. I expect to get the proof within the next hour. But no one must know of my visit here. You will accordingly let me pass but make no entry in your records. I expect to return within twenty-four hours. You will remain here to ensure my return is speedy and also unreported. Do you understand?'

'Sir, I have very precise instructions. No one is to be permitted to pass here without the necessary papers. I must phone my superiors to get permission.'

'Superiors? Who could be superior to the Führer himself? I have shown you my authority. I have warned you of the consequences if you hinder me. But if you insist, I will get you all the authority you need. I presume this phone will be able to reach the Führer's headquarters. You may speak to him yourself.'

Schneider snatched up the phone and waited for the operator to come on. He saw surprise on the young man's face.

'Get me the Führer's headquarters in East Prussia at once.'

It was a preposterous request from an obscure guard post, just as Schneider had been banking on. He was told it would require some considerable time for the connection to be made.

'Time is the one thing I do not have. Very well, then. Can you get me the Reichsführer any quicker?' Schneider kept his eyes firmly on the young man and raised his eyebrows in a gesture that said, *It's your last chance to see sense.* 'Maybe he will suffice?'

Doubt was creeping onto the officer's face. He clearly didn't relish speaking to Himmler any more than Hitler.

The operator was telling Schneider that connecting with Himmler would also take some time, and Schneider said, 'Fifteen minutes? That may well be too long.'

He stared at the worried man opposite. He could see sweat on his upper lip, and the eyes were now in constant nervous motion. One more push should do it. He reached for his holster, undoing the leather cover over the pistol.

'You leave me no alternative. I think you have just signed your own death warrant.'

The young man cracked. Any sane person would in those circumstances. Clearly, Schneider had all the authority in the world. He reached out, took the phone from Schneider, and told the operator it was all right, there was no need for the call. Two minutes later, Schneider was driving over the border into Basel. Into Switzerland. He wondered what the young officer would be thinking. Should he tell his superiors about Schneider, just to cover his own back? But then he would have to admit to breaking orders. Such a course of action could and probably would be fatal to him. That was how it worked in Nazi Germany. Schneider decided that, sooner rather than later, the officer would report what had happened in a way that tried to put him in the best light, and that report would eventually reach Himmler. It wouldn't matter by then. If he kept it totally secret, as Schneider had demanded, that would be better. But he had only done this to add to his air of authority, of menace. All that had mattered was getting over that border.

Unlike almost every other country in Europe, Switzerland had stayed neutral throughout the war. It was good for business. The Swiss border guards were happy to let Schneider and Anna enter. It was a fairly normal occurrence for senior SS and party members to enter the country, given that the vaults beneath Switzerland's banks were overflowing with Nazi plunder. As the guards were checking the car, Schneider wondered absentmindedly whether it was possible for all the inhabitants of a country to remain morally neutral in the middle of a world war. Surely the people must know right from wrong. But people think within the limits of their knowledge. His own conversion had been very recent, and it had taken Auschwitz to achieve it. He was in no position to judge others.

Schneider told the Swiss border guards that he was going to a bank in Basel and intended to return to Germany the next day. He was granted the necessary visa – for payment of a fee, of course. If you had money, you could do anything in Switzerland. Anna was introduced as his wife. The Swiss guards gave a knowing look, but again the payment of a fee solved the problem.

In less than ten minutes they were in the city centre. They found a small, quiet hotel and booked a double room. Payment was requested and made in advance.

Schneider wanted to get out of that bloody uniform. He had noticed the way the Swiss looked at him in the street. In Germany, no one in their right mind stared at such a uniform. Here, the locals very deliberately did just that, to show it carried no power in this country. Some even smirked. It was easy to be brave when you were neutral.

He removed the hated tunic and the rest of the paraphernalia and changed into a sedate lounge suit. Anna was sitting with the metal box on her knee. She hadn't opened it. Every now and then her hand would play with the metal clasp holding it closed.

'Go on, then. It's what we came here for.'

'I'm afraid of what I may find.'

She pushed the box to him as if it might bite. He prised open the lid and took out the surprisingly small stack of papers inside. They were in three separate bundles. Schneider looked at the topmost, the one he had seen when he had found the box in the altar. It seemed to be made up of government documents. He put it aside and looked at the next bundle. This seemed to be made up of typed sheets of paper, each with a name at the top. Schneider rifled through them. They were Heydrich's notes on the secrets of many of Germany's leading bankers and industrialists. Mistresses, homosexuality, pederasty and financial irregularity. Heydrich had used them to control these individuals. But they were of little value to Schneider.

The third bundle contained five separate files. He

looked at the first. It bore the name 'Adolf Hitler' on its cover. Inside, it contained details of the death of Hitler's niece, Geli Raubal, his genealogy and a medical report from Austria, and something about a home in Vienna. None of it made any obvious sense to Schneider. He looked at the next file. It was marked 'Hermann Göring'. Inside were details of morphine shipments and artwork. There was also something about payments into Swiss bank accounts. It suddenly struck Schneider what he had. These were the darkest secrets of the Nazi leadership. Secrets that could destroy the others before Hitler. And then Hitler himself. No wonder Himmler was desperate to get his hands on these. They were dangerous to him in someone else's hands but priceless in his own. Schneider checked the names on the other three files: 'Heinrich Himmler', 'Josef Goebbels' and 'Martin Bormann'. It was the full set of all the leading Nazis. He settled down to read them in detail.

The five files were made up of a mixture of documents and notes written in Heydrich's own hand. Each was no more than five or six pages thick, but those pages could be more devastating to the Nazis than an atom bomb. He started with Hitler himself. The first page was an autopsy report on Geli Raubal, who shot herself in 1932, just a year before Hitler came to power. Schneider remembered that at the time, when the German press was still free, there had been allegations made against Hitler. Some had suggested he had killed his niece himself – his pistol was used – while others said he had ordered her death. Hitler himself had an alibi, as he was driving to Hamburg at the time of her death. He had apparently been devastated and still mourned her to this day. It was rumoured that the room where she had died had been kept as a shrine that only Hitler himself was allowed to enter.

But the autopsy report showed she had been three months pregnant at the time of her death. This information had never reached the press and had been totally suppressed after Hitler came to power. Heydrich's note gave the reason for this: Hitler had been the father of the child his own niece was carrying. Schneider knew that while such information might have prevented the Nazis gaining power then, its only use now could be to embarrass Hitler. And that could only be abroad. With German radio and newspapers so tightly controlled by Goebbels, it would now never reach the German people.

He turned to Hitler's genealogy. He realised that neither he nor the German people knew anything about Hitler's background. He was a man of mystery who had appeared from nowhere to become the Führer. But everyone must have parents and other relatives. Schneider studied the chart. It showed Hitler had a sister and a half-sister. It showed his parents and their relatives in Austria. Nothing appeared that important until he noticed that there was a red asterisk against the name of Hitler's paternal grandfather. He turned to Heydrich's note and read that an investigation carried out after Hitler came to power showed that his father had been illegitimate and that it was only some years after his birth that his 'father' had acknowledged paternity. The belief among many at the time had been that Hitler's father was actually the son of his mother's employers. She had worked as a maid for a well-to-do family that had also paid maintenance for the child. It was a typical story that probably happened all the time in such circumstances, except for one thing: *this family was Jewish*. Schneider considered what it would mean if this became public knowledge. Probably not a lot, especially as there was no real proof.

The third sheet was merely details of Hitler's existence in Vienna before he came to Munich. It seemed he had lodged in a hostel for down-and-outs, and had made a meagre living by painting and selling postcards. Again, it might embarrass Hitler if this became known, but little else. Schneider was starting to think that maybe Heydrich's secret papers were not going to live up to expectations.

He put down Hitler's file and picked up Göring's. It showed he was a drug addict, addicted to morphine. And since coming to power, he had stolen artwork from across the whole of Europe. Goebbels' file disclosed he was a serial womaniser who had impregnated several of Germany's leading actresses. Bormann's file was the thinnest, containing only some sketchy details of fraud involving money from the building of the

Berghof. Schneider turned to the last file, Himmler's. This was also pitifully thin. Himmler appeared to have a mistress. That was it.

Bitter disappointment welled up in Schneider. Was this all there was? Was this what he had risked his life to find, in the hope that somehow it would be a magic weapon? He threw the papers on the floor at his feet. His mind was reeling. Surely there must be more. Weren't these people murderers on a scale never seen before? How could their sexual or financial behaviour compare to that? Then it came to him, and his despair was complete.

Schneider realised that all these people must have been involved in horrific crimes. But these were only crimes *outside* Nazi Germany. Heydrich's files contained nothing about these because such information would have no value inside the country. So, he had concentrated on their personal failings and peccadilloes. These might have been useful to Heydrich, but they were worthless to Schneider. Unless the other two bundles of files offered something better, he would have nothing to use at all.

He was just about to put the useless file down when he noticed a small letter clipped to the back of Himmler's file. He almost didn't look at it, but more in desperation than hope he peeled it off. The letter was meaningless to Schneider. It was the one Heydrich had obtained from the Hungarian, and Schneider had no idea who B. was. Clearly, neither did Heydrich. A short note summarised Himmler's involvement and suggested that the Reichsführer may be committing treason, but B. had to be identified first. That was all. It all added up to nothing.

Schneider felt drained. All his plans, all his hopes, had been dashed. There was nothing he could confront Himmler with. He hadn't really known what he had expected to find. Evidence of criminal activity, of murders probably. Instead, it was only tittle tattle, gossip. He pushed the files aside. Anna had fallen asleep on the bed. How could he tell her what he had found? Maybe he should leave her here in the safety of Switzerland and go back and kill Himmler. All his life he had been an upholder of the law, and now here he was thinking of committing murder. But was it murder to kill someone like Himmler? Deep down he still knew it was. What would Father Stein have told him to do? Forgive? But how would that achieve anything? He had walked into the gas chamber forgiving his killers but still the killings went on. So, was it not right to kill the killers, to prevent even more deaths? But Schneider knew he could never be what he wasn't.

Suddenly, with a flash of insight, he realised what he had been doing wrong. Instead of thinking like a normal person or a police officer, he had to try and think the way that a Himmler or a Heydrich would think. Both of them thought these papers were priceless. How would they use them? What did it matter to them if there was proof or not? If Hitler got to know about Himmler's action, that might be enough in itself. Law courts and evidence weren't relevant in their world. Power was everything, and Hitler was more powerful than Himmler. That was all that Himmler feared: that the papers would find their way to Hitler.

But there was another factor. Himmler couldn't know what the papers contained. How real was the danger? That would have been how a master manipulator like Heydrich would have used them. Veiled threats, hints and suggestions only. Always pushing to get that little bit more power, always looking for a weakness. Schneider knew he was no Heydrich, but now he felt there was still a way to use these papers. He needed help to see that way clearly.

A new plan started to form in Schneider's mind. It took him time as he wasn't used to thinking that way. As a police officer, he sometimes felt he could get inside the minds of criminals. Was this really so different? By the time Anna awoke, it was complete. It was also late in the evening. They had dinner together and in the deserted dining room he told her what he intended to do. She didn't like it, as he knew she wouldn't, but she saw it was the only way.

That night, for the first time, they shared a bed and their bodies. It had been natural and spontaneous, a new experience for both of them. It was an unspoken lifetime pledge, but both knew that lifetime together could be short, so no words about a future were wasted. What would be be would be.

The next morning, Schneider made a phone call to an old friend in Switzerland. He and Schneider had worked together in the past, and he was one of the few men whose word Schneider would trust absolutely. He had been head of the Swiss Special Branch but had retired two years ago. His principles hadn't allowed him to carry on working for a government that turned a blind eye for the sake of making money. Now he lived in a remote village, tending his goats and making cheese. But Schneider knew his men still kept him informed of what was happening in the world he had left behind. The call was short and cryptic, as only a call between two minds that understand much more than is said can be. It was two old friends arranging to meet socially, nothing else, and a bit of local knowledge. Nothing for any eavesdropper on the line to wonder about.

Schneider and Anna drove to the bank his old friend had recommended. He paid the necessary fee and was shown into a private room. An empty safety deposit box was brought in, and they were told to ring when they were finished. Schneider had the impression he had entered a church rather than a bank, judging by the silence and sense of reverence that imbued the whole building. Perhaps this was Switzerland's true god. He put all of Heydrich's papers in the box and locked it. He gave the key to Anna and rang the bell. The immaculately dressed official reappeared and checked that the box had been suitably locked. He removed a card from one pocket and a fountain pen from the other.

'All that is necessary now is that you remember the number of this box. Two six three. Do you wish to write it down? I suggest that if you do, you do not put down anything other than the number. But that is a matter for you, naturally.'

Schneider told him he would remember.

'Then all that remains is to agree the access password. What would you like that to be?'

This was the ultimate in Swiss banking security. No names of clients, no details of what the box contained. Instead, all that was required to get access to it was the key and the number. But before that, you had to give the bank a password. Anyone armed with all three requirements would get such access. That was the strength of the system as, without any one component, access would be denied. Schneider had also seen it was the weakness. For anyone with these three items could access the box. And there were lots of persuasive people in Germany. He wondered how many of the victims of Auschwitz had handed over such information. He knew anyone could be coerced eventually, even himself. So, Schneider had thought of a further safeguard.

'My friend will give you the password after I have left.'

If this arrangement seemed unusual to the Swiss banker, it didn't show. It was all part of the customers' service. He left and two minutes later Anna joined him. Now only she could access the papers. No matter what was done to him, Himmler couldn't force the password out of him, and without that no one would get access. Anna would never return to Germany. It was a certain safeguard but also put him at terrible risk. For he could never reveal the information, not even to save his life. This had been the part Anna hated most.

They drove out of Basel and headed for the meeting with Schneider's friend. Soon the Alps loomed over them, heavily shrouded in snow and mist. The road climbed continuously but had been kept open. Banks of snow piled along the roadside testified to the Swiss work ethic. Higher and higher they climbed until they came to a series of hairpin bends. These had defeated even the Swiss road clearers and almost defeated Schneider. Somehow, with the tyres slithering wildly, he made it round the last bend and drove into the village.

Kandersteg lay at the end of a valley, with that one road the only way in or out. The village looked as if it had lain undisturbed by the passage of time for over a century. Large wooden houses lined the almost deserted main street. Some of them were adorned with Christmas lights, safe from bombers in their neutrality. Schneider followed the road into a small town square. He turned left onto a track and followed this out of the village. They drove towards a vertical wall of mountain that seemed to hem the whole village in, but between the village and the mountains lay the very narrow pastures that allowed the village to exist. The short, hot Swiss summers produced all that was needed to survive the long winters. His old friend had taken an ancient farmhouse with its own tiny meadow for his goats. He had seen the car coming and was already waiting for them at his door.

Norbert Sutter looked every inch the Swiss peasant. He was attired in leather trousers and two brightly coloured woollen shirts. His hair and beard were almost pure white, and neither had seen a comb nor scissors for several weeks. His face was ruddy, beaming in welcome. Anna felt the effect was like being welcomed into Santa Claus's house, until she noticed the eyes. They were smiling in genuine welcome, but they also held a keen glint that spoke of a very sharp mind behind that hairy disguise.

He welcomed them profusely and insisted they have some coffee immediately. He fussed in the kitchen and proudly produced a spread of his own bread, butter, honey and cheese. Both of them realised how hungry they were and were able to do it full justice. After honour had been satisfied on both sides, Norbert cleared the remains way. All through the meal, the talk had been light, recalling old friends and incidents. Schneider had told Anna that Norbert Sutter was the police officer he admired most. He had described him as totally honest, totally dedicated and simply the best detective he knew. He could have been describing himself. It was easy to see why this synergy existed between them. Now, as if by some mysterious unseen signal, the humour stopped.

'So, my old friend, what can I do for you?'

Schneider told him everything, every detail. Even Anna had never heard everything before. It took him a long time. Sutter sat and listened in silence, sucking on his pipe. Schneider's story was clear and logical and required no clarification. When he had finished, he asked a simple question.

'What do you think I should do?'

Sutter was seemingly lost in thought. Then he began to speak, and Anna saw the real man behind the peasant façade.

'You have seen things no man should ever be asked to see. You know who is responsible for these things. You believed you would get evidence that would destroy them. But it has turned out to be less than you hoped for. You now fear for the life of Anna Weiss but are prepared to sacrifice your own if need be. Am I correct so far?'

Schneider looked as if a weight had been lifted from his shoulders. His old friend would analyse the whole matter clearly and dispassionately. His own brain was now too fogged with emotions.

'Do not worry about Anna. She will stay here as long as is needed to keep her safe. Should you sacrifice your own life? Only you can decide that, Rolf. It may

300

be that it is the right thing for a man to do. But if I may give my view here, it would only be right if it stops the horror you have seen. I do not believe it will, and another life will have been thrown away uselessly. So, we return to these papers. Slurs, immoral behaviour and lies. But isn't the whole of your government built on these things? You are right when you believe they are useless to you. Such information is only of value in its threat, not in its reality. And therein lies your remedy. Only we three know what these papers contain. Do you not think that Himmler and the others have even deeper secrets they wish to conceal? Perhaps Heydrich had discovered these, perhaps they are held in the papers as well. It is the threat of the papers that is your weapon. And you still have that.'

Anna was fascinated to hear such a simple yet brilliant analysis of the use of power. In some ways, she was reminded of Heydrich himself. As his secretary, she had been privy to some of his plans, which had carried the same logic. But his was cold and self-serving, whereas here it was offered freely, for the benefit of others.

'But what can I do when Himmler asks for proof? I don't have anything.'

'You haven't changed, Rolf. Still that chess player's mind, always analysing. But in chess nothing is hidden, so you have to play a new game here. What does the poker player do? If he is bluffing and his bluff is called, he raises the ante. You can do the same. We

know Himmler was to do something with this mysterious B. I believe he may well have been planning to
overthrow Hitler, but we have no proof. Perhaps he
still is. But whatever it is, it is important and very dangerous to him. That is your weapon. He cannot know
what Heydrich found out, so you bluff him. Maybe
he will even reveal more himself. Think of how often
we have used this on criminals, letting them think
we knew much more than we did, with just the use
of one or two snippets of information. Himmler is a
criminal, treat him as such.'

Anna interrupted. She saw where this was going.

'But that would mean facing Himmler again,
putting yourself in his hands. And what is it you are
trying to achieve? To find out who killed Heydrich,
just because you gave your word? To find out about
some stolen gold?'

'I did give my word and I will keep it. As for the gold,
I know why Himmler didn't want me to investigate
further. That gold was torn from the teeth and fingers
of his victims at Auschwitz. I don't know if Auschwitz
is the only place this is happening, but I will find out.'

Sutter cut across the growing tension between
them.

'So, Rolf, you have gone from being a police officer
sworn to uphold the law to becoming some kind of
political activist. Your heart is burning with the injus-
tice and inhumanity you have seen. That is natural.
But what do you intend to do about it? Do you plan to

302

kill Himmler? If you do, you will die for nothing, for another will take his place. All that can help is if the war itself is shortened. Can you do that?'

Anna thought Sutter was on her side. But she didn't realise it was his way of challenging his colleague to even greater efforts.

'I don't know if I can or not. I only know I have to try. These papers were forged in evil. Everything I have seen in the last week has been evil. What was it somebody said once? Something along the lines of "For evil to triumph, it is only necessary for good men to do nothing." I will not do nothing. I'll find a way to use these papers to make a difference.'

'Even if it means your own death?'

Schneider looked at Anna. His look was all the answer she needed.

'Remember, Rolf, you are a gambler who is bluffing. Do not push him so far that he really asks to see your cards. And there may be more happening here than you can know. Find out everything you can before you make your final decision.'

A few hours later, Schneider was on his way back to Germany. His old friend had given him his word to look after Anna until he returned. No one had said 'if'. Schneider was grateful for that.

– **17** –

Berlin, 22 December 1942

Himmler had laid his plans carefully. No one could have suspected what he had in mind. Everything could be explained away, right up to the last minute. He trusted B. as much as B. trusted him, so he wouldn't be the first to act. As always, he would watch and wait and strike only when he was certain. At the back of his mind, a nagging worry refused to go away as he wondered what he should do about Schneider. He had eventually pieced together everything that had happened. The journey to Auschwitz and the old priest. The visit to the church and the time spent alone there. The sudden flight to Switzerland with Heydrich's former secretary. He didn't know how he had done it, but somehow Schneider must have got Heydrich's papers. Had they been hidden in that church all the time? Never one for self-recrimination, he still bitterly thought of how the papers had been in his hands all along if only his men had searched the church properly. He glanced at their files lying on his desk. They had already paid for this incompetence, but that didn't matter now. All that mattered was what Schneider intended to do with them.

Could he get to him in Switzerland? Of course he could. But would he get the papers? If he killed Schneider and didn't get them, who would turn up with the papers next? Most worrying of all, he didn't know what the papers contained. But there was one thing in his favour: he sensed Schneider would contact him. The idea of Schneider, of anyone, trying to bargain with Hitler was inconceivable. No, it had to be him, and Schneider must want something to have gone to all this trouble. He had no idea what he might want in exchange for the papers. But if he could only delay him until after Christmas Eve, it wouldn't matter. And then he could deal with him properly, and at his leisure.

*

Schneider had left Kandersteg in the small hours of a bitter winter day. Sutter left them alone for what they both knew could be their final goodbye. Anna realised that Schneider felt this agony as much as she did and that any more words, any more emotion, would be superfluous. They had loved together long into the night in the tiny bed Sutter had provided for them. She kissed him briefly, avoiding his eyes, and told him she would see him soon. He told her to close the door to keep the heat in and, wordlessly, she obeyed. Neither saw the tears of the other as Schneider started the car and headed back to Germany.

Three hours later, he passed through the same border crossing. The young officer was still there but tried to avoid Schneider's gaze. Schneider knew what this meant; he had made his report. Schneider couldn't blame him in the dog-eat-dog existence in Germany, and even thanked him for all his help. He promised him the Reichsführer would hear of it.

He drove to Stuttgart airport and was back in his Berlin office by early afternoon. He had made his plans as carefully as he and Sutter could before leaving Switzerland. Now to see if they worked. He picked up his desk phone and made the first of the calls he needed to make. It took some time but eventually he got what he needed. Another piece of insurance was now in place. He sat for five minutes staring at the phone, allowing his mind to go over one last time what he was about to do. Then he picked it up and asked for a meeting with Himmler as soon as possible. His call was returned less than two minutes later. The Reichsführer would see him immediately.

The room and its occupant looked as pristine and unchanging as ever. Himmler sat behind his desk, staring at him with the same impenetrable gaze. But some things had changed. There was a tension in the room that was almost palpable. Schneider could feel the hairs on his neck start to rise, as if the very air itself was electrically charged. This was to be a showdown, and possibly a final one for him. He had been searched before being allowed in and his pistol was removed.

He mused that it was as well he hadn't had to rely on his plan to kill Himmler. It would have failed.

Himmler made no pretence any longer. 'I think this game has gone on long enough. Please tell me what you want.'

Schneider was too experienced from long years of questioning prisoners to be tricked into showing his hand too soon. He remembered what Sutter had said about poker.

'Perhaps you would like to elaborate, Reichsführer.'

'All this about trying to find out the truth about Heydrich's death. These journeys from one side of Europe to the other. I know what you have been trying to do, and I warn you now that it is more dangerous than you can imagine. Nevertheless, if you tell me everything, I may be the only person who is in a position to help you.'

Schneider considered what Himmler had said. It was really nothing. Sutter was right, Himmler still didn't know for sure if he had the papers and had no idea what they contained. It was time to push back.

'You are mistaken, Reichsführer. I have been investigating that death and have made some very interesting discoveries. Perhaps I should be saying to you that I am the only person who is now able to help you. Is there anything you want to tell me about his death?'

It was outrageous, a police officer daring to suggest to the head of the SS that he might face criminal proceedings. It just didn't happen in Germany. But Himmler didn't find it amusing. He removed his glasses and rubbed their already immaculate lenses. He stared myopically at Schneider.

'You are either a very brave man or a fool. I could have you shot now, immediately, and no one would ever challenge me. Give me one good reason why I should not do that.'

'I will give you two. I still have the Führer's authority. I know that is meaningless to you, but before I came here, I arranged to meet with him again to report on my findings. *All my findings.* Don't you think he would find it strange if you had me shot just before such a meeting? But you haven't become the second most powerful man in Germany today by risking anything, and I am a risk. So, I will give you an even better reason. As you already suspect, I found them. I have Heydrich's secret files.'

Now it was out in the open. And he had mentioned the meeting with Hitler as well. That was his insurance against Himmler just having him killed now. It all added to the pressure on Himmler, but then his whole life had been pressure. He didn't crack.

'How do I know that you have these papers? And even if you have, why do you think I would be so interested?'

'The proof of both is in what I am about to tell you. How else could I know about your mistress, for example? Do you want me to give you details?'

Himmler blanched. Only a very few people knew about this. Schneider must have something, after all.

'But that isn't really all that important on the scale of things, is it? Not when compared to your dealings with . . . shall we stick to "B." for the moment? I am sure you don't want his name mentioned even here. Do you?'

Involuntarily, Himmler's eyes searched the walls of the room as if half expecting to see someone listening there. Himmler's expression was all the confirmation that Schneider needed that he had hit his target. He waited for Himmler to recover from the shock. It was the moment of truth that Sutter had foretold. Himmler now had to raise or fold. Who was bluffing the most? If possible, the tension in the room had grown even higher. Their eyes bored into each other's, trying desperately to see into the mind behind. Somebody had to call or fold. Seconds seemed to stretch into minutes. Himmler folded first. His voice almost squeaked when he spoke.

'What do you want?'

'That depends. If I give these papers to Hitler, you're a dead man. You know that. But yours was not the only file. I have files on Göring, Goebbels and Bormann. What would they be worth to someone like you? I could give you this country with those files. As for what I want, that's simple. I've seen what is happening to the Jews, and I've been to Stalingrad. Germany is going to lose this war. You know that as well as I do.

So, if I give you the files, I want to know what you will do with them.'

Himmler was astonished. He had thought he was going to be blackmailed for money or something as mundane. But this really was a man of principle, after all.

'You overestimate my power. Only the Führer can make decisions about the direction of the war.'

'I can give you a file on him as well. The information it contains will allow you to . . . ah, *persuade* him also, I'm sure.'

Himmler's mind was racing. This could tie in very well with his own plans. After they were all dead, these files could remove any doubt from the German people's minds that he had done the right thing. Sadly, some of our leaders fell prey to human weaknesses and, for the good of the German Reich, these people have now been removed. And he would have the evidence to support that.

'Where are these files now? How do I know they are safe?'

'Oh, they are very safe. I don't suppose I need to say it, but if you won't help, others might. And don't forget B.'

What did he know about B.? Himmler pondered whether to probe a bit deeper but decided against it. He couldn't know everything: only two people knew that. Could this man really only be interested in stopping the war? Would he hand over the papers for that?

Desperately he tried to calculate what Schneider knew, but it was impossible without further information.

Himmler reached for the phone. 'I am not to be disturbed for any reason for the next hour.' He nodded towards the seats in the corner of the room. 'We might as well be comfortable. I think it is time for you to tell me exactly what you want from me, and for me to find out exactly what you have to offer in return.'

It was just as Sutter had said, two poker players alone in a room, each trying to bluff the other. But the stakes were higher than any game ever played before.

*

The meeting lasted well over the hour Himmler had set aside. When it finally ended, both Himmler and Schneider thought it had gone well. Both felt they had got the better of the other. They had agreed to meet again on Christmas Eve. Each had his own reasons for choosing that date.

Schneider had started the meeting by telling Himmler that he wanted the answers to certain questions. He warned Himmler he already had much of this information from Heydrich's papers, and if he lied then he would never get the files. If anything happened to Schneider, Hitler would have the files the following day.

Himmler couldn't know what Schneider had got from Heydrich's files nor what plans he had for getting them to Hitler. He suspected it was a bluff, but he couldn't

311

be certain. He had to tread carefully for now. But he was also sure that Schneider's knowledge couldn't be complete. If it was, why ask questions? So, he could test the limits of his knowledge with his answers. Bluff and counter-bluff, until someone made a fatal mistake.

Schneider began. 'I want the answer to three questions. One: who killed Heydrich? Two: why did you stop my investigation into the gold thefts? Three: I want to know everything about Auschwitz.'

Himmler peered from behind the pince-nez, his expression unfathomable. Time passed as he weighed the questions, trying to judge what Schneider already knew and what he didn't and why he wanted the information. He decided Schneider had deliberately left the most important question until the end. That was interesting. Why was he so concerned about the fate of the Jews? Perhaps he had something to work with there.

'Who killed Heydrich? It all depends what you mean by "kill". Some might say he killed himself by his own arrogance and stupidity in not making adequate security arrangements. Others, that it was the British secret service and their proxies, the Czech assassins. But he was a man surrounded by enemies. Who do you think killed him?'

Schneider stood up and headed towards the door. 'I told you I wanted the truth. Goodbye.'

He had raised the ante sharply and without warning. Himmler had tested his mettle and got his answer.

'Please, Schneider, sit down. I was only musing out loud. I will tell you what you already know. Heydrich was killed by the Czechs, but they were under the direction of Standartenführer Heizmann. He planned the ambush and made sure it was successful. That was why he went to such lengths to ensure the terrorists were all killed in the church. That is the truth.'

'And who told Heizmann to do this? He wouldn't have done it without orders from very high up.'

Himmler seemed shocked. 'You think it was me? You do not know how much I valued Heydrich, not just as my associate, but as my friend and even my protégé. I give you my word I will not rest until I find out the truth also. That is why I was so concerned about your appointment. I didn't want the real killer alerted that I was still investigating. Let him think the investigation was over and then I would have him. Whoever he is, he is brilliant. He used my own liaison officer in Prague to try to implicate me. That is why Heizmann is still alive and free. He is my only lead.'

On the face of it, Himmler seemed to be taking an awful gamble. If Schneider knew for certain that Himmler was the one who had ordered Heydrich's death, it was probably the end of their meeting. But cold logic told him Schneider's information could only come from the files, and the files could not contain anything about this. If Heydrich had known about the plan to assassinate him, he would still be alive today; and he, Himmler, would be dead. Even Heydrich couldn't add to his files from beyond the grave. Himmler waited for Schneider's reaction.

'And you still have no idea who gave the order? The truth now.'

'If I did, I would have had him arrested by now. I am telling you everything I know.'

Schneider seemed to accept it, and Himmler thought he had won round one. Schneider was still just a gullible police officer when all was said and done – he actually believed what people told him. Himmler had never suffered from that particular weakness. It was going well.

But Schneider also thought it was going well. He knew instinctively and absolutely, even without proof, that Himmler had killed Heydrich because of B. But he hadn't expected Himmler to admit that. He just wanted to push him on something that would make him nervous, and to see how easily he lied. And if he now felt more confident in his ability to deceive Schneider, so much the better.

'What about the gold?' Schneider asked.

'I think what you wanted to know was why your investigation had been stopped. That is simple. It was an embarrassment for me and the whole SS. I could not have anyone outside the SS knowing this. So, I dealt with them myself.'

'Do you really expect me to believe that? I know they were still working in the same jobs after you stopped me.'

Himmler looked surprised. 'Did you think I would have acted immediately? I wanted to find out if there were others. I had techniques available that perhaps you did not. And I got them all. They were a disgrace to me, to the SS, to Germany. To steal from your own country in time of war is totally and utterly without excuse. I will not tolerate any dishonesty in the SS.'

Now it was Schneider's turn to be surprised. Himmler almost sounded as if he meant it.

'So, what did you do?'

Himmler again looked surprised. 'All of them, from the lowest to the highest, are dead.'

'Prove it.'

Himmler moved back to his desk. He picked up the phone. 'Tell me the names of those you uncovered,' he said to Schneider.

As Schneider recalled them, Himmler repeated them into the telephone. When Schneider stopped, Himmler told his listener to bring him at once the personnel files of those he had just named.

Both men waited in silence. The files would determine what happened next. The SS filing system was efficient, and when the Reichsführer said immediately, he meant it. The files arrived in less than ten minutes. Himmler nodded that Schneider should check them himself. Every officer was dead. No reason was given other than they had been found guilty of treason and the death sentence had been imposed by the Reichsführer himself.

'Are you satisfied, then?'

'Why does it not give a reason?'

'My dear Schneider. It is a blot on our SS. We do not want it recorded for posterity. Their deaths are enough for our records.'

Schneider realised that Himmler was telling the truth. Men who had stolen some gold for themselves were guilty of a crime and were executed. But others were overseeing the extermination of an entire people from whom this gold was being systematically stolen on behalf of the whole German race. They were being rewarded. In Himmler's eyes, they were just doing their duty. For a moment, Schneider was transported back to the smell and sound of the gas chamber in Auschwitz. He wanted to strangle Himmler with his bare hands. Wouldn't that be the best thing to do now? He even felt his muscles starting to tighten and could almost feel his hands squeezing the life out of that scrawny little neck. But he controlled himself, as he knew he must. He wanted the answer to his third question first.

'So, tell me about Auschwitz.'

Himmler knew this was what Schneider was really after. He frowned. 'You have been there yourself. What more is there to tell you?'

'I want to know the whole history. When did it begin? Why did it begin?'

The 'why' registered in Himmler's mind. Curiouser and curiouser. This Schneider clearly had some real concern about the Final Solution.

'It began the day we took power. Do you wish me to reacquaint you with all that the Jews have done in the past? The steps that had to be taken? The biological threat? You are a police officer. You accepted the Nuremberg laws outlawing marriage and sexual relations between Jews and Aryans. The removal of their citizenship. You must remember Kristallnacht – the aftermath? You accepted the laws removing the Jews from the civil service, the law and medicine. You accepted their wearing the yellow stars. Auschwitz is merely the continuation of our programme of purification – a programme you supported.'

Schneider knew Himmler was baiting him, trying to provoke him into revealing what he already knew, why he was so interested. He knew he couldn't take it. No one who had seen Auschwitz could. Once again the gentle face of Father Stein came to him. If he could endure Auschwitz, Schneider could endure this.

'My views are irrelevant to this meeting. Tell me how the gassing started.'

'I know you have never been interested in politics, so perhaps you need a little of the background first. It was always our intention that the Jews and racially impure degenerates be removed from our society. We must achieve racial purity for the Aryan race. So, we did this. When they lost their rights as citizens, did you hear any protests? Were people marching in the streets to object? Of course not. The German people supported us. Then the other nations of Europe started to threaten us. Do you remember what the Führer said in his speech in January 1939? He said that if the Jews started another war, they would be the ones to suffer. We had plans to ship the entire Jewish population to Madagascar. They could have made their Jewish homeland there. But before that happened, the war started. It was impossible to move the Jews anywhere except to the east. First, we moved them to the General Government, what used to be Poland. After we conquered western Russia, we found millions more there. What were we to do? We had war on two fronts, we were blockaded, and food was rationed. Should we feed and clothe these enemies of the Reich? Tell me, Schneider, what would you have done in my position?'

'The only reason these people were your enemies was because you said they were. I knew a lot of Jews before all this started. They were as German as I was. It was you who decided they weren't.'

'Clearly, you do not understand politics at all. Consider this, however. If the Jews are so wonderful, why didn't other countries welcome them? We wouldn't have stood in their way.'

'And would you have let them take their possessions and valuables with them?'

'Ah, Schneider, Schneider. You really are a sentimentalist. Don't you think they should pay for the wrongs their people have done to Germany? But we could talk all day about this, and we would never agree. So, shall I continue with how the Jews ended up at Auschwitz?'

Schneider was finding it more and more difficult to keep himself under control. How Himmler could sit and talk about the extermination of a race as if it were some domestic political problem to be solved was almost beyond his tolerance.

'Get on with it. And remember, the truth.'

'There isn't really that much more to tell. At first, some of the Russian Jews were shot. But it was haphazard and not really effective. We recruited Latvians and other Balts in the north to do this. Then we set up Einsatzgruppen, mobile killing squads, to take a more systematic approach, but it took a terrible toll on our men. Some ended up in hospitals, others became alcoholics. We had to find a better way, a quicker, more effective way. So, we tried various gasses until we discovered Zyklon B. The rest you know.'

There it was again, this strange dichotomy that Himmler seemed to find so normal. He could extol the mass slaughter but be concerned about the health of the killers just because they were his men. And he was still not telling Schneider everything he wanted.

'I want you to tell me the rest. Do I need to mention Heydrich's papers again?'

Himmler laughed. 'You seem to think these papers are some kind of magic talisman, something good that will drive away what you think of as evil. But don't you know Heydrich was the man who thought up the Final Solution to the Jewish question? Don't you know we called it "Operation Reinhard" in his honour?'

Schneider was shocked. All along he had thought that Himmler was the driving force behind Auschwitz. He let his guard slip.

'You're lying.'

It was all Himmler needed. He immediately realised there were serious gaps in Schneider's knowledge. Incredulous, he also seized upon the fact that the Jews were very important to Schneider. Could he be Jewish himself? Himmler made a mental note to check Schneider's heritage after this meeting was concluded. But for now, he had the advantage.

'I am not lying. You can check the details yourself after this meeting. Your letter from the Führer will be authority enough. Heydrich had a meeting in January of this year when all the details about Auschwitz were finalised.'

Schneider was finding it difficult to keep his mind clear. Could it have been Heydrich, not Himmler? But even Heydrich wouldn't have had this power. Only someone at the very top could do that. He needed time to think. Himmler was as dangerous as a rattlesnake. If he made one error, he would strike.

'I know all I need to about Heydrich's involvement. Now, finish telling me about Auschwitz.'

'You have seen its size. We needed somewhere where we could proceed on a much quicker basis. So, we set up Auschwitz and the other extermination camps. Soon all the Jews will be gone.'

Schneider had what he wanted. Germany, his own

country, a country he had served for years, was systematically slaughtering millions of innocent people because of their race.

'Let us presume for now that I believe you. If I give you these papers, how would you use them?'

Himmler tried to guess what this man wanted. He could give him Heizmann. And he had already proved that the gold thieves were dead. So, what did he want with regard to the Jews?

'You said Germany had lost this war. I would not quite go that far but would say that we will lose this war unless it is stopped now. If I had the papers, and they are all you have said they are, then I would use them for this purpose.'

Both understood what 'use' meant. Himmler would become the leader of Germany.

'And how would B. fit into this?' Schneider asked the question as if he might know at least part of the answer.

'I don't see why that should alter. The papers only make my part easier.'

Schneider realised Sutter had been right again. Himmler had been plotting to overthrow Hitler, and still was. He asked his last question. 'And the Jews?'

Himmler peered at him as if trying to understand something that was beyond him. 'As I told you, Hitler said they would be punished if they caused a war. If the war ends, there would be no need for further punishment. I personally hold no ill will towards them. I give you my word on that.'

Himmler had pressed him for an answer, but Schneider insisted on time to think. He wanted to go back to Switzerland – to see Anna and hear Sutter's wise counsel – but knew this was impossible. He would only ever return to Switzerland once more in his life, and now was not the time.

So, they had gone their separate ways, to make such plans as they could. Schneider said he was to see Hitler on Christmas eve, in two days' time, and would make his final decision then. Himmler, with absolutely no hint of subterfuge, said he also was to see the Führer that day. They arranged to meet again then.

Schneider knew Himmler would much rather have taken him off to the torture chambers below SS head-quarters, but he was safe for the moment. But only for as long as the papers were beyond Himmler's reach.

As soon as Schneider had gone, Himmler immediately put his plans into action. Certain elite SS units were given instructions. Standartenführer Heizmann received an urgent call from him. And finally, he asked the Gestapo to let him have everything they had on a Chief Investigator Rolf Schneider. Almost as an after-thought, he added the name of Anna Weiss.

18

Obersalzberg, 23 December 1942

Everything, even a war, winds down for the Christmas holidays. In Berlin, now bombed both by day and night, the Christmas spirit was strained almost to breaking point. But even there, families were trying to make the most of what celebrations they could muster. Carefully hoarded scraps of food were replacing the traditional goose. A rare piece of fruit served as a child's gift. People prayed to their god for peace. Publicly, at least, they claimed they were still praying for victory.

Both Himmler and Schneider had left all this behind them. The Obersalzberg was covered in crisp virginal snow. The war hadn't touched it, and the town of Berchtesgaden had even managed to put up some Christmas decorations. An SS brass band was playing carols in the town square. Food was more plentiful in the country, and the people – in their undisturbed ignorance – still believed in the final victory. Schneider saw the belief in their eyes as he was driven through the town on his way up to the Berghof, and he found it depressing. Could these people really not be aware of what was happening? Didn't they ever wonder what happened to their former neighbours who had now mysteriously disappeared? Yet hadn't he been like them until a few days ago? Could he really blame them now?

He had spent last night going over and over the meeting with Himmler in his mind. He had joined the rest of Berlin in the bomb shelters and returned to his still undamaged flat in the early hours. Still sleep eluded him and he tossed and turned, trying to make a final decision. By morning, he was no closer to it. He knew what he had to do, but still he hesitated. He didn't know why. Fear? He knew that wasn't it. Doubt? He had never been surer of anything in his life. He got up, shaved and left his flat for the last time. Without Anna it seemed empty and cold, and he was glad to be leaving it. He still couldn't decide what to do. He would simply have to wait for matters to take their own course. It was an old habit of his when an investigation refused to yield any leads. There was no other way.

*

Himmler had also left Berlin that morning. On the flight south, he studied the papers rushed to him by the Gestapo. Schneider really was a man without a blemish in his past, unless you considered his complete disinterest in politics to constitute one. His work, his personal life, his family background all contained nothing to interest the Gestapo. So, why was he doing what he was doing? Himmler was intelligent enough to accept that some people may well act in an altruistic fashion. But these were rare individuals, and Himmler did not believe someone like Schneider could suddenly change in this way. Yet something was now causing him to act the way he was. His record spoke of the long and dedicated service of a professional police officer, not of an idealist. So, something must now be driving him in this mania about what was happening to the Jews. Could there be more to his relationship with Anna Weiss than the Gestapo surveillance indicated? Was there something there?

He picked up her file and studied it for a second time. Still it suggested nothing. Her position as Heydrich's secretary meant she had been fully vetted. Himmler knew from long experience that Heydrich was as adept at using people as he himself was. Had he discovered something that gave him a hold over her and made her something more useful than a mere secretary? Carefully now, very carefully, Himmler studied Anna's file for a third time.

It took in most of the flight and several radio calls to Berlin, but by the time the plane touched down at Munich he had it. He knew Anna Weiss was Jewish. So, it was as simple as that. A man falls in love, he forgets his duty to his country, he forgets everything. Himmler felt disappointed. In a way he had hoped for something more from this man. He contacted Heizmann again with new instructions. Hopefully, by the time he met Schneider he would have a new bargaining chip. He spent the rest of his journey checking the plans he had made about B. As before, he couldn't see any flaws. Now it was only a matter of waiting.

*

Both men had arrived within an hour of each other. Schneider was accommodated in the large hotel specifically built to house those who were visiting the Führer. Himmler had the honour of a guest room in the Berghof itself. Both knew they could be summoned to see Hitler at a moment's notice. Since the growing crisis on the eastern front, his daily routine, if he had ever really had one, had become even more disjointed. He rose late in the morning and wasted more time on lunching with his secretaries. He held military conferences at all hours of the day and night, expecting his generals to be instantly available. In the evening, he liked to relax with the chosen few he felt comfortable with. They watched films together or listened to his interminable monologues. These evenings became feats of endurance as they usually ran into the early hours of the next morning. Hitler was almost nocturnal and expected everyone else to be the same. He had reluctantly left his headquarters in East Prussia to come here. He would stay only two days as things were reaching a critical point at Stalingrad. He couldn't know that a strange fate was drawing him to his favourite mountain to meet two other men who now held history in their grasp.

Surprisingly, Schneider was summoned before Himmler. He was driven down from the hotel and went through the same strict security routine as on his first visit. His report was to be verbal and brief. He had been warned that Hitler's time was very short. As he waited in the Berghof, Bormann appeared.

'So, Schneider, you didn't think it was necessary to advise me of what you are going to report to the Führer. I hope for your sake that you know what you are doing. That piece of paper will not protect you from me. And just as soon as the Führer is finished with your services, you will be mine.'

Schneider stared at the ugly, puffy face pushed pugnaciously towards his own. Whatever happened, he wouldn't ever need to fear this man again.

'Fuck off. Your time for threatening me is past.'

The effect of the words was electric. Bormann flinched. No one ever spoke to him like that. He too knew about the Heydrich papers. Did this policeman have something on him? Sweat immediately lined his greasy forehead. For the first time in years, he felt icy fear clutching at him, but there was nothing he could do about it at that moment. He would have to bide his time for now, but woe betide Schneider when his time came. He nodded towards the door into Hitler's study.

'The Führer will see you now.'

Schneider still didn't know exactly what he was going to do. He would give a brief report culminating in his discovery of Heydrich's secret files. What happened after that would depend on Hitler. He was shown into a surprisingly small study. He was determined to resist giving the Hitler salute, but the necessity faded as the old man behind the desk shuffled towards him. For a moment, he thought his sight was failing him. Surely this was not the same man he had seen only a few short months ago.

Adolf Hitler was hunched as if from some crippling spinal defect, or from a burden beyond bearing. The hair was now clearly white in areas, the thin lips almost bloodless. The hand that reached out shook with a visible and constant tremor, and its grip was almost imperceptible. The face was lined and tired, like that of the very old nearing the end of a long struggle with some terrible illness. But the eyes were the worst. Those crystal-clear blue irises remained. But now they were surrounded by the bloodshot whites of an acute insomniac and circled by deep, grey bags. The man before him was old, terribly old. What had happened to him?

Even the voice had lost much of its power. That deep resonance was still there but now it was muted and soft, like that of an old man recalling his youth to other old men, in the twilight years of memory. Schneider couldn't stop himself: he just stood and stared. But Hitler seemed unaware of the image he now presented, or of its effect on Schneider. He mumbled a few words of welcome and returned to the seat behind the desk. He asked Schneider for his report. Already, something was gnawing at the back of Schneider's mind. He played for time.

'I have completed the investigation into Ober-gruppenführer Heydrich's death. I have found several defects in the original report. I will give you the essential elements of my findings. Heydrich was assassinated by the Czech resistance with the help of the British. I have no evidence that there was any help given to them by anyone in Germany or the German forces. I also discovered that Heydrich may have kept secret files on the leaders of the Reich. It was imperative, in my view, that these files be discovered, to ensure they did not fall into enemy hands. I consequently carried out a full investigation as to their whereabouts.'

Hitler seemed to show interest for the first time. The voice regained a little of its strength. 'And what did you find out?'

'I discovered that the files did exist. I traced a possible source of information to the eastern front. I went to Stalingrad and interviewed this man. He—'

But Hitler was on his feet, the quivering hand held up to silence him. 'You have been to Stalingrad? And you have returned. You know my generals tell me it is lost, that it is impossible to save it. And yet you, not even a soldier, are able to get there and back again. I knew I was right, that it could be saved. All this talk of starvation and surrender. I know my troops will fight on, and we will succeed. Didn't you see this when you were there, Schneider?'

The voice had risen in desperation. Schneider was no psychiatrist. He didn't know if this was sheer delusion or someone trying to convince themselves and others that things could be as he willed them to be. Schneider remembered the real Stalingrad, a city of lost souls and men, devoid of all hope, but he said nothing of this. That could only send Hitler into a rage, and he wanted to mention another name to him first.

'I agree, *mein Führer*. Your soldiers are fighting on, and victory will still be ours. I have seen this with my own eyes.'

He felt stupid even as he uttered these platitudes, but they seemed to be enough for Hitler. He sank back in his seat, reinvigorated that he had once again been proved right and his generals wrong.

'After Stalingrad, I had another interview with someone who had seen the secret files. I found him in Auschwitz.'

As he said the name, he watched Hitler's face as he had never watched a face before. The next few seconds would tell him everything he needed to know about what to do with the papers.

The name didn't seem to register with Hitler. Schneider repeated it. 'I said I found him in Auschwitz.'

'And what did he tell you?'

Clearly, the name meant nothing to Hitler. Schneider didn't think Hitler was another Himmler, who could hide all emotion from his face. On the contrary, he was a man driven by his emotions, by his hatred. But Schneider had to be certain.

'Do you know where Auschwitz is?'

Hitler was becoming irritated. His only interest was in the papers. 'Somewhere in Russia or Poland, I presume. What significance does that have?'

'It's where they send the Jews.'

'So, it is one of the resettlement camps out in the east. I cannot be expected to know all their names. Are you saying this man you interviewed was a Jew?'

'He was a priest, an old priest. Now he is dead. He was gassed along with a lot of other people.'

'And did he tell you about the papers before he died?'

Schneider was getting nowhere. He had to ask the question directly. 'He told me about them just before he was killed. Why are so many being killed there . . . *mein Führer*?'

He added the honorific reluctantly. He knew he wasn't dealing with a Himmler, who was deadly but rational, but someone who could easily have him killed on a whim without even thinking about it. And he had annoyed him. The Führer of the German Reich and conqueror of most of Europe and Russia wasn't used to being questioned in any way. Hitler struggled to his feet, life flashing back momentarily into his eyes.

'There is a war on. Thousands of my best young

men are dying. I cannot allow our enemies to live as we die. So, Himmler has made arrangements for all of them to be transported east. Is this where they are going, this Auschwitz?'

Schneider believed him. He didn't know the name or the details. Nor did he care. What was worse: to give the order to murder millions and leave the whole thing to others, or to actually organise it yourself? To be so detached from it that you didn't even know the name of where thousands of people were being killed every day, because of you? Schneider knew he would never have an answer, and he didn't need one. Both Hitler and Himmler were guilty of genocide in their own ways. Schneider could do business with Himmler; he was rational. That would clearly be impossible with this wreck of a man before him.

'Excuse me, *mein Führer*. I am not a soldier like you. The sight of death is still new to me. Please forgive me.'

Hitler seemed to calm down. 'So, where are the papers?'

'Heydrich kept them in a Swiss bank safety deposit box. Only he had the password and knew which bank they were held in. Without the password, those papers will remain sealed in that box for ever more. I do not believe they are a threat to you or to Germany.'

'You are certain of this, Schneider? There is no possibility of anyone else finding them? You do not know what they contain yourself?'

'No, *mein Führer*. Their contents were known only to Heydrich. When he died, they were lost for ever.'

'Perhaps not for ever, Schneider. When I have finished in the east, then I will have time to consider matters a little closer to home. The Swiss think those mountains will protect them. Nothing will protect them from my armies. And then I will find those papers. But that is for the future. In the meantime, I thank you on behalf of the German people for your efforts in this matter. Your work is now concluded.'

Again, the weak handshake and, with a supreme effort, Schneider left the room without giving the Hitler salute.

He was spared another run-in with Bormann and went back to his room. Now he had to wait for Himmler. He phoned his liaison officer in the Berghof and was told the Reichsführer had now been summoned to a meeting with the Führer. He intended to see Schneider that evening, however, and would send for him then.

To pass the time, Schneider decided to take a walk. He needed to clear his head, and he knew it was probably the last time he would ever see Germany or breathe pure German mountain air. His pass allowed him into all areas of the Obersalzberg, save only the area around the Berghof itself. It was a crisp Alpine afternoon. The temperature was well below zero and the snow sparkled under the large but impotent winter sun. He wrapped up well and set off. Sentries were everywhere. Not only was Hitler in residence, most of the Nazi top brass were also on the mountain. Absently, he wondered why it had never been bombed by the British or Americans. They knew the whole complex was here as, before the war, Hitler had brought many foreign visitors to the Berghof. Schneider still remembered the news pictures of Chamberlain making obeisance to the Führer there and claiming 'peace in our time'. If they decided to bomb it that day, they might end the war in one go. But he knew it was only wishful thinking, that he had to go on with his own plan.

The paths had been cut through the tall pine trees that shrouded the mountain slope below the complex. He could walk to Berchtesgaden if he chose, but that would take far too long. He wanted to be ready for Himmler's summons. Every ten yards or so, a sentry would magically appear from the darkness of the trees and then disappear again. Stone pillboxes dotted the path. Clearly, Hitler took good care of his own security. He heard the sound of marching and had to move aside to allow a column of SS through. It must have been a handpicked squad, for every man was at least six feet tall and clearly athletic. They carried large packs on their backs, and rifles and machine pistols over their shoulders. They ignored Schneider, keeping in perfect step. Their officer gave him a curt nod as he passed.

Something, almost at the subconscious level, registered with Schneider. Perhaps it was his years of police work that had disciplined his brain to recognise anything unusual. And something was unusual here, but he couldn't quite figure it out. He looked at the backs of the disappearing SS men but nothing specific struck him. He continued with his walk and thought no more about it.

He walked on for another fifteen minutes or so and then turned to go back. The sun was disappearing behind the mountains and the temperature was plummeting towards arctic levels. He had already passed several sentries when it struck him. When he came to the next sentry, he stopped.

'Which regiment do you belong to?'

The sentry came to attention. Anyone with the authority to wander the Obersalzberg required to be treated with respect. 'The Leibstandarte Adolf Hitler. We act as the Führer's bodyguard.'

'And no other regiment would do this?'

'No, sir. We are his lifeguards. That is why we are the only regiment to bear his name on our sleeve.' He held out his arm to show Schneider the silver ribbon bearing his regiment's name.

Schneider thanked him and hurried back to the hotel. What he had noticed on the other SS regiment's sleeves was the standard of the Totenkopf, the Death's Head regiment. And their first loyalty was to Himmler, not Hitler. It had also been that regiment's band playing in the town square when he arrived. Himmler appeared to be building up the presence of his own loyal troops in the area. Suddenly, it hit him like a splash of cold water to the face. Himmler was planning a coup. All the Nazi leaders were here on this remote mountain top. They were effectively cut off from outside help. Himmler would only need a small number of his own troops to capture or even kill all of them. After that, all the SS troops on the mountain would follow his orders as the new leader of Germany.

Schneider had to admire the plan. It was so typical of Himmler: cold, logical and completely unexpected. It was bound to succeed. Then an even more terrible truth dawned on him. If it did succeed, Himmler wouldn't need Heydrich's papers any longer. Schneider pounded his head with his fist. He wasn't cut out to deal with political intrigues on this scale. But he alone had to decide what to do now, for there was no one else. He had to make the right decision, not for himself, but for the tens of thousands already heading to the extermination camps in the east. His first inclination was to run, to try to get back to Switzerland. Let Hitler and Himmler fight it out. But without a pass, without Hitler's letter, which had already been taken from him after the meeting, he had no chance of getting across the frontier. He knew that wasn't the right thing to do anyway; it was only his desire to live a little longer. He could still influence events.

But what to do? He could tell Hitler or even Bormann of his suspicions. They would no doubt think him deluded, but in Nazi Germany, they would check. That should be enough to stop Himmler and probably to finish him. He reached for the phone then stopped. Maybe it was already too late. Even if he told them now, Himmler might have enough men here to go ahead anyway. He wished he understood politicians' minds better. What should he do? His brain felt as if it was about to explode.

Then he remembered a chance remark he had overheard when leaving Hitler's office. One of the secretaries had commented about the Reichsmarschall only arriving tomorrow morning because of bad weather. Schneider had his breathing space. Himmler wouldn't strike until Göring was here as well. After all, wasn't Göring Hitler's chosen successor? For the coup to succeed, Himmler needed to get him as well. Now Schneider only had to work out how to turn this to his advantage. He lay down on the bed and closed his eyes. He always thought better this way. When the phone rang, an hour had passed. Himmler was ready for him now. He hoped he was also ready for Himmler.

337

19

Obersalzberg, later that day

Himmler appeared not to have a care in the world. His greeting to Schneider was almost warm, as if they were old acquaintances. He even indulged in a little small talk. Schneider was instantly worried. Himmler wasn't a man; he was a calculating machine who didn't do anything without some purpose. Schneider knew he was about to get some bad news.

'So, Schneider, have you come to your decision about the papers? I understand you had your meeting with the Führer earlier today. As I haven't been arrested yet, I must presume you did not give him this . . . ah . . . information you have about me.'

Himmler was actually smiling. He was finding it hugely amusing. Schneider decided to hit back.

'Is that why you have so many of your own men here? Were you worried I might tell him that?'

The smile froze on Himmler's face. 'What do you mean "my own men"?'

'I saw the Totenkopf regiment in the village and here on the mountain. Is that usual?'

Himmler was wary but reasoned he was still safe. It was too late for Schneider, for anyone, to interfere now. 'My compliments on your excellent powers of observation, Schneider. But you worry unnecessarily. I thought it prudent to have extra security, with all the leaders of the Reich being in one place. Did you think I had some other motive?'

Himmler stared quizzically at him, watching for any reaction. To sit or to raise. The poker game between them was starting again. In a way, it had started as soon as Schneider had been appointed to investigate Heydrich's death and had never stopped since. Both men knew this was the end game. Schneider decided to bluff and to raise again.

'You forget, I know about your correspondence with B. It's still not too late for me to stop you.'

Himmler's mask slipped. He had become too used to instant obedience and couldn't tolerate a direct threat. The thin lips curled back into a fearful snarl. So, there was some emotion there, thought Schneider.

'I think you overestimate your strength. If I had you shot this instant, do you think your papers would bother me then? By the time they were used – assuming there is actually something there to use – it would be too late. I think you have unwittingly given me the answer of how I should deal with you.'

Schneider didn't know if he was bluffing or not. A man like Himmler wouldn't hesitate to kill him if he thought it was the expedient course of action.

Schneider tried to remain calm, to hide his true feelings. It was like being in a room with a tiger that might pounce at any moment. So, he played his ace. He could only hope it wasn't too soon.

'You cannot act until tomorrow at the earliest. I know that Göring won't be here until then. And if I don't make contact with my associates tonight, the papers will be with Hitler before you can act.'

It was all nonsense and bluff. Himmler would almost be certain of that. But he couldn't be 100 per cent certain, and that alone would be enough to check him now he was so close. Schneider fervently hoped so, for he had no other card to play if Himmler raised the game again.

'My dear Schneider, I was only making a small joke at your expense. Why should I think of killing you? I hope we can come to an amicable arrangement about the papers. And as for your so-called associate, I now understand much more about your motives and hers. Being Jewish must be a terrible burden to bear.'

'I don't know what—'

'Please don't try to deny it. I know all about her background now. I suppose that was why Heydrich kept her. Her secret meant she was his tool, although as you probably know, there are some who say he had Jewish blood himself. Personally, I never believed those rumours. You have seen what Heydrich has organised for the Jews out east.'

The threat was implicit but clear. Anna was in

danger. With a sudden clarity, Schneider realised that was something he couldn't allow to happen. He realised if it came to a choice between Anna and people being exterminated in Auschwitz, there could be only one winner. It was something he couldn't rationalise because his feelings for her went beyond that. He just knew he would do anything to protect her. His emotions had been torn asunder. From the guilty years of self-denial, through the awakening rage and anger at Auschwitz, he had finally reached a level that surpassed all other feelings he had ever known. The simple and overwhelming love of one human being for another that outweighed everything else in the balance. As quickly as this realisation dawned, he also saw its danger. This was his one Achilles heel, and if Himmler ever found out, he was lost.

'Leave her out of it. I still don't know why you and the rest of the Nazis hate the Jews. Maybe you can hate something as a concept or a thing, but to take that hate and apply it to every individual man, woman and child is something I cannot fathom. But it doesn't matter any more. If I give you the papers, what guarantee do I have that you will stop the killings?'

Himmler pursed his lips, thinking. As was his habit at such moments of tension, he started to polish his glasses.

'I can give you my word, my oath as an SS officer. But I suppose that would hardly satisfy you. So, what else can I offer? Nothing, except for one thing. The reason you are talking to me and not the Führer is simple. You have correctly deduced that the Führer will never stop this war until he has won. We both know that will not happen now. So, you are talking to me as the only rational hope for stopping this war. I am rational. It would be madness to continue and risk the complete destruction of Germany. So, that is your guarantee, is it not?'

'And what if the Allies refuse to accept your terms? I know they have been calling for unconditional surrender.'

'That is true, but it only applies to the current leadership. I have already made informal contacts, which lead me to believe that a successful negotiation of the end of hostilities is possible. Nobody wants to fight a war. And remember B.'

Himmler had thrown it in so casually. Now he was studying Schneider to see his reaction. What did he really know about B?

Schneider thought he might have a future as a poker player, after all. He kept any suggestion of lack of knowledge from his face. 'I hadn't forgotten. But any plan might fail, even B's.'

'He is even more careful than me, and with good reason. At least the Führer trusts me, as much as he trusts anybody. So, you can be certain that his part of the plan will work.'

It was a clue, and Himmler had made a mistake. This was back in Schneider's domain. That great police mind started to work. It felt good to do what he had been put on this Earth to do, as no one else in Germany could. In less than a minute, he had B.'s identity. And more than that, he saw the great weakness in Himmler's plan. He wondered if Himmler had also seen it. But his face gave nothing away.

'You're right. I have to trust you because there's no one else.'

'Trust is, however, a two-edged sword. I also have to trust you to deliver the originals of Heydrich's papers. I want your word that no copies have been made and that you will never reveal their contents. I should say that after tomorrow, your knowledge of B. will be irrelevant, as far as I am concerned.'

'And what guarantee can I give you? Presumably my word will not be enough?'

'Strangely enough, I would almost be happy to rely on your word. I know you keep it. So, give me your word. But I will add a penalty clause if you like. If you break it, Anna Weiss will pay the price. Do you understand?'

'There is no need for threats. I give you my word I will never reveal the contents of the papers, nor will I keep any copies.'

Schneider knew he could keep his word, for it did not prevent Anna from revealing the papers' contents. If only he had realised, Himmler must have known this as well.

'Excellent. It only remains for you to hand them over.'

'As you undoubtedly know, the papers are in Switzerland. I will return there now and hand them into the German consulate in Basel. I presume you have someone there who can take them on your behalf. After I have given you the papers, I have no protection against you. It would be foolish of me to return to Germany.'

'You really do not need to fear for your safety, Schneider. However, I can understand your reluctance to come back here. Particularly as we now know about Miss Weiss's racial problem. But I do not want anyone getting their hands on those papers, unless it is someone I trust.' He tapped his fingers on the desk, his forehead creased in thought. Then he smiled; an answer had occurred to him. 'I will send one of my men to Switzerland with you. He will take delivery of the papers directly from you there. That way, we are both safe.'

A warning bell was sounding furiously in Schneider's brain. What was Himmler up to? He knew things weren't as Himmler was portraying them, that a danger was lurking. But he couldn't work it out; it wasn't something his police brain could solve. He had to agree, and Himmler picked up the phone.

'Send Standartenführer Heizmann in.'

Himmler must have noticed Schneider's look of surprise. It seemed to please him, and he became almost like a schoolmaster talking to a struggling student. 'Yes, it is him. He is one of my most trusted men. At least, that is what he thinks. This way I will find out who he is really working for, who told him to have Heydrich killed. I always like to kill two birds with one stone if I can. I think you deserve to know as well, after all your efforts.' Himmler's smile grew wider. 'Perhaps you want to leave me a forwarding address?'

Schneider ignored the jibe. He ignored the clue Himmler had unconsciously given him. He fell into the trap.

'But if he gets these papers, how do you know he won't pass them on to someone else?'

'That would be stupid, and he is not stupid. He will read them and then plan to pass the information on to his real master. So, he will bring them back to me. He won't risk any delay or a phone call on an open line from Switzerland. I will have an escort waiting for him at the border to bring him directly to me. All I need do then is to monitor his phone. The first call he makes will be to Heydrich's killer.'

Schneider could admire the plan as a professional. It was brilliant. Build up Heizmann's confidence that he was absolutely trusted. And then when he least expected it, the roof falls in. Except for one thing. Schneider knew that Himmler had ordered Heydrich's death. But that was only based on his instincts. They had never failed him in the past, but did he *really* know? Maybe the experiences of the last few weeks had dulled his instincts; maybe he wasn't the man he had been. Could it be that Himmler was telling the truth, that he really hadn't ordered Heydrich's death? It was the only explanation that appeared to make any sense to his increasingly confused mind.

'But he will still know what the papers contain.'

Himmler gave him a knowing look. Heizmann would never get the chance to pass his knowledge on. Schneider understood.

Himmler smiled. It was like playing with a child. What would Schneider think if he knew what he had just told him was complete and utter fiction? He had a very different purpose in mind for Heizmann.

Heizmann entered, and Himmler made the introductions. Schneider couldn't help but feel sorry for the man. But then again, he was also the man who had arranged Heydrich's death and killed the Czech assassin. Schneider decided he was beyond trying to apportion blame in this world. Perhaps it could only be truly meted out in the next.

The meeting moved quickly to a close. He told Himmler he no longer had the Hitler letter. Himmler said he would arrange the necessary passes for the trip to Switzerland. He wanted Heizmann back with the papers as soon as possible tomorrow and asked them to set off immediately.

'I do not suppose we will meet again, Schneider. I think it is better that way.'

Schneider sighed. The veiled threat right to the end. The sooner he got to Switzerland, the better. But before he could relax, he had another problem to deal with. How was he going to deal with Heizmann when he found out that Schneider couldn't get access to the papers?

Heizmann had stood quietly by as Himmler made his farewells. Now he led Schneider to the car that was already waiting. It took less than five minutes for Schneider to collect his bags. Heizmann drove the large, powerful car expertly down through the series of hairpin bends that led from the Obersalzberg to Berchtesgaden. Schneider let him concentrate on his driving. Already the roads were covered in a skin of ice that demanded total attention. They passed through the final security check point just outside Berchtesgaden, and Heizmann accelerated to as fast a speed as he dared on these roads. He spoke to Schneider for the first time.

'I will drive to the Swiss border. You can give me directions after that.'

It was a statement that neither required nor requested a response. Schneider studied the man beside him. He had an almost animal quality to him. It was like being in the car with a wolf which at any moment could turn and savage you. Schneider saw the large muscular arms and chest that spoke of his physical prowess. But there was something else, almost like a scent that poured off this man. It was the odour of the hunter in the jungle, of the top predator, that warned everything that crossed its path to beware. Himmler had given off a coldness, as if he had no feelings at all. This man gave off a heat, a heat that spoke of his pleasure in killing, and killing as painfully as possible. If he had still been a police officer, Schneider would have wanted this man committed to the nearest psychiatric hospital. He had seen many psychopaths in his long career. He thought back to the young man who had jumped from his window earlier that year. But he had been driven to the brink of his sanity by something outside himself. This man's psychosis came from deep within. Schneider realised he was afraid of him.

He would have been more afraid if he could have read the man's thoughts. Heizmann was what he was, but he was also very intelligent. He had served the Reichsführer well, and in return Himmler tolerated his more bizarre tastes. He had been given very specific instructions about his job. He must, under all circumstances, recover the papers. He could use such means as he determined necessary to achieve this. His second priority was the death of Schneider. Himmler could not have someone with his knowledge on the loose. After the papers were recovered, Schneider became a risk that had to go. His last task was to find the Jewess, Weiss. She too had to die. Who knows what she might know? In any event, she was a Jew. Himmler had told him he could do with her what he wanted before she died. Heizmann had admired the photograph Himmler had shown him. He was already looking forward to making her acquaintance.

The fastest way to Switzerland was along the German autobahns. So, Heizmann took them back towards Munich and then along the shore of the Bodensee. They reached Schaffhausen in the early hours of the morning. Heizmann's papers saw them past the German border guards, and the usual payment for visas saw them into Switzerland.

Heizmann drove until they were out of sight of the border post. 'Where do we go from here?'

Schneider had dreaded this moment coming. He had thought of taking him to Kandersteg, where at least Sutter would be there to help him. But that would expose Anna's whereabouts to Himmler. And he knew he didn't want this brute of a man anywhere near her. At some point on the journey, he had finally made up his mind. He didn't know when or how he had finally arrived at the decision, but he now knew he wasn't handing over the papers to Heizmann. That was another reason for keeping Anna's whereabouts secret. So that left him alone with Heizmann. It was him and no one else. He had, at best, until the banks opened before Heizmann became suspicious. Schneider knew what he had to do, but couldn't. He would keep him driving for now.

'Take the road to Bern.'

'Is that where the papers are?'

'Just drive. I'll tell you what you need to know when you need to know it.'

There was no sense in showing someone like

Heizmann fear. But Schneider knew a predator like him could probably smell it, perhaps even expect it as his right.

'And is that where Anna Weiss is?'

A shudder ran through Schneider when he mentioned her name. But it made up his mind about what he had to do. He had finally reached the last card in the deck.

The roads in Switzerland were even icier than in Germany. It was dark and Heizmann was unfamiliar with them. Even his driving skills were being tested to the limit. It was going to take a long time to get to Bern.

Schneider must have dozed off. The tension, the sheer never-ending strain of the past days and weeks had finally taken their toll. He was exhausted both mentally and physically. He was woken by Heizmann shoving him roughly.

'Bern is just ahead. Where do I go there?'

Schneider looked at his watch. It was almost six o'clock. Time had run out for him, and fear gnawed at his reason. Despite himself, despite what he had promised to do, he knew he needed help. He couldn't deal with this man alone. Only Sutter could help him now, but he couldn't expose Anna to the man beside him. Instinctively he made a decision that kept his options open for now.

'We don't go into Bern. Take the road for Spiez and then after that to Kandersteg.'

'I thought the papers were in a bank?'

'I never said that. They are somewhere very safe. After all, had you ever heard of Kandersteg before I told you just now?'

Heizmann made no reply. He started driving again. It would take less than two hours to reach Kandersteg. Schneider's brain was racing, but it wasn't getting anywhere.

Kandersteg, Christmas Eve

Afterwards, Schneider would never know if he could have done it if Heizmann hadn't started talking to him. He remembered what Himmler had planned for this man. No one should ever be in the power of that monster. So, Schneider had made a terrible mistake: he treated Heizmann as a human being. Even worse, he believed Heinrich Himmler.

'What do you plan to do after all this?' Heizmann asked. 'Are you going to stay here in Switzerland?'

'I think you know as well as I do that I cannot go back to Germany.'

'You could, you know. I have worked for the Reichsführer for a long time. I think you can trust him.'

Schneider laughed out loud. 'You can't really mean that, can you?'

'I do. Look at us now. He has let you go, hasn't he? He could have kept you there and tried to find the papers himself or used your life as a bargaining chip against the papers. But he trusted you to give them to me. He trusts me to bring them to him. Doesn't that show he can be trusted?'

'And after you bring them to him, what do you think will happen then?'

'What do you mean?'

'Well, do you think he'll trust you sufficiently not to have read the papers yourself?'

'I won't read them. Some people are nosy and learn things they shouldn't. But I know better than that. I deliberately don't find things out. It is much safer that way in my job.'

'And what is your job exactly?'

'I am a soldier. I do whatever I am told to do.'

Schneider said it before he realised it. 'Including killing Heydrich?'

'Why do you think I did that?'

'Listen, there is no need to lie now. I am finished in Germany. But I know you organised the killing and the clean-up afterwards. So does Himmler. But I would really like to know who gave the order – just to satisfy my professional pride, if you will.'

'I don't know what you are talking about.'

Schneider was impressed with the man's ability to stick to a story. He really was a true professional. But then he didn't know what Schneider knew.

'Maybe I can help you. Tell me what I want to know, and I'll tell you something you might want to hear, something that might save your life.'

352

Heizmann was looking at him very strangely. Schneider wondered if he had gone too far, to risk maybe everything to try to help this man. But it was too late now. Heizmann studied him a few seconds longer and then spoke.

'I don't think there is anything you could tell me that would do that. But let's see. The Reichsführer himself gave me the order.'

Schneider retorted immediately. 'I know that isn't true because Himmler told me why he really sent you here. He knows you are working for somebody else, and he intends to trap you on your return. That piece of information will save your life. So, what do you want to tell me now?'

Heizmann was used to Himmler's deceptions. He had seen many people before Schneider fall headfirst into one of Himmler's traps. Heizmann worked for Himmler and for nobody else. He trusted Himmler because he knew his value to the Reichsführer. So, this must be part of Himmler's plan. What an idiot this man was to tell him this. No wonder Himmler had found him so easy to manipulate. A fool like this deserved to die. But then another thought struck him. Even a fool wouldn't tell him this and then give him the papers. So, what was Schneider planning?

They had almost reached the steep road up to Kandersteg. Heizmann slowed even further, his instincts now finely tuned.

'Before I tell you anything else, tell me where the papers are.'

Schneider nodded at the sign up ahead pointing in the direction of the Blue Lake. 'Turn off there.'

Heizmann pulled off the road and drove down to the lake. It lay in a small valley whose natural beauty was concentrated even further by the majestic circle of Alps that guarded it. Early on a bitterly cold winter's morning, it was deserted. Half the lake was frozen, but the other half showed why it had been given its name. It was the bluest water either man had ever seen.

Schneider had thought of the plan at Bern. It was the best he could come up with. He would bring Heizmann here and try to reason with him. He would tell him about Himmler's plans for him. He would tell him the papers weren't there. If all else failed, it was as good a spot as any to dispose of Heizmann once and for all. But he knew he was less than four miles from Kandersteg, from Sutter. Subconsciously, that must have been why he picked this place. It still gave him a second option. It was an option he had to constantly fight against.

When Heizmann cut the engine, the silence was almost absolute, broken only by the plaintive cry of a solitary bird. Heizmann turned to him, more wolf-like than ever. 'And now?'

'Now I tell you the truth. I have already told you what Himmler intends to do to you when you return. If you choose to disbelieve me, that is your own look-out. But I will not be giving you the papers to pass on to him. The papers aren't even here. I only wanted to get out of Germany. I have given you the same chance.'

He studied Heizmann to see his reaction. Anger at being duped? Worry about what he would tell Himmler? What he didn't expect was laughter.

'So, you think you can just walk away and let me do the same. I think it is time I cleared up some confusion for you. First of all, I have only ever worked for the Reichsführer. He ordered Heydrich's death, as I have already told you. I suppose he told you a story about me working for someone else and him trying to find out who it is? He has used that before. It's quite good for making people believe him and maybe even feel a little sorry for me. And it worked a treat on you, didn't it?'

Schneider had received a few revelations in these last few days and now he was getting another. His mind was in tatters. He knew he was out of his depth in dealing with these people, but Heizmann hadn't finished.

'I was given two things to do before I left Germany with you. One was to get the papers back, and that is what I am going to do.'

The gun had appeared by some sleight of hand and now pointed squarely at Schneider's chest.

'If you kill me, you'll never get the papers.'

'I don't think so. You want to know why? Because

someone else knows where they are, don't they? I'll just need to ask your girlfriend, won't I?'

Schneider felt the panic starting to rise. Against Heizmann, Anna would be helpless.

'But you'll never find her.'

'Again, that is possible, but unlikely. For you know where she is, and you'll tell me. Why? Because you are the second thing I have to do. So, it can either be easy or hard. I hope you decide it's to be hard.'

Heizmann licked his lips in anticipation. There could be no doubting he meant every word. Schneider had no option left. He knew it was useless, but he lunged for this monster opposite him.

'You bastard, I'll tell you nothing.'

Heizmann had heard it all before. The pistol cracked against the side of Schneider's head.

When he awoke, Schneider's first impression was one of cold – deep, deep cold. He realised he was lying down and tried to get up but found he couldn't move his hands. They seemed to be stuck to his sides. He lifted his head and looked down at his body. It was naked, which explained the intense cold he felt. He saw the rope running round his chest and arms, pinioning them to his side and the board he was tied to. Heizmann was sitting on a fence smoking a cigarette. He noticed the movement and crushed it out.

'So, you're back with us again. Excellent. I have been busy while you had your little nap. Do you see where we are?'

He pulled Schneider to his feet as if he were a child. They were on the small jetty at the water's edge. He dragged Schneider forward as he spoke.

'Please take as long as you want to tell me where the papers are. As you might have realised by now, I enjoy this. I always have, for as far back as I can remember. It started with pulling the legs off frogs, then crucifying birds and then torturing cats and dogs. I was good at it. I could keep them alive for days, studying how far I could go, where the most pain came from. Then the Reichsführer found me.'

Nothing in Schneider's time in the police had prepared him for this. Consciously, he knew Heizmann was only trying to add to his terror. But his unconscious mind refused to listen. He was terrified. Heizmann set the board down halfway over the edge of the jetty. He picked up the end of the board and plunged Schneider headfirst into the water, using his head to smash through the film of ice on its surface.

Exposure to extreme cold causes a reflex gasping action. The rational brain is unable to prevent this, and Schneider gasped as the water closed over him. The clear blue water poured into his lungs, almost stopping his heart. It was beyond endurance, and so another reflex came to his rescue. He blacked out.

When he came to, he was shivering uncontrollably. He could feel nothing from the waist down. A pool of water had formed by the side of his head where he had coughed and spluttered his way back to consciousness.

And Heizmann was back on his fence, another cigarette between his lips.

'Welcome back. That was an old technique I learned in my Gestapo days before the Reichsführer recognised my true value. I'm sure that a fine, upstanding police officer like you would never have had any experience of such things, so I'll explain how it works. I ask you a question. If you don't answer, in you go. When you recover, I ask you the same question. If you don't answer, in you go. And so on and so forth until either you answer, or I get it wrong and you drown. They say that drowning is a pleasant death. My experiences have led me to the opposite conclusion. Perhaps we can discuss it later, for the great benefit of this technique is that you drown over and over again. It's wonderful, isn't it? So, shall we start? I don't want you dying of the cold on me. Where are the papers?'

*

Three times Schneider was plunged into the icy waters and revived. The last time took several minutes and the appliance of Heizmann's boot to his ribs. Clearly, he wasn't going to live much longer. Despite Heizmann's show of confidence, he couldn't let that happen. His first priority was the papers. He decided to have one last go.

'I don't think you'll survive another time in the water, do you? So, why don't you tell me and save

358

yourself any more suffering. If you do, I promise I won't harm the girl when I find her.'

Maybe it was the mention of Anna that reached far down into what was left of Schneider's sanity. For a moment the veil of pain was drawn aside. Incredibly, the old priest came into his mind again. Was this worth dying for? He knew it was and that he didn't have much more suffering to go. But could he die and leave Anna behind with Heizmann searching for her? He knew he would find her. The SS had plenty of money and that was all that was needed in Switzerland to get someone to talk. Even Sutter wouldn't be able to prevent it. Somehow, he had to stop this man. And somehow, through all the pain, he now knew something else. He needed to stay alive long enough to do one other thing. He croaked to Heizmann, his lungs on fire with the effort.

'No more. No more. I'll take you to the papers. They're with Anna Weiss. But for God's sake, get me some clothing before I freeze to death first.'

Heizmann finished his cigarette. He pulled Schneider upright and cut the rope. He had to support him. Roughly, he dried the almost dead man with an old sheet from the car and pushed him into his clothes. He threw him in the front seat of the car and turned the heater up to maximum. Schneider believed he might live. Heizmann opened the glove compartment and pulled out a bottle. He stuck it between Schneider's chattering teeth and poured neat schnapps into him.

He gagged and coughed, but he felt the life-giving heat. He would live, but for how much longer?

He told Heizmann to drive to the village. A few people were on the streets bundled up against the weather. Schneider didn't have the strength for anything else. He was shivering like a man with advanced hypothermia. He told Heizmann how to get to the farm. The tyres crunched in the snow as he pulled up outside. Heizmann didn't need to threaten any longer. Both of them knew very clearly what would happen if this was another trick. Heizmann pulled him from the car and rammed his pistol into his spine. He kept close behind Schneider when he rapped on the door. Anna opened it, a look of shock spreading over her face when she saw the state of Schneider.

Heizmann thrust him into her, sending them both sprawling. By the time they had untangled themselves, the door was shut and Heizmann had already checked that no one else was hiding in the room. Anna was trying to pull the almost unconscious Schneider into a chair when Heizmann drove the barrel of his pistol hard into Schneider's cheek.

'One chance and one chance only to save his life. Is there anyone else in this house?'

Heizmann had terrorised so many in his life he knew exactly the reactions to look for.

'Please don't hurt him any more. There's no one else here.'

Heizmann heard the desperation in the voice, but

that wasn't what he was waiting for. It was the eyes that held the truth in such situations and, despite herself, Anna's eyes darted to the door opposite. In a flash, Heizmann had her by the throat and propelled her headfirst through the door. For a moment there was silence and then he heard it.

He followed her into the unlit room, his torch probing, the barrel of his pistol following the beam. He saw nothing but still the noise continued, and then his nose gave him the answer. The sweet smell of goats assailed him. Expertly his eyes searched every corner, every shadow, but the small barn held only the inquisitive goats. There was nowhere for anybody to hide. He grabbed Anna off the floor and pulled her back into the living room. Why had she glanced there? Heizmann had stayed alive for so long by always relying on his instincts and by always checking. Very carefully, very slowly, he quartered the room again with his torch, but there was nothing. Maybe he had been mistaken, or maybe this Jew loved goats. Either way, there was nothing. He slammed the door shut and was standing over Schneider as Anna again tried to pull him into a chair.

'So, you are Anna Weiss. Your photograph doesn't do you justice.'

The terror in Anna Weiss's throat silenced the scream that never came. Try as she might, she couldn't take her eyes off this monster. It was her worst nightmare come to life. But Heizmann was a professional, first and foremost. He looked at Schneider.

'Give me the papers and I'll put you out of your misery. But before you go, there's one other thing you should know. I lied about having only two things to do in Switzerland. There is a third. I have to – how shall I say? – take care of your girlfriend as well. And I can tell you, I'll really enjoy that.'

Schneider didn't know what had gone wrong. It had been the last thing he had planned with Sutter. It had even been Sutter's idea. They had tried to plan for every eventuality, for everything that Himmler might try. As a last resort, Sutter had suggested that he could somehow force Schneider to bring one of his men here. Schneider had said he would never do that, no matter what happened, but Sutter maybe had a greater knowledge of men's weaknesses and the depths of terror that Himmler and his minions could mine. So, they had agreed that if Schneider ever turned up here with anyone else, it would be because he was under duress and that person would be an enemy. Schneider had insisted it would never happen, but then he hadn't met Heizmann at that time nor been in the Blue Lake. Sutter had assured him that if it did happen, he would be here to protect Anna. And now, when he needed him most, when Sutter had been proved right about his own weakness, he had disappeared.

Schneider tried to struggle to his feet, but Heizmann back-handed him down again. Schneider had all the strength of a puppy.

'How would you feel if I enjoyed myself with this

Jew in front of you? Do you think you would like that? Well, let's see.'

Heizmann grabbed Anna by the hair and pulled her face close to his. 'Now you're going to find out what a real man can do for you. Take your clothes off.'

Schneider was starting to black out. Blood was pounding in his ears, stars dancing before his eyes. He had caused this because he was weak. Why had he brought this monster here? His last conscious thought was about Sutter. He should be here, he had promised.

Anna was trying to get away from Heizmann's steel grip. He seemed to find it even more exciting. He was talking almost to himself.

'That's it, pretty girl. You keep fighting. I like it better that way. Maybe I won't kill you right away; maybe I can keep you for a few days. We'll see. But for—'

His words were cut off. Some animal instinct alerted him to a hidden danger. He spun round in the direction of the danger, trying to pull Anna in front of him. But he was too late. Sutter's head was poking out of the trap door leading to the tiny storage room above the barn. It was too small for a man to climb through but was just big enough for Sutter's head. And his revolver. He had always been an excellent shot and Heizmann was dead before he had completed half his turn.

*

Sutter used brandy and coffee to warm and revive Schneider. Anna had fainted, out of terror, and needed the same treatment. By the time both of them recovered, Sutter had pulled Heizmann's body out of sight. All three tried to speak at once, in the way that people do who have just survived some dreadful experience together. Sutter held up his hand for silence.

'One at a time. I will go first, as I think you two need more brandy first.'

He refilled their glasses and poured some for himself.

'My God, Rolf, but I never want to do anything like that again. I must have aged ten years in the last thirty minutes.'

Schneider couldn't restrain himself. 'For God's sake, where were you?'

'I was here all the time. We saw your car coming and that you had company. I know what we had agreed. But you never said you were going to bring Himmler's most lethal assassin with you. None of us are any match for him. If he knew I was here, we would all have been killed. I couldn't tackle him head on, so as you were struggling out of the car, I hid in the little room in the barn roof. It's too small for anyone to notice unless they really know the house. And as you now know, it has this little trap door leading back into here. I had just managed to get into it when our friend arrived. We have known about him for years in the Swiss Special Branch. We know he has carried out at least four killings in Switzerland. We'll never know now, but I think he was probably the man who tried to kill your soldier in Stalingrad. His skill and brutality are legendary. I knew I would get one chance, and one chance only. I prayed that Anna wouldn't give the game away before then.'

He turned to Anna, who was now well on the way to recovery.

'I'm sorry I had to let you go through that. But I had to wait until I was sure he was distracted enough to give me a chance. You saw how he sensed the trap door opening. I would only get the one shot. He would have used you as a shield after that. So, I had to make certain his attention was elsewhere for that vital fraction of a second.'

'Don't apologise. You've saved all our lives. I don't think I'll ever be able to thank you enough.'

She rushed over to Sutter and threw her arms around him. The old man seemed almost embarrassed.

'Schneider will only get jealous if you carry on like this. And that's not good for him in his condition. Do you think he's well enough to tell us his story now?'

Schneider was well enough. Quickly he told them what had happened at the Obersalzberg. He left out what had happened at the Blue Lake. It was still too fresh in his mind. But this wasn't a time for telling stories. Time was too vital for that, and his watch had been ruined by the water.

'What time is it?'

'Just after nine o'clock.'

'Sutter, you've got to help me. I've got to get through

to Himmler before it's too late. Is there any way I can do that?'

For a moment, Sutter thought his old friend was still suffering the after-effects of what had happened to him. But his voice carried the desperation of absolute necessity.

'We could go to the police station. I still have enough authority to get you a priority line to Germany. Whether you can get Himmler is up to you after that.'

'He'll speak to me, this morning of all mornings. Let's go.'

Obersalzberg, Christmas Eve

Göring's plane had landed at Munich. He was expected at the Berghof within the hour. Then everything would be in place. No one had apparently noticed the number of aides that Himmler needed for this visit to the Berghof. That very morning, another four had arrived, bringing urgent dispatches to him. Like everyone else, they were searched and relieved of their weapons. But a few were spared the security checks. Himmler was one of these few. His unchecked bags contained enough machine pistols to allow his aides to take over the Berghof until the Totenkopf regiment arrived. Now all he had to do was wait for news. He had told one of his most trusted liaison officers to keep his radio tuned to an unusual frequency. The man was a fluent Russian speaker and understood every word of the news broadcasts he was hearing from Moscow.

More than a thousand miles away, B. was also listening to a radio broadcast. His broadcast came from Berlin.

Kandersteg, Christmas Eve

Sutter's authority had barely been enough to get him his international call. Switzerland was a place of regulation, a conservative country. Anything unusual was to be considered at leisure and proper authority obtained. It was also time to go home and celebrate Christmas. At one point, Schneider had thought Sutter was going to produce his gun again. But the young police officer had been persuaded by the sheer power of Sutter's personality and his well-known reputation. And now the phone was ringing in Germany, at the central Munich telephone exchange.

'This is Chief Investigator Schneider phoning from Switzerland on a matter of the utmost importance. I must be put through to the Berghof, the Führer's residence, immediately.'

In some countries, this would have been considered a crank call. Not in Nazi Germany. 'Please hold for my superior.'

Time seemed to drag but eventually a more authoritative voice came on. 'What is your authority for the Berghof, please?'

Schneider tried for ten minutes. But without a definite authority he was getting nowhere. The best the telephonist would do was contact the Berghof and advise them of his call. If she received confirmation that his call would be accepted, he could phone back later that day. By then it would be too late.

He didn't know where the inspiration came from, but just as he was about to put the phone down in defeat, it came to him. 'Can you put me through to Munich airport?'

'That is not a problem. Please hold.'

He gave his name and asked for the commanding officer. He prayed it was the same one who had already seen his letter from Hitler. It was.

'Has the Reichsmarschall arrived yet?'

'Yes, Chief Investigator. His plane arrived a few minutes ago. He is just about to leave for Obersalzberg.'

'Stop him immediately. That is a direct order from me, acting on the Führer's behalf. Tell him he must speak to me before he departs. Do it now. I will hold.'

He heard the sound of running feet and shouts. Minutes passed in silence. Then he heard heavy footsteps and the receiver being lifted.

'This is Reichsmarschall Göring. What is so urgent, Schneider?'

Epilogue

Reichsmarschall Hermann Göring was unavoidably delayed in Munich that Christmas Eve. It was Christmas Day before he reached the Berghof. He had gone along with Schneider's urgent request. He didn't know why it was imperative he stay away for one more day, but he could guess. He hadn't reached the top in Nazi Germany without having that sixth sense for survival. He knew he had no evidence, no proof, and probably never would have. But that didn't matter. He only knew that he had somehow thwarted Himmler in one of his schemes, and that was enough for him.

Himmler had left the Berghof with his aides. The Totenkopf regiment returned to its barracks. It was as if nothing had ever happened.

Heizmann paid a final visit to the Blue Lake. Weighted with stones, Schneider himself had dropped his body from the rowing boat. But it gave him no satisfaction. And then he and his old friend had gone back to the warmth of the house and Anna. She still didn't know the whole story, so after dinner Schneider had filled in the blanks.

'I knew the moment I saw that gas chamber in Auschwitz that I had to stop it somehow. I was going to give the papers to Himmler so he could get rid of Hitler and stop the war. But in that last meeting with him, I realised he was lying. Not about stopping the war; he would certainly do that if he could. But about the Jews. He would need to carry on until all of them were gone and all trace of the camps had disappeared. It was the only way he could safeguard himself. So, I thought about giving the papers to Hitler. That would have stopped Himmler. Only I was too late. If I had given the papers to Hitler that night, I think that Himmler would still have tried to seize power. He would have been a dead man, so what would he have had to lose? And I think he would have succeeded. He thought the papers would guarantee his success.

'But the only way to save as many people as possible from the camps is for Germany to be defeated. With Hitler leading them, that will happen sooner rather than later because he is already half insane. He interferes with every operation and still believes he has great armies at his disposal. So, Germany will lose the war and only then will the camps close.

'If Himmler had become leader, he would have tried to negotiate a peace. But only until Germany had built her strength up again, and then he would launch an even worse war. And all the time the gas chambers would still be working. So, I decided in the end that no one should get the papers.'

'But couldn't we publish them abroad?'

'We could try. But what good would that do? It wouldn't affect Hitler or Himmler's position in Germany.'

'You could tell them about the gas chambers.'

'And Germany would deny it. They're already at war. What more could they do?'

'But isn't the truth important for truth's sake?' Anna was getting upset. She wanted the suffering of her people to be known.

'Truth is all that matters ultimately. And the truth about the camps will be known after Germany is defeated. But there is another reason for keeping the papers secret. You're forgetting about B.'

Sutter smiled and knocked his pipe into the fire. He had also worked out who B. was. Now he knew why the papers had to stay secret.

'Who is he?' Anna asked.

'B. is Himmler's alter ego in another world. He is none other than Beria, the head of the KGB and one of Stalin's closest advisers. Himmler and Beria had planned to assassinate their leaders and to rule the world jointly. Together they would have turned their combined armies on the West. And that was also why Himmler had to be stopped. That was a much greater threat than Germany alone. But was it ever real? Was Himmler trying to bluff Beria into killing

371

Stalin, or vice versa? Anything is possible. The one thing we know is that Himmler expected it to happen on Christmas Eve. It didn't. Maybe Beria has more loyalty to his leader than Himmler does. Or maybe with two such men, one wouldn't take the risk of striking the first blow. And that was what I was going to tell Himmler if I could have got through to him. I was going to tell him it was all a plot of Beria's to get rid of Hitler and that Heydrich's papers showed this. If he took power, Beria was going to expose everything about the camps to the Allies and show that Himmler was the person responsible. Then he would never get his peace.'

Norbert Sutter shook his head.

'For once, Rolf, I have to disagree with you. You are still thinking as a police officer, albeit a brilliant one. But these people are not your average criminals. Nothing is as it seems. You have drawn a very reasonable conclusion, but I think it is wrong. Let me explain why.

'What would be in it for either Beria or Himmler to double-cross their leaders? Any hint of it would mean instant death. So, what was the great prize that would make these ultra-cautious men risk their own lives? You think it was a plan to jointly rule the world? A pipe dream. Both of these men are also realists and know that will never happen. At best, they might survive. So, what was to be gained? Men like Beria and Himmler could never share power with each other.

It would be like putting two scorpions in a bag and expecting them to coexist peacefully. No, that idea is completely wrong.

'Yet the notes between them do exist, so they were planning something. But the crucial point you haven't considered is that I think each was planning something different from the other. Again, I ask the crucial question, what was in it for each of them?

'For Beria, the idea of him trying to replace Stalin would be impossible. Far too risky and, even if it happened, he would then be a target himself for the other members of the Politburo. All his power comes from Stalin, and Stalin alone. Without him, he would be defenceless against the others. No, Beria's plan was quite different. Indeed, I doubt if it was even *his* plan. I think it was Stalin's plan all along. Stalin wants to get a separate peace with Germany. Russia is being bled dry. Now he knows that the Allies are bound to win the war, but at what cost to Russia? If he could get a separate peace, he could rebuild Russia's armed forces while the West and Germany destroyed each other. Russia would then re-emerge much stronger against the eventual winner.

'Stalingrad is proving to any thinking German who knows the true situation, and that includes Himmler, that the war is being lost, and unless something dramatic happens, Germany will be destroyed. So, a separate peace would also suit Germany. But not Hitler. He would never agree, so that was Himmler's motivation. Save Germany and win the war against the West, while at the same time carrying on with the killing of the Jews, and then no doubt ensuring it was never discovered.'

Schneider knew his old friend was right. He should stick to police work. He wasn't used to the subterfuge and dispassionate brutality of men like Beria and Himmler. Brutality they used as a ready tool for their own purposes without a moment's hesitation or remorse.

'So, you really think Himmler would have gone ahead with assassinating Hitler and the others?' Schneider asked.

Sutter sucked on his pipe. 'Who knows, Rolf? Maybe he was just trying to bluff Beria all along, just as Beria was trying to bluff him. But whatever they were planning, Stalingrad was forcing a decision. Hence the final message from Beria. Once Germany loses that battle, her fate is sealed, and even Stalin wouldn't consider a separate peace then.'

Anna looked confused. She was still thinking back to what Schneider had said. 'I don't remember Heydrich's papers saying it was all a plot of Beria's to get rid of Hitler.'

Schneider and Sutter glanced at each other.

'It never was, but Himmler wouldn't know that. I was still playing poker.'

Realisation dawned on Anna's face. 'Of course. Himmler would never risk his own skin. If the Allies knew he was responsible for the camps, then he would be even more worse off than he is just now.'

Schneider nodded in agreement.

Anna had one more question. 'What do you propose to do with the papers now?'

Schneider guessed that Sutter probably knew the answer already.

'I suggest they stay where they are. Who knows what might happen before this war ends? Maybe the papers will still be needed. Only Anna has the password. I suggest we leave it that way.'

Anna agreed. After the war was over, she intended to do two things. She wanted to visit Lina Heydrich to tell her the truth, the whole truth, about her husband's life and death. And she wanted to return to Auschwitz, to bury the safety deposit box key where so many had died. Schneider would never know, but it was also the password she had chosen in the bank. *Auschwitz*. She had known no Nazi would ever think of that.

*

A thousand miles away, Beria knocked on Stalin's door. It was time to tell him their plan had failed. This time . . .

Author's Note

Germany is my favourite country to visit. I have lots of German friends. All of them abhor the Third Reich and the Holocaust. So how did it happen? It is a question that many people have tried to answer. It intrigued me.

I read extensively on how Hitler came to power, and how the German people reacted or, perhaps more accurately, failed to react to the growing persecution of the Jews. An apparently normal democratic country allowed a few evil men to assume absolute power and instigate one of the worst atrocities in human history. Ultimately, there is no simple answer to the conundrum.

Could it happen again? Could it happen elsewhere? We already see the rise of dictators again around the world. We see democracy again under threat. Constant vigilance is necessary.

I used the character Schneider in the book to demonstrate what happens when people faced with such evil turn a blind eye and try to ignore it. Eventually they are forced to realise their error, but by then it is too late. Perhaps I can only refer to Elie Wiesel's warning that 'to remain silent and indifferent is the greatest sin of all'.

Let us hope that history has finally taught us this lesson.